Working
Weekend

Working Weekend

Penelope Hill

Elsewhen Press

Working Weekend
First published in Great Britain by Elsewhen Press, 2020
An imprint of Alnpete Limited

Elsewhen Press, PO Box 757, Dartford, Kent DA2 7TQ
www.elsewhen.press

British Library Cataloguing in Publication Data.
A catalogue record for this book is available from the British Library.

ISBN 978-1-911409-61-8 Print edition
ISBN 978-1-911409-71-7 eBook edition

Designed and formatted by Elsewhen Press

This book is a work of fiction. All names, characters, places, hotels,
conventions, and events are either a product of the author's fertile
imagination or are used fictitiously. Any resemblance to actual events, fan
gatherings, inns, places or people (living, dead or undead) is purely
coincidental.

To my mother, who took me to my first convention, and to my dearly beloved Robin who accompanied me to many more. Miss you both.

Coffin Con VII

Venue Map - Ground floor

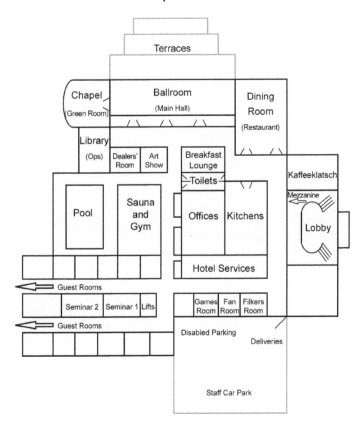

Coffin Con VII

Venue Map - Mezzanine

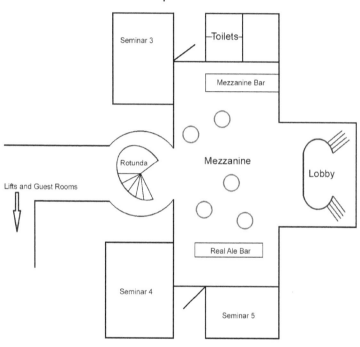

Marcus Holland
Bibliography

Writing as '*Ned Landers*'
The Jackson Hobb Mysteries:
Ill met by Moonlight
A Staging of Shadows
Cobwebs and Lace
Still waters run deep

Travels in Carpathia:
Dwellers in Destiny
Beneath the City Walls
Heir to the Impaler
Walkers in Darkness

Writing as '*Marcus Holland*'
The Stones at Dawn
Golden were the Meadows
Skinwalker
Fair and Faerie
Song of the sea. (A Selkie's tale)

Non-Fiction:
The Fairest Folk
Wolfkin (Shape shifters and lycanthropes
in mediaeval literature)
Blood on their lips (A new look at the vampire myth)

Chapter One

He only just made the train.

There hadn't been much space left in the car park, and he'd had to squeeze his Citroen into an awkward space between a battered van and a shiny, over-sized sports car. He'd only just managed to manoeuvre himself out of the driver's side door, grab his bags from the boot and sprint for the platform. His laptop case had thudded against his hip as he ran, his shoulder bag steadied by the tensioned wrap of his right arm and his suitcase merrily bouncing behind him. He'd practically flown up the twist of the staircase and onto the waiting train, diving in through the first open door just as the shoulder bag finally completed its threatened fall. He let it go, feeling rather than hearing the wince-making thump as it slid down his side and landed on the metalled floor. He couldn't remember if he'd packed anything fragile in it, and – right then – he didn't really care. He took a moment to lean against the glass divider and get his breath back: the train doors closed with an impatient hiss and the floor beneath him lurched with a determined jerk.

If he'd left anything important behind, he was just going to have to cope without it.

"Further up and further in," he muttered, reaching to pick up his fallen bag and taking a moment to identify which carriage he was in.

It had felt like a mad dash all morning. From his reluctant rise – encouraged by Malfeasance's persistent head butts and purrs – through the morning's tedious emails, the hasty 'throw everything in the suitcase' packing, the brief pause to pass an indignant Mal over to his helpful neighbour, to the final fuming through unexpected traffic. Marcus hadn't been having many good days just recently. Today hadn't started out as one, and he wasn't holding out much hope of it getting better.

Despite his destination, and the prospect of a weekend away.

He was, of course, in the entirely wrong carriage, and he had to pick his way past a long line of passengers, trying to avoid committing accidental assault with either laptop or shoulder bag, his suitcase grumbling behind him. He'd just about made it to the door into the next carriage, when his phone rang.

What now? he grimaced to himself, jerking his suitcase past the sliding door and into the rattling space between 'F' and 'G'. The ride was bumpy, and he staggered a little as he hastily adjusted his burden of luggage so he could lean against the carriage wall and grope for his phone.

A quick jab at the screen accepted the call. "Holland here," he growled. "Make it quick. I'm on the train."

"You made it!" The smooth tones of his literary agent oozed out of the speaker like a thick, rich syrup. Cloying and slightly too sweet to be completely additive free. "Well done. Still think you should have driven, but … what do I know?"

Marcus curbed the temptation to say *everything*, and sighed instead.

"Not going there, Francis. What do you want?" He was actually quite fond of the man, but sometimes – some days – he could be a little bit much.

"Just checking in. This is an important weekend for us, you know? You meeting your fans, selling – *signing* a few more books, stuff like that. Just wanted to be sure you were on your way and had everything you need." The assurance was meant to be warm, but Marcus wasn't buying it.

"And?" he prompted. The train rattled over points, and he lurched sideways, having to grab for his suitcase to stop it falling over.

"Well …" The pause was drawn out and deliberate, intended to tease.   Francis probably thought it was good news. Marcus suspected it wasn't.

"I've had an offer for a three book deal."

He was right. Good news for a literary agent. A moment of looming horror for an author.

Especially one that had run out of creative steam.

"Three?" he managed to question in semi-reasonable tones. His stomach had done a three-sixty flip and his heart had just migrated to his boots.

"Yeah. Great news, right? One Jackson Hobbs, another travel thingy, and … one more on whatever you fancy. One of your fair folk things, perhaps.   You win awards with those."

"I know." His voice came out ice-cold and sepulchral. He might manage another Jackson Hobbs if he forced himself – working with his supernatural detective and his slightly off-kilter world was basically write by the numbers stuff. And he might – *might* be able to churn out another Victorian Gothic tale of lost travellers in some remote part of Eastern Europe – Werewolves in Romania, perhaps.   But the Fair Folk stuff was *hard*. It took extensive research and careful crafting, spinning tales of glamour and deception and half-glimpsed worlds, where nothing was what it seemed, and everything had to weave together into a delicate, intricate web.

Finishing the last one had felt a little like giving birth – not the physical experience that is, but the laborious, painful, exhilarating struggle that he'd gone through with Beverley when Molly was born.

He didn't think he could face that again.

"So what d'ya thi…"

He was saved from saying *exactly* what he thought by the train racing into a tunnel. The signal dropped out and he grabbed the opportunity to shove his suitcase and shoulder bag into the storage rack and take at least six steps towards his reserved seat before his phone rang again.

"Gerry says we can have an advance on the first book right away," Francis told him with enthusiasm. "He says he'd rather get the Hobbs first, but I think he'd be happy with that, or something Gothic and vintage if you'd rather. You might even get another trip out of him. He loves the authentic detail, and I could ..."

"Francis. Francis!" Marcus tried to keep his voice steady. "I haven't agreed to anything yet. I don't know if I have one more book in me, let alone three."

"Oh, don't go worrying about that. Every author I have is always telling me the well's gone dry, and it never is. Well," he corrected thoughtfully, "apart from that time with Henry Ess ... but he had a nervous breakdown. That's not going to happen to you."

"I'm glad you think so." He checked the reservation ticket tucked into the back of the seat, dumped the laptop on the table and sank down into the welcome luxury of softly padded fabric. "But – listen – three books? I have a job remember? The University needs me to publish, and I have students to supervise, and a new course to write..."

"And two kids to support," his agent shot back. "Not to mention keeping the Ex happy. Come on, Marcus. Academic papers don't earn you royalties. And you could use the new course work as background for the third book. The way you've done before. This is a great deal. And if we don't take it we'll have to fight much harder for the next one."

"And you hate fighting publishers." Marcus rolled his eyes at the thought. One of the things Francis loved was making deals, and schmoozing while making them. He always tried to stay on the good side of everybody. He even succeeded sometimes.

"I'm a lover, not a fighter. You know that. Come on.

What do you say?"

"I'll think about it." He wasn't willing to promise any more than that. The English countryside rolled by outside the window, looking green and lush in the late morning sun. There was a young woman sitting in the group of seats across the aisle, her fingers dancing on her laptop keyboard, while – further down the carriage – someone else was laughing raucously at something their friend had just said. It must have been a pretty good joke. "Let me get this weekend out the way. Spend some time with other writers. Run some ideas around … Maybe – *maybe* an idea or two will come up. I don't know. We'll see."

"Atta boy." Marcus could hear the grin behind every syllable. "Listen – you have a great time at the convention. Get your fans to buy you a couple of beers, listen to what they like about your stuff, drop a few test hints and teasers and … yeah. We'll see. Twenty percent early advance, remember? You could buy a lot of ice cream and toys with that…"

"Ice cream? Molly's sworn off dairy and you know Reuben's diabetic…" He caught up with his indignant response and cut himself off with a sigh. Francis knew all that. "Never mind. I said I'd think about it. I'll call you after the convention, okay?"

"Okay." Now Francis was laughing at him. He'd never liked being teased as a boy, and he was even less amused by it now. Still, the man was a damn good agent, and he was only trying to do his job. Teasing authors was probably written into his job description. "Don't sign anything I wouldn't. I'll speak to you next week."

Marcus put down the phone and sighed. Three books! He'd been trying to work on one paper for the last few weeks and had found himself struggling to write even half of it. There were words that came, yes, but he would spend hours writing a single sentence, only to find himself deleting it again the following day. Every statement felt trite and obvious. Every argument weak and fallacious. He couldn't find an original thought, or a new angle, and if he couldn't do that for the subject that he loved, then there was no way he'd be able to churn out three books worth putting his name against. Not even his pen name. The fiction might be different in style and approach to his academic work, but there had to be a story to tell for him to be able to tell it, and – truth be told – there didn't seem to be a single tale left in him.

Maybe that last book had scraped out all his creativity and left him empty. Hungry for … something, although he didn't know what.

"Tickets please!"

The conductor was coming down the carriage aisle, punching tickets and checking passes. Marcus took a moment to find the relevant orange and cream piece of pasteboard, and carefully tucked his return ticket back into his wallet before holding out the outward one.

"Thank you," the conductor muttered as he took it, then paused, taking a second look. "This train only stops at Moor Street and Snow Hill," he said. "You'll need to get across to New Street for the connecting train."

"Yes, I know." Marcus had considered travelling via Coventry to avoid the hike, but the timing had been tight and it would have meant navigating the Coventry Ring Roads. "I'm looking forward to stretching my legs."

That was true enough, although there was always the option to grab a taxi if the weather took a turn for the worse. Not that it looked like rain today. Outside, in the passing countryside, the sun was sailing in a sea of constant blue with not a cloud in sight. This was a familiar journey for him, veteran of many an academic seminar and even a guest lecture or two at Birmingham U. It was the second half of the journey that took him past the University stop into the unknown, a local train that passed through exotic places like

'Five Ways,' 'Selly Oak,' and finally 'Westeringford' – one stop on from Bournville.

He'd promised Molly he'd look out for some dairy free chocolate…

The train stopped at Solihull shortly after the ticket collector moved on, which might have given Marcus time to contemplate the rise of sprawling suburbs and encroaching industrialisation, if his phone hadn't rung again.

He jabbed at the screen to silence the sudden burst of Katy Perry. "Holland, here" he sighed. The woman across the aisle gave him a puzzled look, and he turned towards the window so as to avoid looking at her. It wasn't his fault that his daughter liked to reprogram his phone with her favourites. And it was entirely her mother's fault that he never bothered reprogramming it until the day before he was due to see her again.

"Marcus, so glad I caught you!"

"Sharon." Instinct half straightened his spine before he remembered that she couldn't see him, and he defiantly slumped back into the seat. "What can I do for you?"

"You could send me your comments on the Research Council bid," she answered tartly. "It has to be submitted by Wednesday, you know."

"Yes, of course." He hadn't forgotten, as such, but there'd been other pressing paperwork to do, the preparations for the weekend – and that problem with one of the undergrads that had taken most of the day before to sort out. "I'm sorry, I've been meaning to do it, but…"

"No buts," she drawled, probably aiming for amusement and only just managing barely concealed irritation. She was an amazing administrator, and well qualified to be head of the department, but people skills were not well featured in her CV. "We need your contribution, Dr Holland. Your future funding may depend on this."

"I know, I know. I have it with me. I'll look at it over the weekend, and I'll let you have my comments by Monday. Will that be acceptable?"

She sighed. "I suppose it will have to do. Did you file your supervision reports?"

"Yes," he assured her, trying hard to keep his own irritation from showing. He'd finished the undergrad summaries over a week ago, and the notes on his three PhD students had been emailed the day before. "Everything else is up to date."

"Good, good." The train paused at another local station. Several people left the carriage, and an older couple climbed on board, pausing, as they passed him, to wave at someone on the platform. "You're away this weekend, I gather. Some kind of conference, I believe? Are you presenting a paper?"

He suppressed another sigh. There were colleagues at the University who knew all about his literary career. Some of them thought it was funny. Others had been decidedly dismissive. One or two had even expressed envy over the years. But by the time Dr Sharon Powell had stepped in to run the department he'd given up making anything of it, and had long since stopped trying to explain the difference between Academic conferences and genre conventions. She'd undoubtedly read his CV at some point, but – given that his primary specialty was European folklore – she probably thought that the titles in his bibliography were all relevant scholarly examinations, rather than fictional titles and one or two non-fiction pieces aimed at the popular market. He never included the 'Ned Landers' works on his scholarly CV. He suspected he might get struck off – or something like it – if he did.

"Something like that, yes. I'm on my way there now. But I will look at the funding bid, I promise."

"See that you do. Good luck. I hope it all goes well."

So do I ...

He tucked the phone back into his pocket and watched as the outskirts of Birmingham transmuted into the inner city.

He'd turn the thing off, so it didn't interrupt him again, but there was always a chance that his hosts for the weekend would be trying to get in touch with him. He didn't want to develop a reputation of being difficult or unapproachable; he always tried to find time for fans, to acknowledge their engagement with his work. Each book sold was a tiny affirmation of his contribution as a writer, a check mark on his self-esteem. He wasn't self-centred enough to think it meant any more than that, but it was a genuine pleasure to know that others liked what he did, that they were entertained, amused, or even inspired by his scribblings.

Even if some of the hard core fans could be … a little intimidating on occasions.

The train arrived at Moor Street, with its glass awnings and 1930's styling – a setting Marcus had liberally borrowed as a backcloth in *A Staging of Shadows* – so he gathered up his luggage and, once the train had stopped, he got off and made his way out into the city. It was only a short walk to New Street Station, but it meant he could pause to grab a decent cup of coffee, stretch his legs a little, and enjoy the summer air. There'd been suggestions of stormy weather on the way, but the sky was still clear and the sun shone with brilliant indifference. Marcus had just finished taking off his jacket and stuffing it through the straps of his shoulder bag, when his phone rang again.

"Holland here," he announced brightly, his sense of eternal harassment having been somewhat eased by the warmth of the sun and the sweeter warmth of a well-sugared latte.

"Marcus, darling!" Beverley's dulcet tones rang out of the speaker, and his burgeoning good mood collapsed into instant wary tension.

"Hello, Bev." He tried to avoid sounding defensive, but he suspected he didn't quite succeed. Not that Beverley would pick up on it. He'd discovered, quite early on in their relationship, that Beverley rarely paid attention to those sorts of social clues. She could be quite sympathetic and supportive if she *realised* you needed her to be – but you often had to hit her with a metaphorical two by four to get her to stop thinking about herself and get her to notice you. "Something you need?"

The irony in that would also go straight over her head. There was always something she needed. She never called him just to talk, these days. They hadn't really *talked* for years.

"Not me, darling. But – " There was the but. Marcus gritted his teeth and waited for the anvil to drop. " – Dr Paulding's been recommending this place – a special summer camp – for Reuben? It's got hydro pools and state of the art therapy units and…"

"How much?" The interruption was probably rude, but he had a connecting train to catch.

"Oh … no, I don't need money … well, a little more wouldn't hurt, you know? But if I take Reuben there, Molly's going to be all on her own for the summer, and I wondered…?"

"If I could take her? For how long?"

"Oh, just a week or two? Next month, once school breaks up? If you can't, I can find her a summer camp of her own, but that's going to cost money, and I don't think your monthly payments will cover that."

They never did. He wasn't sure quite what Beverly spent his child support on – the children were well fed and decently clothed most of the time, so some of it was being used as intended, but she was always coming to him for that little 'more', asking for extras, wanting help with things. He suspected she thought his meagre royalties were bringing in a fortune, and – with every book he published – considered herself entitled to a larger slice of pie. The pie, of course, was meagre pickings; he was never going to be another George R.R or J.K. even if he had started winning awards for his work. Awards didn't put food on the table, even if they were used to justify upping a book's cover price.

"No, no, don't worry about that. I'd love to have her." The *I'd take Reuben, too, if what you really want is a break* hung between them with unspoken weight. She'd never admit to wanting a break from her beloved, fragile and demanding son, and he'd never quite be willing to admit he thought of the boy as his. Even if he wasn't.

The affair had always been the excuse for the divorce, not the reason for it, no matter what they'd both agreed to in court. There was even a little bit of himself – somewhere, buried deep – that still carried a candle for Beverley. It was conversations like this that reminded him how badly a lit candle can burn.

"Wonderful. I'll get back to Dr Paulding to book us a place, and I'll e-mail you the dates, okay?"

"Yes, that's fine." It was a major imposition, and a typically last minute, leave-you-no-choice one, but he was already making hasty plans in his head. He'd have to rearrange his diary, and if he scrimped he might be able to afford to take the two of them away somewhere, and – *damn.* If Francis wanted another book – or two – or three – then writing it would have to wait. Time with Molly was precious and if Beverley was prepared to gift him with two weeks of it, he'd do his best to make the most of it. For both of them.

"You're an angel, Marcus. I appreciate it, I really do. Have fun at your convention thing. That is this weekend, right?"

"Right." He tilted his wrist to check the time, and caught back a curse. "And I need to go. I've a train to catch. Give my love to Molly and Roo. Tell them I'll see them soon. Bye!"

He was thumbing the connection closed before she could respond. He thrust the phone into his trouser pocket, slung the shoulder bag over his unencumbered shoulder and grabbed for the suitcase, charging down the road and into the station concourse with the hurried pace of a man whose leisurely stroll had suddenly become 'if I don't run I'm going to miss my connection'. There were a few other people hastening through the milling passengers for whom that pace appeared to have taken on a similar desperate meaning, but he weaved his way past them, checked the departure board on the run, and arrived at the relevant platform with a couple of minutes to spare.

Once again he found himself tumbling in through the doors of a train and needing to lean on the carriage divider in order to catch his breath. Unlike his earlier dash, though, his arrival did not go unnoticed. There were several people already seated in his chosen carriage. All of them looked up.

Several of them recognised him.

The recognition varied from a moment of wide-eyed realisation and a hasty, shy – or perhaps embarrassed – look away, to the warm and welcoming grin of an old friend.

"Marcus!" Cordell Deveaux, civil engineer, would-be political activist and author of *Walk with me at Midnight*, surged out of his seat and strode down the carriage to offer a warm bear-hug of greeting. Marcus managed to hug back, a little awkwardly, since he was still encumbered by his luggage.

"Hey, Cordell. Should have known I'd see you this weekend. Couldn't resist the Real Ale Bar, huh?"

Cordell laughed, holding out an imposing hand in an offer to assist with bags and baggage. Marcus handed him the laptop case, since he knew the man would be careful with it. He'd known Cordell for several years, ever since they met at a publisher's tedious soiree and had made a mutually agreed escape to the nearest pub. They'd quickly gone from shared acquaintances in adversity to firm friends, and stayed there ever since. "You know me too well, man. How are things? You found the Holy Grail yet?"

Marcus snorted. "I wish. Naw, things are fine. Francis wants me to write more books, the department wants me to take on more work, and Beverley's ... Beverley. You know?"

"Tell me about it." The laptop case was slid onto the waiting table, his suitcase fitted neatly into the space between two rows of seats, and Marcus found himself dropping his shoulder bag onto the empty seat opposite the one Cordell had been occupying when he'd arrived. "Everybody's after something, these days. From governor to government. Time and taxes – they own us, right? If we're not wasting one, we're busy paying the other."

The train lurched into motion, and Marcus sat down with a thump. Cordell slid back into his own seat with an easy, athletic grace, and laughed at his chagrined expression. It was a deep, personable laugh, and, after a moment, Marcus echoed it with a wry chuckle of his own. Everything about Cordell was always larger than life, from the shoulder length tumble of dreadlocks that framed his generous face, to the width of his grin and the even wider set of his shoulders. He approached life with a breezy confidence that Marcus envied; he treated every stumbling block and obstacle with determined challenge, and if something knocked him down, he simply picked himself up, shook the dust off his shoulders and found another way round the problem.

He was a damn good writer too.

"Is it true someone's chasing the TV rights for *Midnight*?" he asked. Francis had mentioned something about that a few days ago, and he hadn't had time to email his friend to check the truth of it.

"Oh, yeah. We're in 'negotiations'." The air quotes were inevitable. Cordell liked people to be straightforward and honest with him. It was unlikely that any TV or movie executive would meet those kind of expectations. "But the offer's a good one. The guy that wants the option really gets the material."

"You hope." Marcus had had similar approaches, none of which had come to any fruition. The minute anyone suggested casting someone tall and handsome as his short, compact and craggy faced detective, he knew they'd missed the point, and showed them the door. Since Cordell's material dealt with 'Voodoo' magic, interactions with the Loa, zombies, and revengeful curses, it was going to take a very careful and reverent hand to translate it onto the small screen. "They do know it's meant to be a romance, I take it?"

Cordell grimaced at him. "Go on with you," he growled good-naturedly. "Romance. Huh! A love letter written in chicken blood with a pen carved from human bones … I don't do romance, and you know it. Might as well call *Heir to the Impaler* a comedy."

"Some people do." Marcus relaxed into his seat and let the rumble of the train ease away some of the tension in his bones. *This* was why he came to things like Coffincon. It was a chance to catch up with old friends and maybe make a few new ones. An opportunity to escape from the petty worries of the world and to explore the kind of ideas and concepts that challenged the intellect and stirred the imagination. "Have you done a Coffincon before?"

"Couple of years back. Just after *Bone Dancer* came out. It was a good weekend. I'm looking forward to this one. And not just for the Real Ale," he added, before Marcus could suggest it. "Lilith and Mazzy will be there, and I've only got two panels and a workshop, so I'll have plenty of time to kick back and relax. Spanner tells me it's got a decent pool, and there's acres of grounds. So I'll be able to run every morning. You – " he grinned at Marcus across the table, "You're guest of honour, right? You won't have a moment to yourself."

Chapter Two

They got off the train at the Westeringford Station, along with at least two dozen other people, most of whom had the air of convention attendees. Among them were a few obvious Goths, travelling in black, one or two men with impressive – and some not so impressive – beards, others of similar age and type but without beards, some women of various ages, shapes, and sizes, ranging from rain-pipe slender teen to plump and grandmotherly, a lanky student type and his not so lanky girlfriend, and an extremely androgynous couple dressed *exactly* alike.

"Guess this is the right place," Marcus observed dryly, glancing round and spotting some vaguely familiar faces in the crowd.

"Guess so," Cordell agreed, his height giving him a decided advantage in general observation. "Hey – there's Mazzy. And Lilith with her. I'd better go say hello. You walking to the hotel or getting the shuttle bus?"

He'd originally been planning to take the bus, but, looking at all the disembarking passengers, he suspected that it was going to be a little crowded. For at least two trips. "Think I'll walk. It's a nice day, it's not meant to be too far, and since I'm going to be jostling shoulders with all these people all weekend, I can probably skip the *actual* jostling and spare them my company for another hour. Or two."

Cordell nodded understandingly, pausing to give his shoulder a friendly shake before striding off down the platform to meet up with his girlfriends. The train pulled away and once the rattle of carriages had passed, Marcus took a moment to look around. The station was a small, local stop, with a single platform either side of the line, and an arching metal bridge so passengers could cross from one side to the other. Both platforms were bare except for station signs, and lacked anything that looked like a shelter, let alone a waiting room. There were some information boards dotted along each platform's length, and a single gate on the far-side platform with what appeared to be a slope, as well as steps leading down from it. Trees had been planted on the slightly raised banks that the platforms nestled against. They created a wall of summer green that obscured whatever lay beyond them. Somewhere, just glimpsed between the trees by the gate were the barest hints of Gothic crenulations. A large sign next to the open gate announced 'Westeringford Grange and Conference Centre,' along with an equally large arrow that pointed in the direction of the mostly hidden architecture.

The convention progress report had said the hotel wouldn't be far from the station, and it was walkable, provided you didn't mind trudging up a long driveway. Marcus didn't mind particularly, although he did cast a slightly worried eye at the sky. Clouds were beginning to gather overhead, and the sunlight was filtering through them, turning what had been a bright, warm day into one that hinted at coming rain.

The crowd had started to thin out as people made their way along the platform and over the angled bridge. As friends met up and introductions were busy being made they had separated out into little clumps, with the odd straggler drifting in between. Marcus picked up his bags, grabbed the handle of his rolling suitcase and headed after the last of these, amused to note that Cordell was still looming large on the platform, deep in animated conversation with the two women who'd exited from the rear carriage of the train. There was an intimidating pile of luggage stacked around them: much of it, he had no doubt, containing Mazzy's artwork and Lilith's stock. He would have to remember to visit her table over the weekend and find something he could take home for Molly. Something striking and expensive. Not just because Lilith would appreciate the income. Beverley didn't like her daughter wearing cheap or trashy trinkets. He'd have to remember to save the price label, and emphasise the value of hand-crafted goods...

Once over the bridge, and through the gate, he found himself looking at two rather impressive sights. One was the vista that dropped away to the right, revealing a narrow valley in which nestled what had been a town and was now the suburb of Westeringford, a mix of sturdy Victorian buildings, civil-minded architecture, and a number of more modern structures. Behind it, the sprawl of the city lay in a hazy mass, with the factories and industry of Bournville dominating the horizon.

To the left stretched the long curve of a weathered wall, over which hung hints of trees and the suggestion of gardens – and, piercing the wall with determined grandeur, was an over-ornamented entrance way complete with huge wrought-iron gates, turreted gatehouses on either side, and massive, furiously decorated, gateposts. There were carved lions, curved urns, curling stone acanthus leaves, bunches of grapes and what might have been a caryatid or two supporting the jutting slabs on which the lions sat.

There was a sign on the right hand gate that declared: 'Welcome to Westeringford Grange.'

Beyond the gates stretched a long gravel driveway – and at the end of *that* stood the hotel.

"Wow," he heard someone say. Someone else began to sing a vaguely familiar tune.

"There's a light...."

"Over at the Frankenstein place," the rest of the crowd chorused, and the spontaneous melody dissolved into hoots of laughter.

Marcus simply stood and stared.

The photos the committee had sent him hadn't done it

justice. Bits of it had looked familiar of course, since its exteriors had been used as backdrop and scene setting in a number of well-known films, from old-style Hammer Horrors in the sixties and seventies, edgy art-studio pieces in the eighties, at least one Bond movie, and it had even appeared – once or twice – in classic *Who*. But the publicity shots had played down the looming Gothic look in favour of stately elegance and formal, classic, architecture. Even the image on the website focused on the main frontage overlooking the formal gardens, rather than revealing anything about the place as a whole.

Westeringford Grange promoted itself as a development of an old Baronial manor, upgraded into stately home in the early eighteenth century and subsequently refurbished by a wealthy Victorian industrialist.

What they didn't tell you was that he'd used Bram Stoker's architect to do it.

It was *huge*. Three, even four storeys high in places, with bold and brooding Gothic features that would have made Pugin proud. There were turrets and towers and crenulations aplenty, decorating a dark and bulky building that was pierced – there was no other word for it – by row upon row of arched, balconied, and overly ornate windows. It didn't belong in the middle of a carefully landscaped garden, no matter how naturalistically it had been designed. It demanded a bleak and weathered heath to dominate, one wracked by bitter winds and that had wolves prowling across it, ready to howl at the moon in the middle of the night. From this angle it looked like some wanna-be vampire's wedding cake: half castle, half cathedral, all rebuilt ruin, accented with gargoyles and decoratively carved stonework, and shrugging down along the rise of a ridge line with the hunched determination of some mythical wounded beast.

Spanner had been wrong. He'd said it might suit as a location for the next Jackson Hobbs' adventure – but it came straight out of Carpathia via a storm-wracked Whitby Abbey. Hobbs *might* be willing to visit, but Marcus knew which of his characters would really feel at home in the place. He could almost see Faulkner Nettlestone stalking up the drive – his broad brimmed hat pulled low against the wind and his travelling cloak flapping around his ankles – while Manaheim, his loyal valet, struggled valiantly with their cases behind him, muttering appeals for protection to the Virgin Mary with every step.

He, of course, lacked the benefit of a personal man-servant. Appealing to the Virgin Mary wasn't going to help him either, although he might get round to thanking the Fates for seeing him safely to his destination before the day was out. The small crowd had begun to peel off, heading towards the station car park, which lay tucked into the curve of the railway bank to the right of the station. There was a minibus waiting there, its driver already beginning to load luggage and passengers aboard. Marcus eyed the queue for a moment, then resettled the straps of his shoulder bag, checked the laptop case was still tucked in comfortably on the other side of him, and picked up the suitcase, starting down the final tier of the steps towards the road. The bus was going to have to make several trips to ferry the gathered fans and their piles of luggage across to the hotel. Mazzy and Lilith, even with Cordell's help, would probably occupy one trip all by themselves – and he didn't really want to stand around in the middle of a group of fans and find himself pestered with comments and questions. Marcus wasn't ready for all that just yet. He'd walk, and enjoy the view. He looked right and left and then crossed the road, his suitcase bumping in his wake. Three other people had apparently eschewed the convenience of the bus and started walking up the drive ahead of him. None of them looked like anyone he knew, so he let them set their own pace and strolled leisurely in their wake, content to enjoy the remnants of the sunshine while it lasted.

The driveway wound up from the gate and round to a pillared portico on the right hand side of the building, which meant that he was approaching the side of the structure, rather than either of the featured frontages. The main bulk of what he could see was stately and *old*. But it was also easy to see how the buildings on the left hand side – the back part of the structure – had been built on by later architects. Stables and carriage houses and other outbuildings appeared to have been cemented together into a mishmash of styles, the older sections of wall subsumed into a long, three storey block that tried to echo the ostentation of the main house, but somehow only succeeded in parodying it. Each of the deep, arch-topped windows that paraded in an unrelenting line along the top two storeys sported a tiny, railed balcony; they, in turn perched on an attempt to mimic the carved ledges underlining the older window line. It was probably meant to blend the two sections together, but it missed that ambition by a mile or more. At least the old house had a sense of character in its design. The extension was soulless, a sullen, lifeless monolith beneath which the echoes of the original buildings lay trapped and silently screaming.

He wouldn't have been surprised to spot a figure in a straitjacket desperately throwing itself against one of the windows.

He stopped. Sighed, and fumbled for his phone. There'd probably be plenty of time to take pictures in the morning, but he couldn't guarantee the weather and – just at that moment, with the summer sun glinting off the glass – the patchworked walls and their sunken, sullen windows presented all kinds of thoughtful possibilities. This end of the hotel, solid, weathered, and clearly stained with time, would suit Hobbs and his urban magics far more than it would Nettlestone's scholarly sorcery.

"Damnit, Francis," Marcus muttered, lifting the phone to snap a few reference shots of the architecture. "I'm not going to have time for this. Not with Molly for the summer and extra students to supervise in the new term." He took the pictures anyway, turning to add a few more of the looming Gothic monstrosity that was the side of the main house. "Maybe next year…"

The shuttle bus passed him on its way up the drive and several of its passengers waved at him as they went by. He waved back, just to be friendly, although he hadn't recognised anyone he knew. He might not know them yet, but he was pretty sure he'd have made most of their acquaintances before the weekend was over.

The closer he got the more the house and its grounds drew him in, defying his expectations of a slightly faded and seedy hotel on the outskirts of Birmingham. He could see why movie-makers had been so drawn to it in decades past. These days they'd probably build this kind of scenery virtually, handcrafting the details with artistic precision. But a virtual world would struggle to match the authenticity of the place. That intriguing impression of a once stately home, fallen – not into ruin, as such, but a slow and shabby decline – then revived to serve a new purpose, only to fall, and fall again. There were signs of neglect and hints of failing grandeur among the archways and the weathered stones. It wasn't pretty, by any stretch of the imagination, but it certainly had character; it was the perfect setting for a Dark Fantasy and Horror Convention, offering an amusing mix of dramatic location, down to earthy detail, over the top imagery, and loads and loads of atmosphere.

Almost *too much* atmosphere. Marcus paused a second time, struck by an unexpected shiver. He was close enough now for the building to dominate his vision and cast its looming shadow over him. The step from bright sunlight into cooler gloom had been sudden and disconcerting. For a brief moment he'd had the impression of stepping – not from light into shadow – but from day into night.

It would be at this point in the narrative that Jackson Hobbs would growl and step determinedly forward, Nettlestone would frown and check his sword-stick, and Manaheim would change his anxious muttering to a more direct appeal to God. Marcus merely shook himself, dispelling that annoying sense of fancy and settling the pins and needles it had raised across his skin. *There are*, he told himself severely, *no such things as vampires.*

Or ghosts.

Or goblins…

Actually, he wasn't all that sure about the goblins. His doctoral research had suggested that *some* of those old tales had some kind of grounding in reality. Mostly they'd been ways of highlighting dangerous phenomena that their observers – along with those who might have experienced them more directly – had been unable to explain. Stories created as warnings, alongside the ones intended as morality lessons, or ways to reinforce cultural behaviours. It was always dangerous to swim in mill streams, whether you believed in Jinny-Green-Teeth or not. Those who did believe generally didn't go swimming in the first place, which is why they survived to repeat the tales.

But jumping at the shadow of an old house that was nothing more than a faded echo of someone's grand dreams was simply pandering to out-dated instincts that were best reserved for scary movies and late-at-night indulgences in someone else's well-crafted tale. His own tales never scared him, even if others reported finding themselves on the edges of their seats. They amused him, frustrated him, even annoyed him sometimes, but they never, *ever,* scared him.

Most of the time he knew exactly how they turned out – and even if he wasn't sure, he was always confident that he'd find a way to defeat the villain and get the hero to save the day.

He picked up his pace a little, following the line of the drive to arrive at the main entrance to the hotel. That was just as grand as the approach had promised it would be: a pillared, ornate portico jutted out from a single storey installation that must have been added to the front of the house at some early stage of its construction. There were huge, carved pineapples supporting an ornate rail above the portico, hinting at the idea that the wide flat roof might actually serve as an open-air balcony accessed from the upper storeys of the house. He stepped back a few paces to check. Sure enough, he could see the top of what looked like French windows in the wall above and behind the installation, and there were stone steps on either side that led up to the floor above.

"Isn't this place *amazing?*" someone exclaimed behind him, and he jumped. The shuttle bus was turning round at the end of the drive, using the entrance to the hotel car park to assist with the manoeuvre. It must have disgorged its first load of passengers; they were gathering in a gaggle at the foot of the wide shallow steps and gawking at the ornate frontage with a mixture of delight, bemusement, and – in one or two cases – disdain.

"Nah," a young man decided, shaking his head and picking up his suitcase. "It's too – frothy for me. Overdressed."

"Well, I love it," an older woman interrupted him. "Very *Gormenghast*. You can just see Titus, perched up there and scowling at the world and his place in it."

"Didn't they film bits of Wuthering Heights here?" someone else asked. "The Seventies one, with Timothy Dalton in it."

"I don't think so," their companion responded. "There was a TV version that came here, I think. But those doors – they were *definitely* used in *Hands of Terror*. Just imagine. Christopher Lee has walked down those steps…"

The entrance was certainly distinctive. There were a pair of heavy, ornately carved doors caught back on either side, nestling under the portico, each at least eight feet high and five foot wide. Two feet back and one step up, there were a second pair of doors – lighter weight affairs inset with intricate and colourful panels of stained glass. Behind them were a third pair of equally decorative doors, imitating Tiffany, and set back behind a tiled lobby, so that, without a servant on hand to support them, a visitor would have to step forward and let the middle set of doors swing closed behind them before they could open the inner ones. The whole effect was clearly designed to make an impression, although the presence of a cracked pane in one of the middle doors did rather spoil it a little.

The cracked pane was a subtle hint at negligence, which would also explain the scattered weeds along the edge of the drive, and the faded paint on the hotel signage. The place might have made money, once, attracting a lively set of the idle rich to stay in its faded glory, dine in elegant style, and possibly even dance at expensive soirees. But that sort of money was thin on the ground these days, and the people that had it were spending their time in Monte Carlo and Vegas, not living it up a stone's throw from Bournville, or resisting the siren call of the night life of Birmingham. It was probable that the days of largesse were long gone from Westeringford Grange, leaving the hotel to scrape by on business conferences, passing trade, and themed weekends like this one. Marcus could well imagine the place hosting regular murder-mystery dinners, Goth nights on Halloween, and a local wedding or two.

Thinking about it, weddings were probably their most lucrative offering. Who wouldn't want to get married in such Gothic splendour? There was even supposed to be a chapel, somewhere in the building, although he was willing to bet it had been de-consecrated, long ago.

"I don't know about Christopher Lee walking *down*," he announced, picking up his suitcase so he could carry it up the steps, "but I'm going up them. I'm dying for a cup of tea."

His words might have been magic; the whole group surged forward, turning the transition through the two sets of doors into a chaotic dance, complete with twists, turns and the encumbrance of luggage. There was a moment or two of jammed bags and conflicting cases, but it was quickly sorted and they all emerged into the hotel lobby unscathed and still on friendly terms.

For a moment, Marcus thought he'd arrived in Versailles. Or possibly Vegas. There were two matching marble staircases rising on either side of him, leading to a balcony on the second floor. Crystal chandeliers big enough to light entire streets were hanging from the ceiling; there were thickly padded sofas and chairs set around glass topped tables, a bar – closed for the moment – under the staircase on one side of the vast space – and the reception desk under the staircase on the other. Behind both, and along each wall, were a line of glimmering mirrors, each one wreathed in gilt and reaching from just above the floor to a line a good foot or more above a common head height. There was so much light in the room, reflected and then reflected back by the mirrors that it took Marcus a moment or two to realise that the huge windows that faced out onto the drive and the car park were actually covered with thick velvet curtains. Deep dark green ones, subtly figured with tumbling leaves which were outlined by a very fine gold line.

He looked up. The ceiling – two full floors above his head – was decorated in white and gold, with a series of inset painted panels depicting stylised mythological scenes. There were a line of portraits and other antique paintings descending with the stairs, and a gilt covered banister rail ascending them in the other direction. The lobby was tiled with a slightly darker marble than the stone of the stairs, but it was interspersed with inset sections of dark green carpet, laid out in a lattice pattern. It was lavish. It was opulent. It screamed *luxurious*.

It was totally over the top. It must have been incredibly impressive when it was first done. It was still pretty impressive now, but age and use were clearly catching up with it; it was starting to look a little shabby in places.

The staff were looking a little shabby, too. There were three of them behind the reception desk; and two more, one manning the concierge service, and the other helping two tee-shirted individuals unfold a trestle table in front of the pair of doors opposite the entrance. He could tell they were staff, since they were all wearing matching dark maroon jackets, over even darker trousers – or possibly skirts, since he could only see the top half of the two women at the desk. The jacket on the man nearest to him had shiny, slightly worn patches on its shoulders and elbows, signs of long wear and hard use, and it looked vaguely *wrinkled*, as if its wearer had been sleeping in it. Or possibly snatching an illicit nap somewhere.

"Dr Holland?" He turned at the question to find a woman walking towards him, a warm smile on her face. She was one of those women of indeterminable age, well past the first bloom of youth but showing little signs of the impact of time beyond a general sense of confident maturity. There were some hints of silver in her hair, but that could just be an affectation. Marcus had endured a sufficient number of Beverley's fashionable colour changes to know that the art of the hairstylist could be as arcane as that of any literary wizard or sorcerer. He'd never make the mistake of trying to guess anyone's age based on the colour of their hair.

"Hi," she was saying, holding out her hand in greeting. "I'm Abigail. Abigail Sterman? Con Guest liaison, and programme co-ordinator?"

"Oh, yes." He hastily stood his suitcase up onto its wheels so it wouldn't fall over, grabbed his shoulder bag with his left hand so it didn't slide off his shoulder, and held out his right. "Hello. Spanner said you'd be here when I arrived. I might be a little late, actually. I – uh – decided against riding the shuttle bus."

She shook his hand, her lips adding a wry twist to her smile.

"I don't blame you. It's not far to walk from the station – and I won't ask if you found the hotel okay because … here you are, and it is rather obvious when you get off the train. Good journey?"

"Not bad. Glad to get here, though."

"And we're glad to have you. Why don't we get you booked into your room, let you have a moment or two to unwind, and then maybe we can go over your schedule for the weekend?" She reached to grab his suitcase, and waved him in the direction of the reception desk. "We've got ops set up in the library, so we're using the Chapel for our Green room. We can meet up there later?"

He nodded. "Sounds good to me. If I knew where any of those places were, of course."

"We have a map," she said with confidence. "And it's not that hard, I promise. Listen, we've put you in one of the executive suites – guest of honour and all that – so you'll be up on the second floor of the main house, rather than out in the extension. If that's okay? We thought you wouldn't mind being away from hoi polloi … not to mention the room parties, and the ghosts … "

"Ghosts?" he queried, wondering if she meant that figuratively or literally. She laughed.

"Well, I've never seen one, but – there are rumours about this place. Not in the main house for some reason, but – well, it was co-opted as a military hospital in both wars and apparently got turned into an asylum in the early fifties, so the extension … has *traces*. Or so they say. Of course, if you do see someone wandering around in a white sheet this weekend it will probably be one of us…"

He grinned, knowing what she meant. "Con-goer or

committee?" he asked, and she laughed.

"Both of the above. Although I don't think there's any one on the committee who can walk through walls ... um, Jessica?" She waved to catch the attention of one of the women behind the desk. The young woman waved back, an *'in a minute'* gesture, since she was in the middle of getting signatures and handing out keys. "When you're done there, can you register Dr Holland for me? He's in 201. Room and breakfast on the con account..." She paused to give him a questioning look. "You do know you'll need to pay for extras, right? Not that we want to be mean, but – "

"No, no, that's fine." The invitation, and the subsequent discussions, had been very clear about that, right from the start. He was well aware that these sort of fan-run conventions – as opposed to the highly commercial, professional events, where attendance was about using known names and big stars to bring in crowds and part them from their money – tended to be cash strapped and working to a tight budget. Hiring the Grange for the weekend was not going to be cheap. He'd been attending this kind of thing on his own account for years, and he wasn't about to turn into a nightmarish diva and make nonsensical demands like having fresh roses in his room, or insisting on a particular kind of tea. They were paying for his room – which made a nice change – and he didn't mind digging into his own pocket to cover the incidentals.

Especially since he could be pretty sure there'd be any number of fans offering to buy him a drink. Or two.

"Good." Abigail looked relieved. "Great. Now – you stay here and wait for Jessica, and I'll go grab you a map. Back in a mo'."

She hurried away, heading towards the now cloth-covered trestle tables over by the inner doors. Marcus let his shoulder bag slide to the floor and leaned against the desk, taking a moment or two to study the current inhabitants of the lobby.

There were the hotel staff, of course, and the new arrivals, toting cases and carrying bags. There were also a number of what had to be scurrying gophers and con volunteers, some dealers – or possibly exhibiting artists – lugging boxes and dragging loaded trolleys, and a scattering of other 'already booked in and getting into con mode' attendees. They were, it had to be said an eclectic mix. Con-goers came in all sorts of shapes, sizes, colours and ages. Well, not *all* colours – no green or blue – since this was primarily a literary convention, a Dark Fantasy and Horrorcon, rather than one aimed at SF and comic fans. But young faces mingled with the middle-aged, the mature, and even the elderly; their skin tones ranged from washed out white to ebony dark, with tones of tan and several other ethnic shades in between.

He smiled as he spotted a cosplayer or two, clad confidently in character, and then widened it as he realised some of the others were draped in less obvious, but equally well crafted, hall costumes. He spotted three people in high necked Gothic gowns, a couple of leather jackets with steam punk accessories, and one really good Victorian Gentleman, in a fitted morning coat and an embroidered waistcoat.

There was even someone looking suspiciously like Nettlestone – or at least like his picture on the UK cover of *Beneath the City Walls*. Marcus currently owned the original, although he'd never had the heart to point out – to the publisher *or* the artist – that while their version of his determined hero looked fairly dashing waving his revolver about, *his* version never carried, let alone used a gun of any sort, relying on blessed steel, a silver dagger, and a hastily muttered cantrip or two.

Jackson Hobbs, on the other hand…

"Dr Holland?" Jessica had finished with her other customer and had moved across to check him in, a professional smile on her face, and a hint of weariness in her eyes. He didn't blame her. Her job was not the most exciting in the world, and she was going to have to deal with a lot more people before her shift was over. "Room 201? If you would just sign here, and here..." She pushed the relevant form in his direction and he took the proffered pen with a wry smile. She might be bored with requesting signatures, but he was going to get *very* bored providing his all weekend.

The pseudo-Victorian Gentleman had made his way across the lobby – and round the back of the reception desk for some reason. Marcus had assumed the man was a con-attendee, but the way the staff reacted to his presence suggested otherwise. Perhaps he always dressed like that. The antique mien certainly suited him; he had that lean and hungry look that Dickens would have loved, whippet thin and wiry with it, as if he lived on short rations while swearing blind that he ate nothing but a strict and healthy diet. Even his hairstyle looked authentic: it had a straggly, slicked down look, long from the crown, but cut short at ear lobe level. There was also a slight suggestion of longer sideburns feathering his chin and a stately hint of grey at his temples. He looked appropriately dignified and imbued with authority – but while his air of smug and overly-confident presence suited his current get-up to a tee, something about it made Marcus' hackles start to rise. His behaviour didn't help much, either. He paused to loom over the shoulder of the other young lady on duty, standing close enough behind her to ring minor alarm bells for anyone who'd recently had anti-harassment training. The way he reached to lay his hand over hers didn't look threatening, but it was a little too intimate for comfort; Marcus might have given him benefit of the doubt and assumed a close relationship between the two, but he could swear he saw the young woman shiver. "Don't forget to cross-check the card numbers, Alice," the man told her in a soft, dry voice. Somewhere, on some small mental notepad that kept track of that kind of thing, Marcus's inner writer scrawled: *He had a voice grown dusty with age and death...*

"Here you go!" Abigail was back, waving what was clearly a program booklet at him. "Maps in the middle, and these are the up to date times for interviews and panels. Main program will happen in the Ballroom – the chapel's at the far end of that – and all the other big rooms – Art Show, Dealers, ops – are next to it on the ground floor. That's on the garden side of the house, just along from the dining room and the breakfast bar. The secondary program streams are all in smaller rooms on the first floor, and the fan room, the games room, and the workshops are on the ground floor of the extension. Just behind the lifts."

"Right," Marcus nodded bemusedly. He'd barely taken in a third of that. Behind the desk, the slender gentleman in the morning coat had let Alice get back to work, moving across to put his hand on Jessica's shoulder so that he could peer over the other one to examine her work. "I'm sure I'll get the hang of it. By Monday," he added, and Abigail laughed. Out of the corner of his eye he saw Jessica's lips purse in a moment of annoyance – one she hastily suppressed.

"Excuse me, Mr Namon," she said politely. "But Dr Holland is waiting for his key."

"Ah, of course." Namon smiled and straightened, loosening his grip on the young woman's shoulder and dipping his head towards Marcus in polite acknowledgment. "Our Guest of Honour. Welcome to Westeringford, Dr Holland. I hope you enjoy your stay here."

"I'm sure I will." He took the proffered key, smiled at Jessica, nodded to Namon, and then turned to follow Abigail as she brightly announced: "Lifts are this way!"

He took two steps, then he paused, turned, and stepped back, reaching to pick up his shoulder bag from its spot on the floor. As he straightened up, he saw Namon had also turned and was reaching for the edge of one of the huge mirrors; it opened outwards, revealing itself to be the door to a small office, into which the man then vanished, the mirror closing behind him with a soft and subtle click. Jessica's reflection swung into view as the door closed, revealing his earlier guess about the hotel's uniform skirt to be an accurate one. He threw her a little grin of triumph that she had no way of interpreting, and hurried after Abigail, ignoring his inner writer's voice as it stuttered to a startled halt.

What on **earth**, it was busy trying to ask him, *was wrong with* **that** *picture* ...

Chapter Three

He'd had a vague idea of what his room might be like when Abigail called it an 'executive suite.' Something, perhaps, with a smallish sitting room alongside a slightly larger than usual bedroom. Maybe even a bathroom that had a reasonable sized bath in it, instead of a narrow coffin tub under an equally narrow shower. Not that finding a coffin sized – or shaped – tub would surprise him much in this hotel; it would fit well with the grotesquely Gothic exterior and the hints at a history that had 'lunatic asylum' in it. He half expected to find a space furnished in early *Addams Family* waiting for him.

The artistry of the bedroom doors should have given him a better hint about what was to come. They were carved and decorated like the rest of the hotel decor, although the quality of that ornamentation had decidedly improved by the time he'd found his way to the second floor of the main house. The lifts had been housed in the extension, which apparently had four floors where the main house had three – so using them to get to the second floor of the house meant you had to go *up* to floor three, and then descend either a long shallow slope or a short flight of stairs, both of which brought you down half the distance between floor three and two in the extension … and spilled you out into a wide and beautifully carpeted corridor. This led, in turn, to an equally beautifully carpeted and circular rotunda. From that a wide spiral staircase made its way back down to the first floor; above it curved an overarching glass and steel dome that should have been flooding the entire space with afternoon sunlight.

Should have been. But – like every other window he'd seen so far, the glass dome was firmly covered with shutters, and the stairs were lit only by a single, pendulous crystal chandelier, its softer light reflected in yet more mirrors spaced along the passageways. In between them were the bedroom doors, each one delicately decorated with a border of carved and gilded leaves and flowers. They were, Marcus suspected, the original fittings, since they – like the decorations on the dome and the banisters on the spiral staircase – were far more subdued and tasteful than the brash extravagance he'd seen in the lobby. The mirrors here were older, too, with their backings of softly crazed silvering shivering the reflections within them into a slightly softer focus than the polished gleam of modern ones.

That thought would return to haunt him later. For now he merely noted it, far more focused on finding his room within the hotel's maze than worrying about – whatever it was that was currently worrying him.

Room 201 – the number painted on the door was in the same colour and font as the number on the key – was one of the two rooms at the furthest possible distance from the lifts; right at the very end of the passageway on what Abigail had called 'the garden side of the house.' That meant that it sat somewhere above the ballroom, and probably also meant not wanting to go to bed too early on Saturday night, since there was almost undoubtedly going to be some sort of entertainment going on below him. He wasn't particularly bothered about that; he wanted time to catch up with Cordell, along with others of his peers who were also listed as appearing on panels over the weekend. As the hotel was some distance from the Westeringford suburb, the management had agreed to not only provide a range of cheap meals for attendees who didn't want to eat in the main restaurant, but to allow one of the fans to bring in stock for a Real Ale bar and to extend their license to allow him to serve across the entire weekend. He was quite looking forward to downing a pint of Goblin Knobbler – or something like it – later that evening.

The key was an old fashioned *key*, rather than an electronic key card, although he'd seen those being issued for the rooms in the extension. It turned easily in the lock, and the door opened with a slight creak. Two steps later he was standing, not in an executive suite, but a palatial one.

It was a corner suite, with a large, impressively furnished sitting room on one side, and the door to the bedroom – and he hoped, the bathroom, on the other. The space was huge, but rather gloomy, lit mostly by two uplighters, one above each doorframe. One or two smaller lamps jutted out from the walls, but none of them were lit. There was also a ceiling rose, but the room wasn't tall enough to accommodate a chandelier, so the only thing it supported was a smoke alarm, its red light blinking balefully in the dim light. Two massive window bays dominated the otherwise square space he'd entered, set at right angles to each other. Thick, heavy curtains were hanging across both sets of windows, a cascade of dark gold velvet that obscured the glass and came draped with yards of twisted gold cords that dripped with a mass of extravagant tassels. A well-polished, antique table stood in the middle of the room, and a matching desk – gilded and inlaid with assorted coloured woods – occupied the wall beside the door. There were three deep set and well-padded arm chairs grouped round a second, low table with a marble chess board set into it, and several more slender and spindly-legged chairs standing around like guests at a swanky soiree, pretending to be Chippendale furniture. The carpet was thick and luxurious, all the cushions appeared to be hand embroidered, and the various paintings that decorated the walls seemed to be originals, rather than prints.

Marcus wasn't entirely sure if he were supposed to *use* the room, or simply stand there and admire it, the way he would a museum exhibit.

There was, however, no red velvet rope to keep him – or any other casual visitor – from venturing further, so he made his way across the room and looked through the side door. The bed wasn't quite a four-poster, although it had pretensions of being one, with sculptured posts at one end and an abandonment of carved acanthus leaves on the headboard at the other. The huge TV, the side table piled with information booklets, and the fire drill instructions hanging next to the bathroom door helped make the space more 'hotel room' and less *Downton Abbey* set, although the chaise longue he found in the bathroom definitely pushed it back towards the surreal. He dropped his suitcase onto the low ottoman at the foot of the bed, dumped his shoulder bag next to it, and went back out to the lounge. He found a bank of power sockets beside the desk, and a sheet with the WiFi instructions on it on the desk itself, so he left the laptop bag on the seat of the nearest Chipendale-ish chair and went to pull the curtains, intending to let a little light into the somewhat gloomy room.

It took a little fumbling with the cords before he found the right one and pulled, hard. The velvet swung back, but there was no immediate flood of light. Instead he found himself staring at the inside of yet more sturdy shutters.

What is it with this place? he wondered. Birmingham zoning regulations hadn't included blackout requirements since the end of the last big war. A bit more fumbling around the window frames located a little handle which – turned with all the effort required for a mechanism that clearly hadn't been used for years – managed to crank back the shutters and reveal the sun.

Well, reveal the rain, actually. The threat of unsettled weather had turned into a miserable drizzle, little droplets landing to fizzle against the now exposed glass before slowly sliding down into the guttering.

For all that, the illumination in the room improved dramatically. It improved even more when he'd tugged back the curtains and cranked back the shutters on the second window. The first had revealed the vista of a landscaped garden, with hints of formal terracing descending away from the house before merging into a wider view of less formal trees and rolling lawns. That ended – somewhat abruptly – in the sweep of a high wall, and beyond it, a tumble of houses and more industrial buildings, the suburb clearly having crept up over the years to devour much of the Grange's original land.

The other window looked out onto the roof of what had to be the chapel. Weathered gargoyles and other grotesque statues crouched along the edges of a boarded over and plastic-clad arched roof, a single, weatherworn cross emerging from one end of the structure and an equally corroded weathervane – shaped something like a fish, or a whale – from the other. Rusty scaffolding poles poked up on either side of the building, suggesting either an abandoned attempt at restoration or some kind of emergency stabilisation. It couldn't be too insecure, since Abigail had mentioned using the chapel as the con green room, but it did suggest that the hotel might not be making the kind of money it needed to keep itself in good repair.

Looking back into the room merely reinforced that opinion. In daylight, the palatial splendour turned out to be somewhat faded and worn. The paintings were starting to look dingy, patinated with age. The carpet showed signs of wear, and the armchairs – while clean – had faint stains on their upholstery. It definitely wasn't Versailles, no matter how much it pretended to be – but it was a good step up from basic Travel-Lodge, and a long way from some of the student accommodation he'd had to endure at certain academic conferences he could mention.

He sighed, stretched, and went to prepare himself for the rest of the day.

– * –

Half an hour later, a much more refreshed and immediately recognisable Marcus Holland could be found striding along the second floor corridors, heading towards the spiral stairs. He'd made himself a cup of tea – a passable brew, with decent milk, thank you Westeringford Grange – and got changed, shucking his day-to-day sweatshirt and jeans to don his usual convention gear. He wasn't entirely sure when the habit had started, but he'd been 'dressing' for these events long before he'd been published, let alone gained any notoriety for it. The outfits had become slightly more elaborate over the years, but the basics were still the same: dark grey slacks and sturdy trainers; crisp white shirt, complete with silver armband rings pushed up on either arm; and the fancy waistcoat, which seemed to be getting fancier and fancier every year. He'd started off buying them in second hand shops, and at flea markets. He still did that sometimes, if he saw one he liked the look of. But then artists and crafters had begun offering to design for him, and he'd taken up the offer more than once. He made a point of paying good money for them, rather than accepting them as gifts, and he'd rarely been disappointed. In fact he now had so many that, whenever he was asked to help conduct a fan auction, he'd started to donate one in order to support whichever charity they had chosen.

If there was a fan after the one he'd chosen for this weekend though, they were going to have to wait a long time. Mazzy had designed it for him, and Lilith had made all the accoutrements – the buttons and the charms, and all the other bits and pieces. Neither of them had seen it finished yet – there'd been a very skilled lady by the name of Alison who'd done the embroidery and assembled the garment – and he was looking forward to seeing his friends' reactions when they finally got to see the fruits of their labours.

It was swirled in silver, smoke, and steel grey, with rune engraved buttons and tiny magical symbols stitched along the borders. It had a pocket on the right hand front, just the right size to hold his 'Ticky' – the sturdy steam-punk pocket watch that he'd been presented with at the last Steamwheeler con in Western Australia – and a second, slim compartment on the inside left that took both his wallet and his phone without spoiling the outer line. He loved it. He felt good in it, and hopefully he looked good in it too, although he really wasn't much of a judge of that.

That used to be as far as he went – a fashion statement, rather than a hall costume or a cosplay – but these days he'd added one more accessory to complete the look.

Jackson Hobbs' bowler hat.

He'd never wear the thing anywhere *but* a convention, of course. The rakish look it gave him would not go down well in staid, or even in revolutionary academic circles. He might – one day – be persuaded to wear it for a TV interview or in a documentary exploring his work, but since neither of those ideas were likely to happen in the near future, he was sticking to a strict 'con-wear only' plan. He'd been given it – by a fan – a few years before, and had worn it that first time, mostly because Cordell had dared him to do so, and – being drunk at the time – he had foolishly agreed. After that, it had become a tradition, an expectation from his fans – and others – and a means of separating out this particular aspect of his life from all the rest.

After all, he might – *might* – have been known to wear one of his waistcoats to a family wedding. But he'd have never, ever, worn the hat.

It was working man's headgear, sturdy enough to be stood on – at a pinch – and solid enough to use for knocking on doors or knocking *out* thugs, henchmen, and creatures of questionable humanity. Not that Marcus had done any of those things, of course, but Jackson often had, and – should he ever get round to writing more of the man's adventures – probably would do so again. He'd also used the small and battered raven's feather tucked into the band to scrawl a hasty counter to a spell or two, and the band itself really did have the names of seven goddesses inscribed on it – although not in blood, and in enochian script, rather than the more Lovecraftian *lost runes of the elder-tongue* that he'd invented for Jackson on one bored and rainy day.

It sat quite well on his unruly mops of curls, concealing some of the burgeoning gray that Molly loved and Beverley was always telling him to do something about. He'd threatened to shave the whole lot off, once, and she'd spluttered and protested about the idea for days.

He paused, just before he reached the rotunda, to carefully adjust the angle of the hat in the nearest mirror. He was about to make an entrance, which would either be a signature moment, or something completely ignored by busy people intent on other things. In some ways, being ignored would be better, but he was supposed to be on stage this weekend. The title 'Guest of Honour' carried a certain number of obligations, after all.

"I trust your room is comfortable, Dr Holland?"

He jumped in startlement, turning to discover the Victorian Gentleman standing – not that far away – in the Rotunda. He'd been nowhere in sight a moment ago – not even in the mirror, which surely he must have passed … Marcus shook his head, and made an effort to paste a friendly smile on his face. The man must have come up the stairs while his back was turned, that was all.

"Yes. Thank you. Very comfortable. A little ostentatious, but…"

"The hotel was refurbished to reflect the house in its heyday," Namon smiled. It didn't quite reach his eyes, but was disarming enough for Marcus think that his earlier impression of the man might have been a little hasty. "The original 'Lord of Westeringford' was quite an ostentatious man. His son…" the smile grew a little wider, "was a much more sensible character. Saved the family fortune after his father nearly squandered it away. He's the reason so much of the original house has survived."

"It's um…" Marcus glanced around the rotunda, considering the decorations with an appraising eye. "… quite impressive. I'd open a few of the shutters though; let in a little light. If this was built when they only had candles, it would have been designed to make the most of the sun."

Namon's smile dimmed a little. "Alas," he said, "what was *done* and what is now necessary can be a long way apart. Sunlight," he explained, "damages our antiques, and fades our furnishings. We act to preserve our interests and protect our investments; I am very… insistent on that."

"Oh." There had been a hint of supercilious admonishment in the man's tones, and it made Marcus feel about two feet tall. "Well, that makes sense. I suppose. I – uh – don't want to sound rude, but – you are?"

A look of momentary chagrin chased across the man's face, quickly replaced by the return of that well practiced smile. "I'm sorry," he apologised. "We haven't been formally introduced, have we. I am – Isiah Namon. Owner and manager of the Grange. Your host for the weekend, you could say. Mr O'Toole's told me so much about you I – I'm afraid I assumed familiarity. Please forgive me for my forwardness."

Wow. Namon didn't only look the part – he'd got the speech and the manners to match.

"No worries. Spanner sent me so much stuff – about the con, and the hotel, and things – I must have missed … *wait* a minute!" Revelation dawned, and he mentally kicked himself for not remembering earlier. "You're Spanner's vampire, aren't you. He told me he'd found someone to … of *course.* I'm sorry, I should have remembered … you look amazing."

"Thank you." Namon bowed, a brief and amused dip of his head. If he'd been wearing a hat, he'd have probably doffed it.

"No – " Marcus was laughing at himself. He'd totally

forgotten Daniel's daft idea – and he *had* thought it daft when he'd been told about it – but here was the villain himself, looking every inch the relic of a long-gone time, and perfectly cast to lurk at the edges of the event and add a soupcon of wary terror to the whole event. "Thank *you* for doing this. I wasn't convinced, but – are you really the owner of the hotel?"

"I am." Namon inclined his head again, amusement dancing in his eyes. "And it's my pleasure. So nice to become involved in an event like this. Usually I'm just standing on the sidelines, observing life, rather than … participating in it. I do – " He paused and smiled, a little more genuinely this time. " – come out of the coffin, every Halloween? We have such lovely young people come to enjoy the atmosphere. I do my best to make it – an experience for them."

"Well," Marcus held out his hand. "It's good to meet you Mr Namon. And I'll try not to give your secret away … too soon."

Namon chuckled softly. "Just as well," he said, grasping the hand with his own and giving it a firm shake. "Because otherwise I would have to kill you, wouldn't I?"

His grip was firm and confident, and the impression of long and bony fingers lingered in Marcus' hand after they let go. The man had to be an incredible actor: the subtle hint of menace in the remark was hard to shake. It was meant – he knew – as a joke. But, just for a moment, an icy chill had crawled up his arm and down between his shoulder blades.

"Don't do that," he laughed, a little uncomfortably. "Spanner needs me to present the awards on Sunday. Not to mention all the other things he's got me down to do."

"I'm looking forward to it," Namon assured him. "You'll see me around, Dr Holland. And do let me know if you have a problem with the room, or anything. I like to take good care of my guests."

"I will." Marcus started to watch him walk away, heading into the corridor towards the lifts, then looked down as his watch announced the time with a quiet *ching*. Four quiet *chings*, in fact.

"Damn," he muttered. Abigail would be waiting for him, and he'd managed to leave his program book back in the room. There was no time to go back for it. He had a vague idea of where the chapel was, but – if he got lost – he'd have to ask someone to point him back in the right direction. Namon would know … he looked up, to find the man had seemingly vanished. Into one of the bedrooms, he guessed. He was the manager. He probably had a master key. *Just have to wing it,* he decided, and turned to hasten down the stairs.

The spiral spilled him out at the back of a wide mezzanine; there was a built-in bar area on one side, some trestle tables being set up on the other, and the rest of the space was filled with a scattering of tables and low, comfy chairs. Artworks and antiques provided discrete decoration, along with a few tubs of greenery and a few floor to ceiling columns, which were probably less about period style and a lot more about holding up the floor above. Several people in Coffincon tee-shirts were putting up posters on doors, and a few other people were sitting about, in among the pot plants and the pottery.

He spotted Cordell holding court with a group of fans and fellow authors, and he waved, earning himself a flurry of waves in return.

"I'll save you a seat," Cordell called as Marcus charged past. "And a pint!" His friend's words followed him down the stairs into the lobby, and he hoped the man had caught his vague gesture of acknowledgment, since he really didn't have time to stop and chat. There must have been another train come in, as the lobby was filled with a swirl of new arrivals; he negotiated gaggles of people and suitcases with muttered apologies, loped past the now operational registration desk, and turned right under the stairs, following the sign that said 'Ballroom and Dining Room'.

Three hasty steps later he tripped and went sprawling, cushioned in his downfall by the thickness of the carpet and a hasty grab at the pile of boxes that seemed to be in his way. They also went sprawling, the top one falling open to spill a glistening of assorted plastic bags across the floor.

"Bugger," he said, with feeling. The tumble had winded him, and he stayed where he was for a moment, trying to regain his breath.

"Are you all right?"

The voice was soft, melodious, and – on first impression – decidedly female. He looked up, his eyes rising from the elegant, sandaled feet of his inquisitor, up the flounce of a gypsy skirt, to meet a pair of dark brown eyes smiling down at him from the frame of a very attractive face. Her wide sensuous lips were curled with amusement, and her skin was as warm and dark as her eyes, her African heritage written with confident surety across every curve of her features.

"Uh…" He thought about it for a moment. His shin was throbbing and his arm was protesting the way he was lying on it, but he didn't seem to have broken anything. Other than his sense of dignity, that is. "I think so. Would you – um – help me, here? Please?" he added, with a hint of wounded chagrin. He waved a vague hand in her direction and she laughed.

"With pleasure," she announced, reaching down to help him get up. Her hands were warm, and her grip was surprisingly strong; he was back on his feet almost before he realised it. "Alright?" She let go for a moment, then returned to steady him, holding out his hat as she did so. "I think this is yours."

"Thank you," he breathed, retrieving his bowler and taking a moment or two to consider his rescuer. She was slightly shorter than he was, but not by much. Her figure was more athletic than slender; she had curves in all the right places, and her arms – bare but for a cascade of bangles that jangled a little as she moved – were toned and muscular, as if she worked out on a regular basis. Her hair was short, dark, and had the same hint of curl as his own. It was cut and styled in a way that perfectly framed her face.

Her con badge claimed her name was Ashera, and identified her as one of the dealers. Which probably explained all the boxes.

"You're welcome," she said. "It's been a long time since a man has thrown himself at my feet like that."

He grimaced. "Sorry. I was hurrying and I..." He suddenly realised that he'd been responsible for scattering her stock over the floor, and started to drop down, intending to help gather it up. "Heavens – let me help you with this..."

Ashera caught his arm, halting his descent. "Don't worry about it, Dr Holland. There's no harm done, and I can manage. You need to get to your meeting."

"Yes. Yes, of course, but..."

"No buts," she told him firmly. "You asked for help, and I have provided it. I will go *on* providing it as long as it's required – which, right now, means that I need to get *you* to your meeting. Because you're late, am I right?"

"Right," he agreed reluctantly, carefully stepping away from the flood of bags and bracelets. It looked as if she made – or at least sold – jewellery, although her work was nothing like Lilith's intricate steel and silver ware. There were glimmering beads, bone white carved pieces, and the deep gleam of gold lying among the sprawl of cellophane and paper. There was also – he noticed – a carved scarab beetle pinning her con badge in place, and two more, lapis lazuli blue, and clinging, one to each ear. "Well – maybe I can buy you a drink, later. I owe you that much, at least."

"That would be wonderful. Now – *go.*"

He went, sent on his way down the corridor with an encouraging push. Others had stopped to help Ashera gather up her stock, but he still felt guilty at leaving her to deal with his mess. At least his shin had stopped throbbing and the pins and needles in his arm were beginning to fade. He'd have to be more careful: he could have done himself a lot more damage than he had going over like that, and the last thing a con needed was having their guest of honour rushed to A&E simply because he hadn't been watching where he put his feet.

The corridor turned sharply left as it reached the Dining room – which, of course, turned out to house the hotel restaurant – then, after a short stretch turned again, first right, then left, widening out to become an impressive gallery, in which a number of large ancestral type pictures were hanging. On his right hand side, three large and imposing pairs of double doors were spaced evenly along the length of the hall, some of the paintings that hung between them being vast wall-sized canvases of battles and historic moments. On the other side there were several more doors, and – at the end nearest the restaurant – a glass partition, which separated out a cafe style area with what looked like a breakfast bar at the back of it. The big, double doors opposite had a large poster stuck on them, declaring that what lay beyond was 'The Ballroom. Formal gowns are optional.' Below that was a list headed 'Saturday' with a timetable of events on it, starting with the opening ceremony at 10am, and ending with the Midnight Masque that began at eight with the grand reveal planned – unsurprisingly enough – for midnight.

"No entry before tomorrow – oh, hello, Dr Holland." The bored gopher on guard at the door straightened himself self-consciously as Marcus approached and tried to look conscientious. "Abigail said you'd arrived. Do you want to get through to the green room?"

"Yes please – thank you, Barry." He'd always appreciated

having name badges to refer to, whether it was at cons like this, or at other more formal events and conferences. Barry smiled.

"No problem. Just through here – " He pushed at the heavy door, opening a gap just about wide enough for Marcus to enter. "– and it's right up at the end, under the Clock. Watch out for the cables – the tech guys are still setting up for sound tests."

"Will do," Marcus assured him with an ironic grin. He'd already had one fall today. He wasn't going to make *that* mistake again. He slipped under Barry's arm, through the gap – and stepped into the ballroom.

Which was just as overblown, overwhelming, and over the top as the rest of the place. It was not as big as some halls he'd been in – the one they used for graduation ceremonies back at the University was much larger, for a start. But it made up for its compactness in a myriad of ways, from the line of curving archways that ran down either side, supporting an upper gallery and sectioning off the doors and the terrace windows from the main floor, to the elegant and equally arched ceiling that rose above them. His room wasn't just over the ballroom, it was *right* over the ballroom; he wouldn't be entirely surprised to find there was a hidden staircase in the ornate corner turret, leading directly from the gallery and up into his room.

He might even look for it when he got back up there. It would be quicker than taking the lift.

On the wall at the far end – past the dangle of yet more crystal chandeliers – and right under his temporary sitting room – there was the Clock. It was no wonder Barry gave it an audible capital letter; it was so large and imposing that it really belonged in a church tower somewhere. Maybe it had come from one, originally. It was certainly set in a heavy, wooden frame, and didn't look out of place above the stone archway that framed the chapel door. Its hands, and the raised numerals around the dial, were gilded and gleaming. The plate behind them looked like polished marble, and the frame around it was decorated with a parade of heraldic animals. There was a stylised sun placed above the twelve, and the moon, in its three phases, was set at the other quarter points.

It was also – he tugged out his pocket watch to check – running ten minutes late, which meant...

The minute hand clicked over to point directly upwards. There was a soft whirring noise, and then the clock struck, sending four momentary chimes ringing out into the room. It was an unexpectedly gentle sound. Marcus, who had braced himself for a discordant clang, relaxed with small smile of delight.

"Lovely, isn't it?" One of the techs – who was halfway up a ladder and wrestling to connect a cable to one hanging down from the gallery – paused to throw him an equally delighted grin. "Apparently there's a set of tubes – like those wind chimes things – hanging behind it in the chapel roof? The striking hammer moves round every quarter hour so you get four different notes at different times of the day. Clever stuff."

"It certainly is. Do you know if Abigail's still in the chapel?"

"Yeah. I think she's briefing the timekeepers. You looking for her?"

"She's expecting me."

The tech jabbed his finger towards the stone arch and the waiting wooden door within it. "Thataway," he advised and went back to wrestling with his cables.

Marcus went 'thataway.' The doorway led to the Chapel: a space that, while not quite as Gothically overblown as he'd been expecting, still managed to impress. It was, like the ballroom that fronted it, two storeys from floor to ceiling. Unlike the ballroom, however it was principally stone built, a construction of rounded pillars, carved niches, and arching curves. The floor was paved with what looked like genuine, rather than pseudo medieval tiles, and the outer walls looked to be of a similar age. Halfway up, the supporting pillars became fluted arches, underpinning the roof. This, in turn, had been cut away to make room for a square based cupola, although the final design was difficult to make out, as the whole upper half was draped in thick velvet curtains. More of them hung across the walls, turning what should have been quiet, contemplative space, into something vaguely theatrical in nature. Big, twisted top tassels hung from long braided ropes that looped across the curtains and wrapped themselves around big metal hooks, sunk into the stones. Only the lower half of the space where the Altar must have been set was clearly visible – and the back of that was covered with plain wooden panelling, rather than the painted icons that must have originally taken pride of place. There were several hanging lanterns, lighting up the space, but no lectern, or pews, or any other church furniture or fittings. Instead there were a few trestle tables and several fold-up chairs scattered around the floor. In the middle of all that was Abigail, who was busy handing out timing sheets and room numbers to a gaggle of chattering gophers, half of whom lost their voices as soon as they realised he was also in the room. He ignored the slightly awed glances and found himself a seat by the nearest table. Abigail merely rolled her eyes and came over to hand him a sheet of his own.

"Thanks for coming, Dr Holland. That's your schedule, but don't worry too much about remembering it. Pete here has volunteered to keep track of it for you – he'll go through it with you now, and if you've any questions, just ask me."

'Pete' was a young man in his mid-twenties who wouldn't have looked out of place among Marcus' students. He sat down on the other wide of the table from him and smiled, a little nervously.

Marcus smiled back. "Hi, Pete. I'm Marcus. Don't worry. I don't eat gophers. Not even the ones charged to get me to particular places at particular times. In fact, I appreciate them. Greatly." He glanced down at the sheet in his hand; Abigail had kindly, and very carefully, marked each of his items with a bright yellow highlighter pen. "You keep me on schedule, and I'll try to behave. Most of the time," he added, and grinned.

Chapter Four

As it turned out, there was only one thing he was scheduled to do that evening – and that was to have dinner with the Con committee, so that was hardly going to be a chore. The stuff for Saturday wasn't that onerous either – he wasn't expected to do much more than turning up for the opening ceremony, being present for the first of his two signing sessions, and then joining a panel in the afternoon. So that would give him plenty of time to visit Mazzy in the Art Show, catch up with Lilith and see what the other dealers had on offer, and generally hang around and be sociable all day. Sunday would be slightly harder work; the second signing session in the morning, another panel, and then his Guest slot in the afternoon, from two to three. After that would be the awards, a short break to allow buyers to collect the art they'd successfully acquired in the auction and those less successful to make one last visit to the Dealers' Room, and finally the closing ceremony at five o'clock.

After which everyone could go home, vow 'never again', and then remember that they'd already booked for next year.

Rinse, repeat, and re-run, at several events across the country, and throughout the year.

He didn't think he'd ever be able to explain – to friends, colleagues, even a therapist or two – quite why going to these sort of things helped keep him both grounded and sane.

He'd certainly never been able to explain it to Beverly. Although he did have hopes that – one day – Molly might understand.

Pete wasn't due to be on duty until the following morning, so they agreed a time to meet after breakfast, and Marcus headed back to his room, remembering that he had to look through the funding bid, and determined to get it out of the way before the weekend monopolised his time. He paused on the mezzanine to tell Cordell he'd join him at the bar after dinner, paused a second time to look over the almost assembled Real Ale bar – the barrels now stacked behind or standing on the white draped trestle tables – and then headed for the foot of the spiral staircase, smiling and nodding at various friends and acquaintances as he passed them.

The last of these – friend, rather than mere acquaintance – was busy navigating her powered wheelchair down the lower corridor, probably on her way to the bar from the lift.

"Hey, Mary," he smiled, stepping over to greet her. She smiled and quickly shifted the wheelchair into its parking mode so she could let go of the controls and throw her arms wide in welcome.

"Marcus!" she carolled brightly, breaking into a wide grin. He grinned back and bent to reciprocate the proffered hug. He had a lot of admiration for Mary, who never let the little – or even some of the big – things slow her down. "Let me look at you," she commanded, pushing him out to arm's length so she could admire his new waistcoat. "Niiiice. Very nice. That a new one?"

"Mumhuh." He sat himself on the nearby stair so they could converse without him needing to loom over her. "Mazzy's design. She hasn't seen it yet."

"Oh, she'll love it. *I* love it. So – how've you been?"

"Not bad." He ran a quick mental check: they'd last seen each other at Eastercon earlier in the year, so she was reasonably up to date with his news. "Work is work and – Francis is pushing for another book. Or two."

"Same old, same old, then? We gonna see more of Jackson this year? Other than his hat?" she teased. Marcus sighed.

"I don't know. Maybe. Maybe not. Can't write a book that … isn't there."

"It'll come." She sounded a lot more confident about that

than he was. "You'll see. One of these days, right when you least expect it, Ned Landers is going to wake up inside your head and start dictating a horrifying tale of danger and death and insidious evil ... "

"Did that in book three," he reminded her. "And four." His brief, wry smile turned into another sigh. "I really don't know, Mary. I don't feel like there's anything left for me to tell."

She reached out and patted his arm in sympathy. "That's probably because you're trying too hard," she advised. "You know how it is. If you can't make something work by charging it head on, then you just have to figure out another way. That's how I do it."

He curled his hand over hers, returning her gesture with a moment's acknowledgment of his own. Her fingers were gnarled and bent, and they trembled under his touch. "I know. But you're Mary. You make it look easy."

"The hell it is," she snorted. "At least you understand some of it. A lot of people just don't – well – get it. Like this place – all atmosphere, set dressing, and lip service. Those main stairs? They're big enough to take a chair sized stair lift, but ... noo. Folk like me have to go all the way out to the lifts, and all the way back again, just to get to the bar. I *earn* my rum and coke, mister, don't you ever think otherwise."

He squeezed her hand and let it go, knowing better than to argue with that. "I'll buy you one, later," he offered. "I've got a little work to do, and then dinner with the committee – but I'll be hanging out with Cordell this evening. Come over, and join us."

"I will." She started to curl her hand around the chair control, then paused. "Maybe this place will inspire you," she suggested. "It's calling out for a story, don't you think? An old house, filled with memories and secrets? Something *evil* lurking in its heart, like a hungry spider, drawing

63

everyone who dares to cross the threshold into its web..."

He'd have smiled at her dramatics, at the deliberate relish with which she chewed at the idea, but somehow her words had hit a nerve, sending a sudden shiver through him. The same shiver, perhaps, that had caught at him while walking up the drive, earlier.

"Don't," he managed to deflect with a weak grin. "I need story ideas. Not nightmares."

She laughed and drove away, waving at him over her should as she went. Marcus took a moment to centre himself, then stood and climbed up the stairs, trying to shake off the discomforted feeling. He wrote dark fantasy – *horror* stories – for Aradia's sake. There was no way that he should be letting an old house and a few unsettling moments spook him. Mary was right. He should be using those kind of things to inspire new work.

Not make him start looking over his shoulders at shadows ...

He pushed the matter to the back of his mind and went back to his room, dropping Jackson's hat on a side table, tugging the laptop out of its case, and spending several moments sorting out cables and checking connections. The WiFi worked on his second try – he'd mistyped the password the first time – and he linked across to the University intranet, pulled down the latest copy of the funding paper, and started working his way through it. It was just as turgid and filled with business-speak as he'd expected it to be, and he found himself procrastinating with a whole series of momentary distractions.

Six pages in, he got up to make himself a cup of tea, and drank it while wandering round the room and studying all the paintings. He paused between pages eighty-six and eighty-seven – bored with wrestling with 'public benefit' – to hang up some of his clothing in the wardrobe. He'd barely sat down again – reaching page one hundred and two – when he remembered about the potential 'secret' stair, and started to get up to look for signs of a door, somewhere in the corner between the two bays.

Stop it, he told himself severely. He was acting like one of those cartoon characters that Molly liked to watch, investigating mysteries that always turned out to have some mundane explanation. A house like this *might* have a few hidden servants' passages and well concealed doors, but he knew – more than most – that that sort of thing was usually introduced into a story to solve the writer's problems, not the architects. He also knew he was restless, and it wasn't just the tedium of the paperwork. There was something nagging at him. He didn't know what it was, and couldn't even *start* to put his finger on what had triggered it. He forced himself to go back to the desk and made a determined effort to complete the task in hand. Whatever was bothering him would just have to wait.

He waded his way through the rest of the paper, adding his comments and suggestions – the shareable ones – to the notes already on the file. There were the seeds of a good project in it somewhere, and he hoped that jumping through all these hoops might give it a chance to see daylight. Which was slowly fading into evening warmth as he typed his final comment, hit the button to save the file, and sent a note to Sharon to let her know he'd done what she'd asked.

Then he shut down the laptop, grabbed for his hat, and went to dinner.

– * –

Dinner was fun, but maybe not quite as relaxing and enjoyable as he might have hoped it to be. For one thing, the atmosphere was far more subdued than usual. That was partly due to the general atmosphere in the restaurant, which had an old-style, 'best-behaviour' vibe to it – all silver service, deferential waiters and the sense of requiring

decorum along with your dining. But the con committee –
usually, at this point, pumped full of expectation and walking
the inevitable knife-edge between the sense of 'this is going
to be great' and 'oh god, what are we doing?'– just seemed to
be drained and tired. They had been working all hours in the
past week or two, Marcus knew, but – even so, it didn't feel
right. Not for the night *before* the con.

Spanner – otherwise known as Daniel O'Toole, the con-
chairman, fanzine editor, and a long time veteran on
convention committees – seemed particularly morose. He
spoke only when directly addressed, and rarely interjected a
comment or joke, even when the opening was obvious.

Marcus even leant across at one point and asked the man if
he were all right.

Spanner sighed.

"I dunno," he admitted reluctantly. "I've been a little – off,
just recently. Tired and shivery, like I'm going down with a
bug, or something." He stabbed his fork into his steak, and
stared at it as if it concealed the secrets of the universe. "I
usually get the con-crud *after* the con," he groused, showing
a little more of his usual spark for a moment. "But – hey," he
concluded, giving himself a small shake and making an effort
to smile, "tomorrow's going to be great, right?"

"Right," the rest of the committee – plus guests – agreed,
aiming for confident certainty and not *quite* getting there.

Someone must have opened an outer door somewhere,
because the faintest shiver of colder air wafted across the
table and set the candle flames dancing. Marcus glanced
round, grateful for that brief cooling flutter; the restaurant,
with most of its tables occupied, all the windows heavy with
curtaining, and the residual warmth of a summer's day
lingering in its corners, was feeling rather stifling.

He didn't spot any open doors, but he did see Namon,
standing by the door nearest to the kitchens and deep in
conversation with one of the waiters. He had his hand on the

young man's shoulder and appeared to be offering a sympathetic ear for some personal problem or other; the waiter was slowly wringing a serving napkin between his hands.

"Hey," Marcus confided quietly, leaning in to attract Spanner's attention. "I met your 'vampire' today. He's good isn't he?'

Spanner looked briefly startled, a real 'deer in the headlights' look chasing across his face. "Vampire?" he asked a little shakily.

Marcus's amusement faded a little, his brows creasing in a baffled frown. "Yeah. Took me a moment, but I figured him out … " He nodded pointedly in the relevant direction. The waiter was nodding slowly, as if agreeing to some instruction he'd received, and his manager was smiling with obvious satisfaction. Namon glanced up as Spanner turned and smiled, tipping his head in acknowledgment of being both seen and recognised. Spanner, in turn, visibly relaxed, clearly realising what Marcus had meant. "Oh. Yes, right. Isiah introduced himself? He is good, isn't he."

"The Victorian manner was a nice touch." Marcus returned Namon's nod, and the man smiled before returning his attention to the waiter. The smile was probably meant to be a friendly one, but Namon's angled face and narrowed features lent it an oddly hungry edge.

"Georgian," Spanner corrected distractedly, still half watching the pair across the room.

"Really? I thought…"

"Oh," Spanner turned back towards him, leaning in to impart his wisdom in a conspiratorial manner. "The *costume* is Victorian. But the vampire's supposed to be Georgian. Like the house. It's all part of the schtik. Hiding in plain sight, that sort of thing."

"So," Marcus considered this slowly, "he's a Georgian vampire, disguised as a Victorian gentleman … so that he can blend in with people in the *twenty-first* century?"

Abigail, who was sitting next to Marcus on his right hand side, snorted with sudden laughter. *"No,"* she interjected warmly. "He's disguised as a Victorian gentleman so that everyone *thinks* he's into steampunk. Dressing up as Dracula would be far too obvious. Besides, the Georgians helped re-invent the Gothic, but nobody ever makes that connection. How many people know that Frankenstein was written in 1818, long before Victoria came to the throne? Well," she added, giving Marcus an apologetic look, "apart from our learned guest of honour, that is."

He laughed. "Guilty as charged," he said. "Actually, I suspect a lot of people at the con probably will know, but it's a good misdirection. If you're trying to spot a vampire that's trying to *hide*, you won't be looking for one wearing velvet and a silk cravat."

"Unless you're looking for Lestat," Babs Kincaid quipped from further down the table, and everybody laughed.

"I think it's a great idea," Armin said. He was sitting between Spanner and Helen Rowe, the con's guest artist – which had meant the Marcus hadn't seen much of Helen during the meal as she was small and petite, and Armin was … Armin – sturdy, solid and blessed with unmistakable presence. Which was probably why he'd got the job of overseeing con security. Very few people would want to argue with a six foot plus Sikh who also happened to be a police Sergeant. "I'm still not sure about asking people to give up their holy symbols, though. It feels… disrespectful to me."

"We went over all that," Spanner said firmly. "It's *not* compulsory so they'll be able to say no – just … if they don't want to hand something over, they'll be asked to not … wear it or openly flaunt it. Out of respect for our special 'guest'. Look," he went on, as Armin was still appeared to be unhappy. "It's all to help the charity, right? The Goth girls and the vampire hunters hand in their crucifixes tomorrow, and then they make a small donation to get them back on Sunday. Most of these people don't wear this stuff for religious reasons, Armin. They wear it as part of their look."

"Give it up, or cover it up," Andrew Wallace piped up from further down the table. "Come on, Armin. It's just a bit of fun. We'll even be asking the Wiccans to hand over their pentagrams, and there's no *way* I want to be upsetting the Wiccans. Because – curses and stuff, right?"

Marcus half opened his mouth to respond to that, and then closed it again, deciding that this was neither the time, nor the place to start a theological discussion about the potential consequences of negative hexing. Personally, he'd be much more worried about upsetting a practitioner of Vodun than he would a Wiccan, but the young man had a point. Besides, the idea of staging a crucifix collection in order to allow the 'genuine' vampire to move freely around the con was an inspired one. It would add veracity to the conceit, and give the attendees reasons to be talking about it. And there was no way they could collect *only* crucifixes without raising accusations of bias: the Ankh, the Star of David, Thor's Hammer, the Pentagram, even the Ying Yang symbol would have to be included. The only one they might sensibly omit from any 'symbols that might repel vampires' list would be the *Sigil of Baphomet* – and that only because, given that the Church of Satan promoted rational opposition to faith, it was not, strictly speaking, a holy symbol at all.

Acting almost without conscious thought, he took a moment to run his thumb along the line of his watch chain, and dipped his fingers into the pocket to check that his own, tiny, pentagram was still dangling at the end of it, right next to his watch. There was no way he'd give that up, since Molly had bought it for him at a Beltane Festival event they'd gone to a couple of years ago; but he could – and would – be discreet about letting it show over the next couple of days.

Dessert arrived in a flurry of assorted cheesecakes, chocolate mousse, fruit salad and meringue. Spanner, Marcus noted with slight concern, had barely touched his steak, and he pushed his portion of cheesecake away half eaten. That could simply be due to last minute nerves, since – while he'd been on con-committees before – this one was the first one where he'd stood up to be chair. But it might also suggest that he really was going down with some sort of bug or other, and if he missed some of the con because of it, that would be a shame. Nobody else seemed all that worried though; he suspected that everyone more or less expected their chair to look a little hassled and stressed the night before the con.

He thought he might feel that way, if the job were on his shoulders.

As Guest of Honour, he had a much easier job. All *he* had to do was smile, and turn up to events on time – and that was with Pete's help, and Abigail's oversight, not to mention having all the fans around to remind him of where and when he needed to be. He'd known he'd be standing at the centre of attention when he'd said 'yes' to the original invitation, and his current vague nervousness about that was merely a matter of cold feet and a natural reticence to make anything 'all about him'. But he was hoping, just a little, that this 'guess the vampire' game Spanner had come up with would provide enough distraction to let him slip out of the spotlight from time to time.

After dessert came coffee, and the conversation slid, inevitably, into the minutiae of convention planning and last minute hiccups. Helen excused herself with a warm smile and a round of good-nights, and – after a suitable moment or two – Marcus did the same. He left them discussing whether seminar room three was going to be big enough for the panel on 'Outer Beauties and Inner Monsters,' and made his back to the main stairs, in search of Cordell and his promised pint.

The bustling chaos that had filled the hotel earlier in the day had now faded to the soft stirrings of evening activity. The doors to the Ballroom were firmly shut and unattended. So were those to the Art Show and the Dealers' Room. There was still a drift of people entering and leaving the restaurant, but the corridor leading to the lobby was mostly empty. This was the calm before the coming storm; although there had been a steady stream of arrivals throughout the afternoon, only about a third of the attendees had signed up at the registration desk before it closed for the night. The rest of the convention wouldn't arrive until the morning. At which point it would be bedlam.

At least until they'd all checked in, signed up, and sorted themselves out for the day.

Somewhere – faintly – he could hear a vague hint of music. It grew louder as he neared the archway that led into the lobby, and – as he started to turn that way, he nearly ran into someone, carrying a tray laden with drinks. The man – wearing a tee-shirt emblazoned with a *Vertigo* logo and the languid image of Gaiman's 'Sandman' – grinned at him from behind his beard. Marcus grinned back and stepped aside, watching as he carefully made his way across the carpeted floor and manoeuvred his burden in through a door further down the passageway. Shared music and laughter tumbled out as the door was opened, then faded back into a soft murmur of sound as it shut behind him.

" … *In the coffin, his silk lined coffin, the vampire sleeps all day…* "

Marcus shook his head with amusement and headed out into the lobby. He knew better than to show his face in the filker's den – he'd be there half the night, probably being serenaded with clever and entertaining tributes to his work, among other things. That was something else that Beverly had never understood – why anyone would want to parody well-known songs with lyrics about imaginary characters or movies and TV shows, let alone write original music that honoured them with serious intent. He, on the other hand, had always appreciated the creativity involved. A good filk song could inspire helpless laughter or reduce a listener to tears. Sometimes it might even be the same song.

The lobby was less brightly lit than earlier in the day; the flare from the central chandeliers had been dimmed to provide a more restrained illumination and the dancing reflections from the mirrors had softened into a gentle shimmer of light and colour. There were still one or two late night stragglers booking into the hotel, a gaggle of customers gathered by the lower bar, and a few small groups of people seated among the sprawl of padded sofas and chairs. The soft murmur of various conversations barely generated a background hum; the whole place felt hushed and almost reverent.

Jessica was still on duty behind the hotel desk. She looked tired, which wasn't at all surprising, since it must have been a long day. He threw her a sympathetic smile as he passed, admiring both the artful way the mirror behind her concealed the entrance to the office, and the attractive way she was reflected in it. It was clearly a much older mirror than the ones on either side of it, the faint crazing in its depth more obvious in the dimmer light. He half-turned and glanced over towards the bar on the other side of the lobby, spotting the matching mirror – and presumably the same hidden space – behind it. The mirrored doors must have been part of the original structure of the house; their ornate frames were a match to the ones he'd seen up on the second floor. The other mirrors were less heavily decorated, styled to imitate rather than match exactly; whoever it was who'd done the renovations Namon had mentioned had clearly been working to a tight budget.

Up on the mezzanine the conversations – and the company – were somewhat livelier. Real Ale was flowing with measured generosity, and there was laughter echoing round the pillars among the murmured words. Cordell was holding court with his usual expansive grin and he waved Marcus over as soon as he saw him arrive.

"Hey," he drawled, pointing to the trestles with their burden of ale casks and glasses. "There's a pint over there got your name on it! Bob!" he called, turning the point into a wave to attract attention, "give my man a drink, willya? My tab, okay?"

"Okay," Bob waved back, stepping behind a pile of casks for a moment, then reappearing with a clean glass and placing it under the nearest spigot. He pulled the pint as Marcus approached him, a smooth, confident motion that spilled liquid gold into the glass and generated the minimum of wasteful froth. "There you go, Marcus. Pint of Red Legging to start with. Ease yourself into it."

"Thanks, Bob." He took the pint, took a cautious sip, and then another, deeper swallow. It was good stuff, rich in taste and mellow on the tongue. "Cheers," he offered, and Bob smiled, moving on to his next customer. Marcus weaved his way to where Cordell was sitting, Mazzy tucked under his arm on one side, and Lilith on the other. The three of them had – an *interesting* relationship, which seemed to suit them pretty well. As far as he'd been able to ascertain – without asking any of them the direct question – Mazzy and Lilith were together, and Cordell was a very close friend with occasional benefits. Usually at conventions, but not always, and sometimes on other occasions, such as when one of the girls had to be away and the other was left minding the store.

It was an arrangement that appeared to work well, for them, at least, although Marcus sometimes wondered whether Mazzy had initially encouraged it in order to completely outrage her parents. He'd heard her stories about how they'd been unhappy about her moving in with Lilith, and how they thought she really needed a man in her life. He could just imagine how her turning up one day with the tall, handsome, and decidedly Jamaican, Cordell on her arm might have persuaded them to rethink the matter. After that, Lilith – despite her openly embraced alternative lifestyle – might look, to them, like a far more acceptable partner for their precious daughter.

Marcus didn't particularly care one way or the other. He thought of them as friends. He liked all three of them, and who they slept with – or not – was none of his business.

"Hello, Marcus," Mazzy got up as he arrived and gave him a friendly hug. "Let me look." She pushed him out to arm's length and studied the effect, smiling as she did so. "I told you that colour would suit you. Alison's done a grand job. Look, Lilly – " she tugged him over a step or two so Lilith could see. "Whatd'ya think?"

Lilith, who was dark where Mazzy was bright, and as sultry and as languid as her name suggested, gave him a long appraising look from under her lashes. "He'll do," she concluded after a moment or two, and smiled.

"Hi, Lilith," he said, bending to press a quick kiss to her proffered cheek. "Thanks for all the silverwork. I think they make the piece."

"Of course they do," she laughed. "Can't wear a waistcoat without buttons, can you?"

"I could," Cordell said, then grimaced as she jerked her elbow sideways with a forceful flick. "But I wouldn't." His hasty addition raised a smile all round; Marcus slipped into the chair opposite the three of them and raised his glass.

"To friends," he proposed. "May we always appreciate them."

"I can drink to that." Cordell reached for his own pint and lifted it to chink the rim against Marcus'. Mazzy and Lilith followed suit – although Mazzy was drinking wine and Lilith had something fizzy that sparkled in the light.

"So," Mazzy demanded, after a suitably convivial silence,

"What's eating you these days, Marcus? Work? The Ex? The kids?"

"All three," he admitted. "Well, the first two definitely. Molly and Reuben not so much. Although I have to take Molly again for a few weeks. Rueben's doctor's recommended a summer camp for him and…"

"'Nuff said." Mazzy reached to give his arm a sympathetic squeeze. "But you like having Molly over, don't you?"

"I love it. But it'll mean having to put other things on hold. And Francis is chasing a three book deal, so …"

"Three! You lucky bugger." Cordell eyed him over his pint. "My publishers are 'considering' my next one. But there's no guarantee they'll take it. I mean – they say zombies are in at the moment, but – not my kind of zombie, apparently."

"They'll buy it." Lilith glared at him. "And if they don't we'll just set up a kickstarter and publish it for you anyway. Your fans will love it. Have a little faith in yourself."

"Amen, Sister." Mazzy let go of Marcus' arm so she could jazz hand the hallelujah. Cordell laughed.

"Yeah, yeah, I know. Love you too, guys. See what I have to put up with, Marcus? No allowance for self-doubt or negativity with these two on my case."

"Don't knock it," Marcus advised. "All *I* get is demands to increase the alimony every time I get published. I'd rather have the supportive chorus. Speaking of whom," he said, smiling at Mazzy, "did you being any new pieces this time? They're talking about bringing *Wolfkin* out in paperback, and I might be looking for a cover."

"Ooh." Mazzy sat up a little straighter. "I may have something suitable. I've been working with a Nordic theme for while – I've done work on Fenris, and some wolfraiders, stuff like that."

"Yeah," Lilith agreed. "Those are pretty good. Not as good as her Odin on the World Tree, but that really is a masterpiece. You'll have to drop by the display and take a look."

"I will," he promised, relaxing into his chosen chair and savouring the taste of his beer. If the next couple of days passed as genially as this one had, he decided, he was going to enjoy himself immensely.

Chapter Five

They sat and talked like that for a while, catching up on recent news and discussing all the usual subjects. Marcus finished his pint and went for a refill, taking Cordell's empty glass with him. He was on his way back, a drink in either hand, when a sweep of something deeply scarlet fluttered at the corner of his eye. He turned, to find Ashera walking beside him, draped in a stunning red velvet dress.

"Hello, again," she said, smiling at his expression. "I believe someone said something about buying me a drink?"

"So I did." He smiled back and nodded towards his friends. "I'm just getting the next round. Let me deliver these and I'll get yours when I get the girls. What's your poison?"

"White wine with a spritzer? They've got very nice house white, here. They tell me the owner also owns the vineyard."

"They all do that," he laughed, leading her over to where he'd been sitting. "Guys," he said, "This is Ashera. We ran into each other this afternoon. Well," he corrected wryly, "*I* ran into her. Literally. She was kind enough to pick me up."

"Again, literally," Ashera laughed. Cordell, being the natural gentleman that he was, clambered to his feet and offered her his seat. When she graciously took it, he stepped away to grab a nearby empty chair, brought it back to add to the group round the table and sat down, straddling its seat without bothering to turn it round first. Marcus handed him his pint and took a hasty sip from his own, envying his friend's lanky height, which gave him sufficient reach to put the glass down on the low table they'd monopolised – and to pick it up again, without the curve of the chair back getting in the way.

"One house white – with spritzer," he checked, making sure he placed his glass on a beer mat that was out of Cordell's reach. "One diet lemonade, and ... yours was house red, right Mazzy?"

"Right. Thanks."

He left his friends making Ashera's acquaintance and headed for the hotel's mezzanine bar, which was busily supplying everything that wasn't Real Ale. Not that it was anything like as busy as it would be the following day, but there was a steady-ish stream of customers, and he had to wait a few moments before he was served.

"So was this an orphanage before, or after the Great War?" someone was asking somewhere to his left.

"Before." Namon's dry tones were instantly recognisable. If anything, they were more desiccated than before, a rough edged crack running through otherwise pleasant tones. "There's quite a poignant story about one of the young soldiers who was sent here to recover from his shell shock back in 1916." Marcus turned to locate him, listening, like the rest of the man's audience, with fascinated interest. "How he'd lived in the house as a boy, and had never expected to return?" Namon was sitting with what looked like a group of younger steam-punks, who were hanging on his every word. Abigail was quite right. Where his tailored coat and high collared shirt had made him stand out among the general sweep of tee-shirt and jeans earlier in the day, he now looked comfortably at home; keeping company among the leather gauntleted, greatcoat and/or corseted, pseudo-Victorian cosplayers as if he were one of them. "He must have been badly affected by his experiences, though. He hanged himself, on the Great Oak, out in the park. He's buried out in the little graveyard, the one down by the canal."

"There's a graveyard?" A young woman in a tight-waisted flounce of a dress, that came complete with a matching goggle-accented top hat, declared. "Cool!"

"Would you like to see it?" Namon suggested, clearly pleased at her reaction. Marcus found himself frowning, and he couldn't quite figure out why.

"Now? Won't it be dark out there?"

"Not at all." Namon smiled, knowingly. "It's a summer night, the moon is up, and – the path down to the canal has lamps all the way along it. The gardens are quite beautiful at this time of the night – at this time of the year, that is. I'm told it's very – atmospheric, by the time we get to Halloween."

"Oh," the young lady's companion said, "I've read about that. Don't they hold a Gothic Ball here every year? And there's a candle-lit walk or something?"

The smile widened, deepening Marcus' frown. Maybe it was the way Namon was leaning in towards the two women, a whole lot closer than most Victorians would consider an acceptable distance … He shook his head, turning the frown into an inner scowl at himself. Namon *wasn't* a Victorian gentleman, no matter how convincingly he dressed as one, and his interactions with his current audience were none of Marcus' concern. It probably was a nice night out now the rain had passed over, and extending an invitation to lead a group visit to the hotel's historic graveyard was decidedly in the spirit of the con they'd come to attend. Not to mention being very much in character for the role he'd volunteered to play over the weekend. *Besides*, Marcus considered with momentary amusement – the two ladies he was busy charming were both over twenty, and both clearly very independent and confident young women. If he tried anything *really* inappropriate, they'd probably eat him alive.

When he turned back to the bar, the barman – having dealt with the queue – was also watching his employer, his eyes both shuttered and wary. As soon as he spotted Marcus looking in his direction though, his expression blossomed into a friendly smile. "What can I get you, sir?" he asked.

Marcus pushed his vague unease to the back of his mind and focused on getting his order right. A few moments later, he was making his way back to his group, three drinks carefully balanced on a small tray.

"I think the whole place is ace." Cordell and the girls had been joined by two other authors that Marcus vaguely knew – Jeremy Larksam, an older man with a repertoire of short stories about vengeful ghosts and some longer tales about old sins and the horrifying consequences of trying to keep them secret; and Jasie Hemming-Williams, who'd started out writing horror scenarios for Role-playing Games, had written computer game tie-ins, and had just published her first, original novel. It was pretty good, too. Marcus had picked it up at Eastercon, started reading it on the train and had devoured several chapters before he'd got home. "Stick it out on a Yorkshire moor or a blasted heath somewhere, and yeah – instant Gothic novel. On the outside. But the inside? Way too many mirrors for a self-respecting vampire to be caught dead in."

Larksam waved at the surrounding decor to prove his point. There were far fewer mirrors on the mezzanine than there were in the lobby, or on the upper floor. But there were several floor length ones spaced in-between the seminar room doors, most of them semi-camouflaged by an antique table or a pot plant. They'd probably been installed to brighten what would otherwise be a gloomy and shadowed space – especially since the shuttered roof of the upper rotunda was not letting in the light it had been designed to.

"You may be right," Jasie laughed. "Although I'm not sure that most people are that observant. I think a cunning vampire could avoid *not* being seen – most of the time."

"What do you think, Marcus?" Mazzy asked as he handed her her glass of red wine. "You being the expert on this kind of thing. Would a vampire avoid this place because of all the mirrors?"

He shrugged. "Depends on the vampire." He hovered between the two remaining glasses for a second, then smiled and handed Lilith her lemonade before offering the last glass to Ashera. She took it, thanking him with a soft smile. "Chinese vampires have reflections, but tend to be repulsed or frightened by them. It's a fairly common way to confront or defeat them in the Eastern myths …" He sat back in his chair, reaching for his pint as he considered the matter. "So I don't think you'd run into one of them wandering around here. The Greek and Thracian myths don't really mention mirrors, so it's hard to be sure about the really ancient ones – but then the European *vampyr tales* aren't all that clear either."

"Well, Hollywood got the idea from Stoker, and *he* must have got it from somewhere." Larksam was keen to push the point. "And don't tell me 'he made it all up', because none of us do that. Not really," he added, fixing Cordell with a somewhat patronising glare. "We all do our research, right?"

"We sure do," Cordell responded lazily, not at all fazed by the challenge in the man's eye. "Most of mine at my grandmother's knee. You want the truth, you go to a truth teller." He smiled. "But I don't know nuttin' 'bout vampires," he went on, exaggerating his soft Jamaican lilt into deliberate parody. "All my dead boys get conjured up as zombies."

"They have reflections," Lilith pointed out. "But I think most people would notice if there were a zombie in this hotel."

"I should certainly hope so," Marcus laughed, taking another pull at his pint. He slipped easily into lecture mode, used to this kind of discourse with his students. "So, if you discount the troubled suicide or cursed corpse that doesn't actually *leave* their grave – the ones that simply manifest as an etheric ghostly revenant, stealing life from the living before re-inhabiting their physical corpse at sunrise – then you're left with the type of vampire that Hollywood loves: the living dead, rising from their coffin to feed on the blood and souls of the living. And then, if you postulate that Stoker was right about the mirrors … no, I don't think you'd find one of *his* vampires wandering around the place. Too obvious. Too easy to spot."

"See," Larksam said with a hint of smugness. "Told you so."

"I think," Ashera suggested softly, "that it may depend – not on the vampire as such, but on the mirror."

All eyes in the group swung in her direction. "Oh?" Marcus prompted. "How do you mean?"

"Well," she said, putting her glass down for a moment and steepling her fingers together. "Most people simply assume that – because Dracula didn't reflect in a shaving mirror – he didn't have any kind of reflection. But that doesn't make sense. Everything that exists has a reflection, even if it's only a blurred one – in water, in glass, in any shiny or polished surface. Why wouldn't that kind of vampire reflect in a mirror? They exist. They're not projections or ghosts – they're physically there, just as you said. It has to be something about the mirror that makes the difference. The Greeks, the Romans – they never mentioned the possibility. But their mirrors were made of polished bronze. A base metal, and not a pure one. The best mirrors – the old ones, before modern manufacturing and aluminium foil – were made of glass backed with silver. A precious metal, long associated with purity and sanctified power. What if it's the silver at the back of the mirror that cannot reflect the corrupted, or even non-existent soul of the vampire? And if that's the case, then most of the mirrors around here wouldn't be a threat to them. That kind of vampire would feel safe in the modern world – no worries about film stocks based on silver nitrate failing to capture their presence. And modern mirrors, all shiny and clean and new technology – they might appear a bit blurred, or a little fuzzy, but they would reflect. Only the old, silvered mirrors would betray their presence – or lack of it, it you like. And those would be much easier to spot, and avoid, in a place like this." She looked straight at Marcus as she added: "They'd probably try to stay away from the second floor. Most of the items up there are old, and genuine."

"Wow," Jasie breathed. "That's a great theory." She mulled the thought over for a moment, then perked up, adding: "Mind if I use it?"

"Hey," Mazzy interjected, "don't you dare! Marcus is the expert here – he wrote the book, remember? I think he gets first dibs on something that cool. Don't you? What do you think, Marcus. Marcus?"

Marcus wasn't entirely listening. He was staring at Ashera, trying to shake the feeling they had gone from discussing theory and lore to something far more immediate and relevant. She spoke, not as a theoretician might, but with quiet conviction, offering something drawn – he felt – from experience rather than mere speculation.

"Mm?" He dragged himself away from her intense dark eyes, and smiled round at his company a little bemusedly. "Sorry. What?"

"The theory, man." Cordell was laughing at him. Well, perhaps he had been staring a little more intently at the lady than was polite – but it hadn't been at the glimmering, jewelled Eye of Horus that hung between Ashera's breasts, nor at the breasts themselves, no matter how well her dress accentuated them. He'd noticed all of that and moved on almost immediately. He wasn't that kind of guy, and Cordell knew it. "You wanna use it? Nettlestone might come up with that one, right?"

"Yes. Yes, he – he might." He was still struggling to focus on the conversation, convinced that Ashera had been trying to tell him something important, although he couldn't figure out what it had been. "Or Ackermand. His friend, the alchemist?" The suggestion generated a round of nods, mostly of agreement, although Larksman's was less convincing than the rest. Marcus didn't mind that. He didn't expect *everyone* to have read all his books and be thoroughly familiar with their supporting casts.

He wasn't entirely sure *he* was that familiar with them, some of the time.

"Listen, Jasie," he said, turning to her rather than trying to wrestle with the little nagging voice that Ashera's words had stirred. "It is a good theory, and – I might use it, but … there's nothing to stop you putting your own spin on it. Maybe – acknowledge that you and I heard it together, so if we do both come up with something we won't get accused of plagiarizing each other. If you're okay with that," he realised, turning back to Ashera with a suddenly worried smile. She was the one who'd suggested it…

"I would be honoured if either of you were inspired by my words," she assured them, lifting her wine glass to offer a small toast in their direction. "Wisdom is meant to inspire – as well as inform – or advise."

"I'll drink to that," Cordell declared, reaching for his nearly finished pint to do just that. "You want another, Marcus?"

He thought about the offer for a moment. "No," he decided, a little reluctantly. "Thank you. I'd love to, but – I have to be up for the opening ceremony tomorrow. My days of drinking through the night and bouncing up fresh as a daisy in the morning are long over." He downed the last of his beer in a quick couple of gulps and put the empty glass back on the table. "I'd better head towards bed. You guys have fun, and I'll see you tomorrow, okay?"

He left in a flurry of short hugs and a couple of good night kisses. Ashera had risen to her feet when he did, and she stepped in beside him as he started to leave.

"I'll walk up with you," she offered warmly. "I'm not that

much of a night owl. Good night everyone. It was good to meet you all."

"See you in the morning," Lilith called after her. "Her table is next to mine," Marcus heard her explain to someone as they both walked away.

"Why do I get the impression that you want to get me alone?" he asked her as they left the mezzanine and began to climb the wide spiral stair.

"Because I want to get you alone?" she smiled in response, her eyes crinkling with a hint of laughter. "Not for anything nefarious, I assure you. Just – you asked me to help you, and I intend to do just that. I know that may not make much sense right now, but – I think it will do. And soon. Whatever happens," she said gently, putting her hand on his arm, "no matter what, know that I will listen, I will advise – and I will not judge. You can trust me. I promise."

"Okay," he said, a little bemusedly. Her touch was warm and reassuring; it wasn't a sensuous contact, although it felt oddly intimate and comforting. "Thanks. I think." He paused and added, even more bemusedly. "Have we met before? I – I feel like I know you. Somehow. Is that – weird?"

"Not really." She stepped away from him at the top of the steps, her dress swirling out around her, as if she'd almost moved into a dance. "But you don't know me at all, Marcus Holland. Not yet." She sighed, giving him a look that was somehow part affection, part regret. "In some ways – I am very sorry that you need to. But I am never sorry to make a new friend. Sleep well," she smiled and moved away, heading down the corridor towards a room in the extension – or perhaps in search of the lifts. "If you can," her voice drifted back, sweet and melodious as it was swallowed up by distance.

Marcus blinked. He knew he was tired, but … for one, very weird moment, he could have sworn that – while there was only her, walking up the hallway, the mirrors on either side had flickered with a multiplicity of reflections as she passed.

Trick of the light, he decided. *Or maybe that beer was stronger than I thought...*

He shook his head, turned on his heel and headed towards his room and the promise of a good night's sleep.

— * —

He didn't get one.

He made every effort to achieve it, starting with resisting the temptation to check his emails or to make himself a late night coffee. He went through all the usual routine: hanging up the waistcoat and his shirt so they'd be crease free in the morning, using the bathroom facilities – with the exception of the chaise longue, as he didn't have an immediate use for that – washed, brushed his teeth, and put on his pyjamas. Then he turned off the main light, pulled back the covers on the bed and climbed in, sinking into the deep embrace of a soft mattress, down pillows, and the feather-light hug of a summer duvet.

After the early hassles of the day, the train journey, and two pints of excellent Real Ale, he should have been asleep in minutes.

Sleep, however, did not come.

The bed – and the room that held it – seemed much bigger in the dark, an echoing space that left him feeling exposed and uncomfortably vulnerable. The earlier rain had leeched away the remnants of the day's heat, and while his body warmth quickly created a cosy cocoon, the crisp, cotton sheets felt chilly against his skin whenever he moved beyond it. He could not get comfortable; he piled one pillow onto another to get more support, then pummelled the pile flatter because it felt too high; he rolled this way and that, sinking too deep on the edge of the mattress and then finding the bed springs in the middle too rigid to fully relax. The duvet felt too warm, but without it the room was cold. He got up twice – once to use the bathroom a second time, then again to tug a bottle of water out of the mini-fridge because he'd started coughing and his mouth had gone dry.

His mind was buzzing, wrestling with *something* that would not come into focus; something to do with the hotel, or the convention, or the events of the day. He rolled onto his back and sighed, staring up into the dark while trying to pin down that nagging demand for attention.

Was he developing a fit of nerves about being the 'Guest of Honour' for the weekend? He didn't think so. He'd been flattered to be asked, and honoured to accept the invitation. He'd been to enough conventions to know what the job entailed, and he was enough of an old hand at book signings, panels, and personal appearances to no longer find the experience intimidating. Besides, he lectured for a living, and – unlike many of the students he'd taught through the years – the people who came to conventions generally wanted to hear what he had to say.

His mind skittered on to other issues: Molly, and her brother Reuben, who wasn't actually his child but was still very much part of his family. The boy had been very sickly while a baby, but he was doing much better now that the Doctors had tracked down the cause of his problems. Molly, of course, was the joy of his heart. He'd never quite forgiven Beverley for taking her away from him when she'd left, and he treasured every precious moment he had been able to spend with her since. It would be good to have her for a few weeks this summer. He curled over onto his side and spent a few moments imagining it: trips to the local wildlife park, maybe a longer one to the seaside, and…

It was no good. Thinking of Molly stirred that nagging demand into a sense of shapeless panic, a feeling that he'd missed something important, something that meant she was in danger. Somehow.

"Screw this," he muttered, and got up to pace round the room and stretch everything: legs, shoulders, arms and back. He worked out some of the kinks in his neck and paused to finish what was left in the water bottle. "Work it back," he told himself, getting back into bed and deliberately relaxing every voluntary muscle in his body, starting with his feet. As he did so, he made himself step back through the events of the day, seeking the moment that had planted that tiny seed of discontent. That meant beginning with Ashera's parting smile, which helped with the relaxing, but not a lot else. He recalled the conversations in the bar, and before that, those at dinner, and he was halfway through his review of the report when sleep finally came, immersing him in unsettled dreams. His mind, set on its steady course, continued to unwind the day, twisting him through a maze of hotel passageways and up endless flights of stairs. He was sitting next to Spanner as the man's pale and haunted face began to slowly slough from his skull; horror pushed him backwards from the table, and he turned, finding Namon watching him, his lips curled with amusement. He ran from the room to fall at Ashera's feet, then tumbled away again as she reached for him. Mirrors spun round him as he descended – like some nightmare draped version of Alice – into the core of the rotunda, and when he landed they barricaded him on every side, showing him his panicked race back up the stairs, desperate to reach the shutters, needing to unleash the sun.

Finally, somewhere in the depths of his dreaming, he found himself walking across the hotel lobby towards the reception desk. Jessica was there, in person at the desk, and reflected in every single mirror along the wall. Namon stalked across to join her, his reflection discordant and blurred, following him from mirror to mirror, growing ever more distorted as he reached his goal. He was a shadow that flitted from pane to pane, a creature stalking innocent prey …

… in every mirror, but one.

Marcus woke with a stifled cry, his heart pounding with terror and his mouth as dry as dust.

Somewhere beneath him, the Clock struck four times and then fell silent. Marcus barely noticed it. He was focused on the memory that he'd finally recalled; the moment when he'd seen Namon reach for the hidden door behind the older mirror.

The moment when the door had begun to open – when the mirror had caught and distorted the desk clerk's reflection.

And in which, Namon had not been reflected at all.

Chapter Six

"Shit," Marcus swore, sitting bolt upright and shaking from head to toe.

*Shit, shit, **shit!***

There were too many thoughts colliding inside his head, and he didn't know which of them to pay attention to. He'd spent his entire working life – his *career* – rationalising the fantastic, trying to tease out what he'd seen as truth from all those weird and wonderful tales that mankind had told itself across the centuries. He knew all about the power of story telling, the way that folklore helped structure cultures, providing moralistic warnings about dangerous or unacceptable behaviours, reinforcing societal norms, and giving shape to deep seated fears and the terrors of the unknown. He'd analysed thousands of such tales, tracking common themes, seeking to understand their context, unravelling the way that tales mutated and evolved, changing as the world changed around them. His own work – his fictions, written mostly for intellectual exercise and disguised as entertainment – were simply part of the next step in that process, exploring those old ideas, building on their constantly evolving mythologies and dressing them in newly cut cloth.

He'd studied fairy stories, collected tales of skinshifters and witchcraft, had tracked down obscure legends and unearthed a treasure trove of wild ideas and wilder beliefs buried beneath centuries of folklore and fable. He'd even written the definitive history of the vampire – as definitive as one academic studying such a wealth of material could make it, that is. But he'd never, for a moment, believed that any of it might be *real*.

Vampires were simply projections or allegories – tales told to explain the strange and the otherwise unexplained. They served as bogeymen to scare the childlike and the simple, and as scapegoats for horrors that would otherwise have no explanation in days when medical knowledge was sketchy, to say the least.

And there was one – or something very like one – currently stalking the halls of the hotel.

His world view had taken on a disorientating tilt, and he felt as if he were falling, flailing for balance and not finding it. Not finding it at all.

He knew all the lore – the old and the new. He could discard the modern trappings of tragic, haunted heroes and romantic redemptions. He knew that – if you went back far enough – vampires were bad news. They were always bad news, harbingers of sickness, plague, and death. They were predators or parasites – and sometimes both, the dead clinging to the illusion of life and feeding off the living to sustain it. At best, they were pale, restless ghosts who needed to be put to rest, and at worst, they were hungry, heartless murderers, feeling no regret and even less remorse. They spread contagion and corruption, sometimes unknowingly, and sometimes deliberately, coming to hate the life they had lost while, at the same time, desperately craving it.

Instinct was screaming at him to run. To simply throw everything back into his suitcase and *run*. As far and as fast as he could. But instinct was also warring with cold terror – the shivering voice which kept saying things like '*he's out there somewhere, waiting,*' and, even worse, '*maybe he's right outside the door...*'

Both of those were being battered by what was left of rational thought, which wasn't being all that rational right there and then. Because if what it kept insisting were true – *there are no such things as vampires. There can't be* – then the only other explanation for what he'd seen was *You're going insane.*

He wasn't sure which would be worse – but he could not erase that memory, the stark evidence of something *wrong* which had been screaming for his attention ever since he'd seen it. Nor could he dismiss the other evidence, the slow accumulation of clues which had been adding themselves to the case ever since he'd first seen the man – the creature, the *thing* – in the hotel lobby. So many little hints, observed and dismissed as 'simply getting into character' or else explained away, misread and misinterpreted without the understanding of what might lie behind them.

Jessica's moue of distaste as her Manager had touched her. Spanner's 'touch of flu', and his distracted manner at dinner. The young waiter and the distressed and distracted way that he had wrung the napkin between his hands. The Barman on the mezzanine, watching with disconcerting intentness.

Even their meeting on the stairs – a check, perhaps to assess potential suspicions? Had Namon realised he might have seen the lack of reflection in the lobby glass? He certainly hadn't seen him in any of the second floor mirrors, even though he had to have passed several of them to be standing where he had been. Even that conversation – driven by Marcus's own simple assumptions – could be considered in a different light, now that he knew what Namon might be. What better way to hide in plain sight, that to pretend that you are … what you are? To play on the mythology, drawing on Hollywood's misconceptions and mistakes to conceal the reality of something far, far darker.

How long had he been the spider at the heart of this tangled web? How long had he been using, and abusing, the people who had fallen under his influence? The previous guests, passing through on business. The Goth crowd, gathering to celebrate Halloween, unaware of the predator in their midst? The patients in the asylum, already screaming and disturbed?

The young soldier, who had been an orphan here and chosen to commit suicide, rather than endure the attentions of the Master of the House again...

By the time he'd reached that particular thought, Marcus was feeling physically sick. He threw back the covers and padded, barefoot, into the bathroom. He hit the light switch without thinking about it, and the harsh, bright illumination from the bulb stabbed at him like a dagger. He closed his eyes with a pained blink and staggered across to the washbasin, where he leant forward and retched, bringing back most of the earlier bottle of water, and a good deal of expensive Real Ale.

"Oh, *goddess*," he muttered, sluicing the remnants of the mess down the plughole and grabbing the nearby glass so he could rinse out his mouth. "What the hell am I supposed to do now?"

Guilt was busy clawing at him, reminding him of the two young women that he'd left to Namon's mercies, making him pray, with all his heart, that they hadn't taken him up on his offer. Or that – if they had – they had been able to survive the encounter relatively unharmed. Should he have said something? Stepped in and saved the day? But what would he have said? Would they have believed him? Wouldn't Namon have just laughed off any accusations with the same charming manner he'd been using to ensnare his victims in the first place?

Marcus wasn't a particularly religious man. He'd always thought there might be *something* greater than mankind knew or understood, but he'd never really seen the need to make a huge deal out of it. He leaned – maybe inevitably, given his area of study – towards modern paganism as a reasonable way of defining the divine, finding more sense in aligning his life with the natural rhythms and patterns of the world than he'd ever found inside the boundaries drawn by the more orthodox religions. Molly loved that kind of stuff, and he'd encouraged her a little, enjoying the way she explored the ideas and thoughtfully developed her own. But while he'd probably call himself a Pagan if he was asked to make the choice, he wasn't really a practising one; not beyond a simple acknowledgment of the various festivals, and a willingness to join in with the rites if he happened to be among friends with a lot more dedication than his own.

Right now that lack of specific faith, that failure to find a footing on which to plant himself when faced with something occult or arcane, was adding to the tilted, whirling dance of his thoughts. He didn't own a cross, and he wasn't sure that would work even if he did, given that he was not a Christian to begin with. How could he protect himself? Could he? Could he raid the kitchens for bulbs of garlic? Would the kitchens even *have* garlic, considering how effective most of the folklore tended to claim it could be?

One thought immediately led to another, his mind continuing to whir and stumble in its panicked dance. If he couldn't protect himself, how on *earth* was he going to protect anyone else? His friends, the fans, everyone else in the hotel? All those con-goers arriving for a fun weekend, a veritable feast for any vampire, let alone the one that appeared to own the hotel...

He can enter any room, Marcus realised in horror, hyperventilating a little. The stricture about needing an invitation – the magic of thresholds and household gods, which went back centuries – would have little meaning when the entity you needed to keep out was already *in.* No one needs an invitation when they own the entire property, and you're staying there as their guest.

Get out, a bit of him was still yelling, self-preservation demanding immediate and selfish response. *Get away. RUN!*

He almost did just that – hastening back into the bedroom to grab his case and start stuffing his clothes back into it. But he'd barely filled the first third before a combination of sudden gloomy pessimism, a terrifying thought or two, and a whole load of common sense told him to stop. Running away wasn't going to achieve anything. Other than getting him a reputation of breaking his promises, bailing on people who relied on him, and make him spend his whole life looking over his shoulder until the *next* vampire he didn't know how to deal with came along.

Think this through, he told himself severely, then added, with a hint of hysteria, *What would Jackson or Nettlestone do?*

Wait for me to do a shitload of research, was, of course, the immediate comeback to that. More than one of his books had sat in limbo for weeks while he struggled with plot and figured out how to escape from the corners he was constantly backing his heroes into. He didn't have Jackson's magical allies to call on, or his own personal Manaheim lurking around to come to the rescue – or to *be* rescued, for that matter, although he had more than enough friends at the con to fit that particular trope.

"Self-protection first," he decided, glancing round the bedroom and then out into the sitting room space. There was a pale, silvery light illuminating the otherwise shadowed outer room, slim shafts of moonlight piercing the windows from the garden side of the house. The skies must have cleared after the earlier rain, and the moon was low on the horizon, heading for its rest and leaving the sky free to welcome back the sun.

"Sunrise," Marcus murmured, not sure whether that was a helpful thought or not. Seeing it would certainly make *him* feel better, but he doubted it would do much more than that. He'd already seen Namon wandering around during the day, so he was hardly the sort of creature that lived only at night, or was forced back into the grave at dawn. And the hotel's overabundance of shutters had a perfectly mundane explanation. *Sunlight*, Namon had said, *damages our antiques...*

That spurred another semi-hysterical thought.

I wonder how old he is? How long he's been here?

Spanner had said his 'fictional' vampire was Georgian, the same as the house. Marcus realised that he'd need to research that, at least. 'Know your enemy' was always good advice.

He stepped back into the bathroom to grab the little bottle of massage oil that he kept in his washbag. The mix he used was meant to aid healing rather than provide protection, but without something more specific it would have to do. He tipped a little onto his finger and walked out to the outer room of his suite, carefully using the oil to paint protective runes on both the wood and the door handle. If vampires *were* real, then logic dictated that the symbols used to ward them away were going to have some sort of power to do so. Or not. But it was better to be safe than sorry. He'd done some research on the use of runes on protective amulets when writing *The Song of the Sea*, and while they'd made only a fleeting appearance in the text, he'd not forgotten how to scribe them out.

He marked the door, and then each window, and even the wall in the corner, just in case his suspicions about secret staircases had any truth in it. Then he drew the same symbols at his throat and one on each wrist, just in case. If nothing else, at least he and the room now smelt nice.

Okay... Acting to protect himself had helped calm him a little, even if he had no idea if what he'd done would make any difference. His thoughts were still bouncing all over the place, swinging wildly from unspecified panic, through an undertone of *You can deal with this, you can deal with this,* all way to *It's not true. It can't be true. You're going mad.*

That, of course, was a possibility. It would certainly be a rational explanation, and the most likely conclusion that others would leap to if he started telling them that vampires were real – especially if he went on to suggest that there was one in this hotel, this weekend … and that he knew it because he'd momentarily glimpsed, or rather *not* glimpsed, the monster's missing reflection.

Particularly since he'd spent half a chapter of his book pointing out how much of *that* mythology was down to Hollywood, rather than the older texts and tales.

Even if someone believed him – which they almost certainly wouldn't – they'd only need to hear Spanner's intended announcement about the con having a vampire 'guest' to leap to the other, equally sensible conclusion that he was simply playing along with the pretence, and was somehow part of the act.

Namon, he realised, his stomach sinking even further towards his boots, was not only dangerous. He was very, very clever…

He didn't think – for one moment – that Spanner was anything more than an unwilling, or perhaps a frightened and reluctant, victim, but his collaboration – his support – for that clever and decidedly *evil* plan, suggested that, as many traditions imply, Namon was able to exert some sort of control over his victims. Perhaps through some initial, directed charm and then…?

What? Marcus wondered, thinking about the anxious waiter, and the way that Spanner had reacted to his claim to having met the vampire in the first place. *Some kind of compulsion to obey? Or is it something that fogs the mind, leaving only a vague sense of fear and unspecified unease?*

He rather hoped it was the latter, because *knowing* what Namon was, having been a victim of his hunger and then – frightened, lost, and helpless to resist – being made to help him, facilitating his access to other victims, was not something he'd wish on his worst enemy, let alone a friend.

"I need more information," he decided, speaking out loud in the shadowed sitting room. The moon was sinking below

the horizon and its light – faint shafts of silvery radiance –
was slowly drifting up the patterned wallpaper, leaving the
lower part of the room in darkness. The thought of what
might lurk in that darkness made Marcus shiver. He didn't
want to turn the main lights on, because to do so – without
signalling anyone who might be watching that he was awake
– he would need to close the shutters first. If he closed the
shutters he wouldn't see the sun come up and, right now, he
really needed the reassurance of the dawn.

He headed back to the bedroom for a moment or two,
shucking the vulnerability of nightwear to get dressed for the
coming day. Almost as an afterthought, he slid his waistcoat
on over his clean shirt, not bothering to fasten it yet, but
finding comfort in the gleam of solid silver buttons and the
subtle embroidery that appealed, in twists and stitches, to
higher powers and old, but not forgotten, gods. Then he
made his way to the desk, turned on the angled lamp, opened
up his laptop – and went to work.

– * –

Google-Fu is a powerful skill, but having access to academic
libraries and the archives of innumerable institutions took
remote research to another level. By the time the sun came
up – 5:23 by Marcus' watch, which meant the first creeping
fingers of dawn were quickly followed by five sweet strikes
from the Clock – he'd made progress, and by seven – with
the sun streaming in over his shoulder, warming his back and
settling a little of his still shivering soul – he had discovered
a great many interesting, and disturbing, things about
Westeringford Grange.

According to the Hotel information pack, there'd been a
house on the site since the early sixteenth century. Marcus
had managed to confirm this, identifying that the last
inhabitant of this first house had been rumoured to have been

a pupil of John Dee, Elizabeth's scientific and magical advisor. Shortly after this man's death, the house had been destroyed in a fire. One of the texts he'd found suggested that this might have been arson: there were records that spoke of finding 'unholy' books following the owner's death, and veiled references to unsettling events which had resulted in several other deaths before the fire.

The house seemed to have remained a ruin for several years after that, although there were indications that the land – if not the house – had been appropriated for use as a barracks during the Civil War. The brochure picked up the story shortly after the Restoration, with the land being awarded, by the king, to a Richard Harthorne, the Baron Bowberry, a minor noble who'd served with Charles II while he was in exile. Tracking the history of the Harthornes through a local archive, Marcus confirmed the hotel's narrative, with the Baron having rebuilt the house and his family continuing to live there until 1735, when the last Bowberry died. Since he'd run out of money and had no direct heirs, the estate was sold to settle the Baron's debt. It was bought by one Matthew Wellmore, the son of a wealthy banker and early northern industrialist. It was he who had had the existing house rebuilt in the popular Gothic style, and continued to add to it until his death, some fifty-one years later.

There was a lot to know about Matthew Wellmore. Known in local circles as the 'First Lord of Westeringford,' he had lived an expansive and profligate life in his newly built castle. After he inherited his father's money and businesses, he continued to spend his fortune on parties, pleasures, and the development of his estate; the grounds were landscaped in the popular style, and, when contributing – as part of a local business consortium – to the construction of a canal, he insisted that the work include an additional branch to cross his lands. This was to enable him to transport custom made furnishings for the house, and support the planting of a huge number of mature trees as part of his landscaping projects.

By the time his son, John Isiah Wellmore – born 1757 to Mathew's third wife, Sarah – came to inherit the estate, most of the earlier fortune had gone. John Wellmore was on record as being a successful investor and property owner, with chambers in London, and an early member of the Society of Lloyds.

Marcus had paused there, considering the likely coincidence of the name. This was the first 'Isiah' he'd come across in connection with the house, and in the right time period too: he bookmarked the history texts he'd been tracking and went to look for pictures instead. His first hit wasn't an image from the 1790s – it was a photograph taken in December 1929, showing members of the Lloyds Dramatic, Operatic and Musical Society, taking part in the production of Sir Arthur Conan Doyle's play *The House of Temperley*, at the New Scala theatre.

"Hello," he breathed, staring at the various top hatted gentlemen with interest. None of them were *his* Isiah, but the costumes they were wearing, copies of earlier Victorian finery, looked almost exactly like the clothes Namon had been wearing that afternoon. Not that that was any kind of evidence, but it gave him another potential line of enquiry, if his current one didn't take him anywhere.

The next image, dated 1789, was much closer to the period he needed, but not a lot of help, since it was basically a sketch or cartoon. The men in this were in frock coats and cockade hats, and some of them bore some resemblance to Namon's narrow features, but not enough to be anything more than mere coincidence. A sudden flash of inspiration caught him, and he dropped across to Pinterest, triggering a search on 'Wellmore Family Westeringford.'

He didn't *really* expect that to work, which meant that he found himself sitting back in his chair with wide and disconcerted eyes when it did.

Half the pictures were of the Grange, of course. Others of the local village, both ancient and modern. But one was a portrait of Matthew, round cheeked and well fed in a slightly bulging red jacket and a broad smile, and one was of John.

Painted in 1774, the caption said. John Isiah Wellmore was a dapper Georgian gentleman back then, in a dark green velvet double breasted frock coat and a sober, black cravat. It was a head and shoulders portrait: either his hair had been teased out into ordered curls, or he was wearing a wig, but the features beneath the ornate style were unmistakable. If Isiah Namon were *not* John Isiah Wellmore under another name, then he had to be a close relative. A very, very close relative. The eyes that looked out at him from the screen were calculating ones, slightly narrowed and knowing beneath arched brows.

Encouraged – although not entirely comfortable with this discovery – Marcus scrolled on.

There were more images of the Grange – some from an earlier time, with stable blocks and other outbuildings standing where the extension had yet to be built – another picture of Matthew, one of his tombstone in the local church, and then one labelled *Josiah* Wellmore, an older man in a more Victorian style, but with that same high cheekbones and narrow face. The eyes were more of less the same, too, slightly deeper set and more shadowed, perhaps, but just as compelling, just as intense.

There were no more pictures of the Wellmores, but he wasn't expecting to find any. Victorian Plate cameras used silver compounds to capture their images; no self-respecting vampire would bother posing for a portrait that they wouldn't actually appear in.

"Got you," Marcus muttered, with the satisfaction of a dedicated researcher, finding the evidence he'd been looking for.

He went back to the histories, turning the page in the hotel brochure beside him to correlate what they admitted to with what he found.

John Wellmore had apparently saved the family fortunes simply by not spending any more of it. He'd closed off most of the house, dismissed most of the staff, allowed the grounds to lapse into wilderness, and focused on investing his money in business; recouping profit from insurance deals, buying up property and leasing it out, and extending small loans to local companies. According to the records he'd died in 1846, which would have made him over eighty years old – pretty good going for a Georgian-turned-Victorian gentleman living a frugal and parsimonious life, but, if he were Namon, barely the beginning of his existence among the living dead. It was Josiah Wellmore who'd picked up the inheritance – a great nephew of some sort, a descendant of John's long dead sister, the Hotel brochure said, although Marcus could find nothing to confirm that.

After him, the story grew a little fuzzy. The Grange became a finishing school for young ladies for a while, and then a home for wayward orphans – he found a few pictures of those, skinny waifs standing around in the Grange's dilapidated porch, the ornately carved doors looking stained and weathered, and the glass doors behind them caked with dirt and dust.

"Hospital in the Great War," he read, matching brochure to military records. Some refurbishment in the twenties, and the house leased out for country parties and summer retreats for the flappers and the bright young things – and then a military hospital again, one which had morphed into an asylum, initially for the shell-shocked and those unable to return to civilian life, but then being sucked – no pun intended – into more general use in the fifties.

And after all that – being refurbished as a hotel. Twice. Once in the sixties, enticing the swingers and the nouveau riche, and then again in the late nineties, this time aimed at a business clientele, with what was left of the asylum wards converted into separate ensuite rooms, and the Grange adding 'conference centre' to its name.

Nothing unusual in all of that – except for the number of deaths and other unfortunate incidents associated with the place. That young soldier that Namon had mentioned wasn't the only shell-shocked veteran lying in the little hospital graveyard. Some had died of their wounds, others of unspecified disease, but several were recorded as having taken their own life, both in the First and the Second World War. There'd been three murders, two accidental drownings, four suicides, and six reported nervous breakdowns among the 'bright young things' that had leased the house between the wars. The records of the asylum were harder to find, but a couple of newspaper reports suggested that the inhabitants were 'dour, and sullen' or 'manic and dangerous to themselves and others'.

A little bit of digging suggested that a fair amount of scandal had haunted Westeringford in the sixties, and there were a couple of later incidents, too – the last one only the previous year. A teenage girl had been found floating, face down, in the hotel pool, the morning after the Halloween ball. The evidence had pointed to her having fallen in while drunk, and the verdict had been accidental death.

Marcus suspected there'd been a lot more to it than that.

He sat back, easing the cricks out of his neck and studying the summary of his searching with a critical eye. There was nothing – specific – in that history that screamed *vampire* at him. Nettlestone would be questioning the diagnosis, protesting the lack of the traditional blood drained corpses, and the obvious deaths from unspecified wasting diseases. Nettlestone, of course, was merely a creation blessed with the author's gift of plotting in his favour, and this wasn't the wilds of Carpathia in the late nineteenth century. He was looking at something far more subtle and insidious than the kind of creature he'd created for his exiled nobleman to fight.

This vampire was cunning. Highly intelligent, used to careful planning and clearly capable of both managing his appetite and manipulating his victims so that his presence remained unsuspected, most of the time.

If Marcus had been writing this book, he'd have had John Wellmore discover some ancient manuscript, a lost relic of the Tudor magician's unholy library perhaps, and use it to make a deal with the devil, offering to send him souls in exchange for the gift of eternal life. But this wasn't his plot, he didn't believe in the devil, per se, and if he acted precipitously there was every chance he might end up as a dead or wounded protagonist, slave to the vampire's thrall. Even if he was careful he could still end up in trouble: under arrest, or locked in a padded room somewhere. On the other hand, doing nothing, turning a blind eye and pretending nothing was wrong, was not an option. Namon might have found ways to thrive that meant not having to kill directly, but the evidence was clear: whatever he did, he hurt people, exploited and abused them. Drove them to suicide and madness, somehow. He had to find a way to stop this. Had to protect his friends if he could. Because, if he couldn't, then one day, someone like Namon, maybe even Namon himself, might find and hurt Molly.

There was one small problem with all of that. He might have a better idea of the history now, but he still didn't know what sort of vampire Namon was, let alone how to deal with him.

I need to talk this through with someone, he realised. *If I can. Find a way to get more information. Come up with a plan.*

Cordell might believe him; he'd certainly be willing to listen – or perhaps to play along until he could track down some professional help and get his friend sectioned. For his own good, of course. Marcus sighed. He'd rather not drag his friends into this if he could help it. He'd keep an eye on them, of course. Try and keep them away from Namon and his games if he could. But who else was there?

Who could he trust?

Chapter Seven

"Lords and Ladies, Professors and Adventurers, Goths, Nerds, Steamstokers and sorcerers, living, dead, and *undead*, Gentlefemmes and Gentlemen, welcome to Coffincon Seven!"

Spanner had found something closer to his usual enthusiastic voice somewhere in the night. Perhaps it was because this long planned event was finally happening; perhaps it was a realisation that, in only two more days whatever nightmare haunted him might be over. His eyes were suspiciously feverish, though, so his bounce might have more to do with medication than it did to relief or even sheer adrenaline.

They were holding the opening ceremony in the ballroom; there was a raised dais set up on either side of the chapel door, with a space in between that allowed the guests waiting there – in the 'green room' – to make a grand entrance before taking their seats at the table on their left. The other dais supported a screen and a lectern, allowing the space to be used for both multi-person panels, and single person lectures as the program might demand. For now, the main con guests were sitting at the table while Spanner held forth by the lectern. There was a slide saying *Coffincon Seven: where the dead come out to play* in bold, Gothic lettering splashed across the screen behind him.

Marcus had winced when he'd seen it.

Still, there been a good turnout for the opening ceremony. The registration desk had been doing frantic business when he'd passed it on the way to breakfast, and by the time he'd finished his usual round of hotel bacon, eggs and toast a crowd had been gathering outside the ballroom. He'd smiled and acknowledged the looks of recognition as he'd made his way through it: there were several comments on his new waistcoat, most of them complimentary, and he had had to pause by the fan wearing another handmade variant on Jackson's bowler, just so he could tip his own hat to her and admire her workmanship.

Barry had been on door duty again. He'd smiled as Marcus appeared from the gathering crowd and had pushed the door open so he could slip through it, holding back the inevitable surge as some attendees assumed this meant they could follow him. Pete had been waiting for him by the camera stand at the back of the hall, and they'd walked together up the aisle between the seats and in through the chapel door, exchanging morning pleasantries as they did so.

The chapel had been bustling with people when they'd arrived. Abigail had been hastily instructing some of the volunteer timekeepers who only arrived in the hotel that morning. Johnathan Murray – the head of Tech, who hadn't managed to make dinner the night before, charged past with an armful of extension leads and a cheery 'Morning' as he raced by. Helen was already there, sitting out of the way of the general bustle, along with a man Marcus didn't immediately recognise, but assumed was the con fan-guest, since his jacket was loaded with a fascinating array of con-badges. Pete had guided him through the confusion to join them, and had taken a moment to go through the coming sequence of events. Then he'd had to go, since he had another job to do, leaving Marcus to sit and wait, his body tense and his nerves jangling, as if he were sitting on an anthill.

He'd been intensely conscious – from the moment he'd stepped out into the hallway outside his room – of being in the territory of a dangerous and unpredictable predator. He'd been walking through the hotel with every sense on alert, and every nerve on edge, as if he were some old stag, watching over his herd. He hadn't spotted Namon – yet – but he knew he was there, his presence written on the face of every staff member, in every anxious glance they shared.

He hadn't seen it the day before, but once you knew, it was easy to spot; they too kept watch – on the crowd, on the doorways, and on each other. Like frightened deer they sought protection in numbers, walking in pairs, or gathering in twos and threes, trying to make sure that the youngest and most vulnerable among them was never alone. He suspected they didn't even realise they were doing it; that the vague anxiety that haunted their eyes was never strong or specific enough for them to understand, let alone articulate.

Safety in a crowd, he'd considered gloomily, sitting in his dais-raised seat watching the fans stream in through the ballroom doors and knowing that none of them was safe – nor would be, until they were a long way from Westeringford Grange.

Maybe not even then. Because if Namon really *was* a vampire, who was to say there would not be more of them out there. Somewhere.

Mary had arrived, zig-zagging her wheelchair through the crowd and down the centre aisle so she could park herself at the end of the front row. Marcus had returned the grin she threw him and looked up, trying to spot the rest of his friends in among the gathering. Cordell was easy to spot; Mazzy was with him, but not Lilith. She'd probably decided to skip the opening ceremony, and finish setting up in the Dealers' Room before it officially opened. There was no sign of Ashera – probably for the same reason – and he suppressed a sudden impulse to abandon the formalities and rush off in search of them both.

They'll be okay. They'll be okay ...

He'd taken a final glance round as Spanner had stepped up to the lectern and picked up the microphone, finally spotting Namon, lurking – not at the back of the crowd as he'd half expected, but on the upper gallery. The vampire was leaning on the polished rail, one of those quiet smiles on his face and a shiningly impressive top hat completing his equally impressive outfit. He was in full dandy mode that morning, a black and gold embroidered waistcoat peeking out from beneath his coat, an elegant gold and scarlet cravat tied at his throat, and a long, slender walking stick dangling from his hand. It might even have been a sword-stick, although Marcus hoped he'd never be close enough to confirm the fact.

Spotting him had actually settled some of Marcus' nerves. As long as he knew where he was, had sight of what he was *doing*, then he could be sure that he wasn't anywhere else, doing something unspeakable.

"Just a few domestics to start with." Spanner was in his stride, the presence of the crowd – and possibly the relief of finally getting the con underway – lifting him even closer to his old, spirited self. "There are no fire drills planned for the weekend, so if the alarm goes off, everybody needs to head out of the nearest available exit, and assemble in the car park until the building is cleared for us to return. If you're on the upper floors, then don't use the lifts. There will be people around to help you if you need it." Mary gave him a gnarled thumbs up, and he smiled.

"Now – all the other stuff you need is in the program booklet. Times, locations, and maps. Main program is in here, streams two and three are in the big seminar rooms on the first floor, and the workshops and kaffeeklatsches are in the smaller rooms off the mezzanine. Fan room, games room, and filkers' lounge are all in the corridor by the lifts. Art Show and Dealers' Room across the other side of the hall from here, and ops – if you need ops – can be found in the library. Don't worry if you get lost – somebody will point you in the right direction. If you need help, look for people wearing an orange badge with an orange lanyard. They're our gophers, and if they don't know the answer to your question, they'll know where to go to find someone who does!"

Spanner paused to check his list, in case he'd missed anything. Marcus spotted some of the gophers, Pete among them, moving to stand along the edges of the room. They were carrying small plastic bins and he felt his stomach clench. They were really going to do this...

"Signups for the workshops are on the main registration desk, and you'll find two blue costume tokens in your con envelope. Those are for handing out to anyone in hall costume that you think deserves recognition. Sign them before you hand them over, so we know they've been personally awarded and not just picked up off the floor!" That generated a ripple of laughter. "Hand in any tokens you've been given to the registration desk by Sunday lunchtime, and the person who's earned the most will be awarded a prize ... now then." Spanner paused for dramatic effect. "Let me introduce you to our guests: Helen Rowe, our guest artist..."

The crowd applauded, and Helen stood up and gave a little bow.

"Our Fan Guest all the way from Ohio, David McLaid!"

Another round of applause. David also stood up, clasping his hands above his head in a silent victory cheer. Marcus had heard about the American cons David had been involved with, even though he'd never been to one; his trip to the UK was well earned.

"And our distinguished Guest of Honour, our own Ned Landers, the inimitable Dr Marcus Holland!"

This time there were cheers amid the applause; Marcus rose to his feet with good-natured reluctance – not all of it feigned – doffed his bowler and bent into a sweeping bow. The cheers grew louder. One or two people whistled, and he sank back to his chair, jamming the hat back on his head with an embarrassed grin. It was nice to have your work recognised. Nice to be acknowledged for it, too. But outright adulation was probably taking things a little too far.

Spanner waited for the noise to die down before he continued. "I have one other guest to announce," he said, trying to sound suitably mysterious. "You may all have wondered why we have dragged you to the outskirts of Birmingham, and trapped you in a hotel that's over a mile's walk – or a train journey – to the nearest pizza place. Well, apart from the glorious Gothic that abounds here at Westeringford – and if you join Helen on her guided tour later today you'll get to see all the places you've already seen on film somewhere – this place is home to an old and powerful vampire – and you are all *their* guests for the weekend."

"Yes," he grinned, a little manically, at some of the puzzled looks he was getting. "There is, right now, a vampire walking among us. All you have to do, is work out who they are! Now, if you do," he warned teasingly, "don't go confronting them on your own, in shadowed, dark places. We might never see you again!"

There was laughter at that. People were realising it was meant to be a joke, or perhaps a game. Marcus was clenching his teeth, knowing that saying something – *anything* – at this point would be pointless. The cloak of deception had been cast wide, and trying to tear it away without proof, or the power to deal with what lay beneath it, would be doomed to failure.

"To honour this very special guest of ours," Spanner went on smoothly, "we are asking you to surrender your holy symbols. *Just* for the weekend, of course. We'll make sure everything is labelled, and you'll get all your property back before you leave. If you want to pay a ransom for it, that will be greatly appreciated. Any funds raised will go to the Fan Funded exchange program – the one that's brought David here today – so, as you can see, it'll be in a good cause. If you really don't want to give up your crosses and your pentagrams, that's fine. But if you don't, then – in deference to our special guest – we simply ask that you put them away so they're not openly on show. Wear them under your tee-shirt if you must, or leave them in your room if you can. If you do wear something openly, you *will* be challenged, so hand over or hide those holy declarations and ... welcome to the wicked side."

Don't, Marcus wanted to scream, watching the gophers begin to move among the crowd, offering out little bags and labels to go with them. Too many people were going along with the idea, handing over their treasures and joking with their neighbours about the whole idea. Glimmers of silver and gold began to collect in the boxes waiting for them, the promise of protection, a slim defence against the dark given up on a whim.

Somewhere in the middle of the hall he spotted a dark haired girl, dressed entirely in black, frowning at an approaching gopher. He asked a question. She shook her head – firmly – and very deliberately lifted the silver ankh that hung around her neck to slide it down between her breasts, behind the low cut line of her top. The gopher repeated his question, and the girl lifted the corner of her mouth in a sneer – or what might have been a snarl.

The young man backed away, and Marcus fought down the impulse to cheer. *Good for you,* he thought, making a mental note to track her down and tell her exactly that before the con was over.

"Thank you, everybody," Spanner said, nodding with satisfaction as the now brimming boxes were brought to the front and laid on the dais in front of him. "We promise we'll take good care of all of this. We've asked our dealers, if you buy anything from them this weekend that belongs in these boxes, if they would seal the item up in a bag and hold onto it for you behind their stall. Purchased items can be collected on Sunday afternoon, before the closing ceremony. Our ... friend, will be very grateful for your indulgence."

I bet he will, Marcus growled to himself, gritting his teeth. What had seemed to be an amusing conceit over dinner the night before, was now a deadly and dangerous persuasion, exposing far too many innocents to Namon's influence and appetites. He glanced up, making sure that the creature concerned was still at his place in the balcony. He was; the decidedly hungry smile he wore turned into warmer amusement as he caught Marcus's eye. An elegant hand went up. Namon doffed his top hat in an exaggerated parody of the gesture Marcus had used only a few moments earlier. Vampire bowed mockingly to the author suddenly turned vampire hunter.

And the hunt was on.

— * —

I wonder who's hunting whom? Marcus pondered as he made a mad dash across the hallway. He'd left the ballroom as soon as the ceremony was over and the speakers for the first panel began to step up to the table. The opening moves may have been played, but he wanted to avoid *any* kind of contact with Namon for as long as he could. He needed advice, and he needed support, and he wasn't entirely sure where to find them.

He was intending to head for the Dealers' Room, but he got caught up in the crowd and made slow progress. A glimpse of a top hat coming towards him from along the passageway panicked him, and he dived into the Art Show instead, praying that – if that was Namon – he hadn't seen him, or that, if he had, he had more pressing business elsewhere.

Of course he's seen you, you idiot. Marcus' internal writer chided at him with exasperation. *You're wearing the damned hat!*

The room was larger than he expected. There were glimpses of what looked like wooden panelling on the lower half of its walls, and a faded floral wallpaper covering the rest. The space had been subdivided into a series of smaller spaces by a staggering of standing screens, which gave plenty of places to hang pictures, but also created the impression of entering a complex maze. Helen's work had been given pride of place, hanging in the first section immediately to the left of the door. Somebody else's images were probably hanging on the right, but Marcus didn't see them for a moment or two. His eyes had been caught by the painting that hung directly ahead of him.

It looked like some kind of Tarot card: at first glance a complex and highly detailed version of the Hanged Man. He didn't have time for a second one; the memory of more pressing concerns tugged him away. He hastily stepped round the stand – to find himself standing next to Mazzy, who was busy hanging one last piece.

"Hi, Marcus," she carolled. "Be with you in a mo…"

On the other side of the stand, a figure in a top hat stepped into the doorway. Marcus risked a glance through the gap between the stand pole and the Hessian clad screen it supported, and was in time to see Namon stop dead in his tracks. He glared at the painting with an odd expression, *flinched*, and then turned away, quickly striding out of the room again.

What the ..?

Marcus – stopping only to check that Namon had, indeed left, and not just stepped out into the hallway – walked round the stand again, and stared.

It was indeed a Tarot card – but a quite remarkable one; it depicted Odin's self-sacrifice – reinterpreted, as he'd thought, as the Hanged Man. But every moment looking at it revealed another detail, another subtle reference to several other resurrected gods, elements of their aspects and echoes of their talismans emerging from the design. Runes danced around the border: *nine days I hung upon the world tree,* they said. A spilled wine cup, draped in trailing grapes sat in the lower corner, referencing Dionysus. A scroll in the other corner carried Egyptian hieroglyphs and the cask of Osiris. In the background, a Sumerian goddess with a complex headdress stood in front of an open cave…

"Ishtar, summoning Tannis to return to life from the underworld," Mazzy said with a grin, appearing at Marcus' shoulder. "The feathered serpent is Quetzalcoatl, of course, and the pine tree with the almonds scattered under it is for Attis … the one I had the most trouble fitting in was Ganesha. So I put in Krishna as the wounded deer, and then hung the elephant head among the lanterns on the world tree."

"So you did," he noted, spotting what she meant. "That's clever. It's a lovely piece, Mazzy. Very …" he thought about the look on Namon's face, starting to understand why the crucifix collection had been important to him. "…iconic," he concluded, and she laughed.

"Yeah," she said, dismissively. "It was a thing. I – I might do more, you know? Loki as the Magician, with all the Trickster gods hanging out with him? Or Freya as the Empress; lots and lots of Earth mother stuff to play with there. Come and look at my wolves," she commanded, grabbing his arm to drag him back round the stand. He followed without protest, his mind still weighing up what Namon's reaction to the picture implied. Sacred symbols … did what? Repelled him? Caused him pain?

Whatever it was, it indicated a weakness. One that it might be possible to exploit.

"Fenris, Tyr, and my wolfraiders," Mazzy was saying, pointing at each of her pictures in turn. They were, as usual, lovely pieces of art. She didn't aim for photorealistic imagery; her execution was raw, and it was powerful because of it. He considered all three images, admiring the sense of strength in the figures and the way she'd used both darkness and light to frame and present them. Any one of them would work as a book cover, but he was drawn to the swirl of mist and the hints of moonlight from which the wolf cloaked Viking raiders were emerging.

"That's the one for *Wolfkin*," he decided firmly. "Can I use it, Mazzy? Would you mind?"

"Mind?" She looked at him as if he were mad. "*Mind* one of my pictures being used for one of *your* books? What longship did you come in on? Of course I don't mind. In fact," she said, "I'll give you the picture – as long as the publisher pays me for reproducing it, of course ..."

He smiled. "I'll make sure of it," he promised. She took a moment to do a little victory dance, squeaking in delight – then she grabbed up a pen and wrote SOLD very firmly across the bidding slip.

"Must be my day," she said, coming back to give him a quick hug. "Good news, and – now this. Don't spread it around," she went on, leaning in close enough to whisper, "but ... my next masterpiece is gonna be a *baby*."

Marcus blinked, taking a moment to process that – then pulled her into a warm hug, muttering meaningless congratulations and making *happy for you* noises that made her giggle in response.

Halfway through this process of delight, his blood ran with cold with sudden terror. *She's pregnant* had collided with *Vampire in the building;* he needed to protect her, to *warn* her, and he didn't know how.

"Mazzy," he said carefully, "I'm very, very happy for you – and for Cordell, and Lilith too – but I want you to promise me something, okay?"

"O-kay," she answered slowly, looking at him in puzzlement.

"Promise me, that if you're not here in the Art Show, that you won't be alone this weekend. Not for a moment.

Surround yourself with friends." He paused, and added, trying to convey the seriousness of his request. "Don't even sleep alone."

Her puzzlement took on an exasperated twist. "You guys," she muttered, rolling her eyes. "Marcus, do you think Cordell would *let* me sleep alone after this news? He's papa-bear-ing me, already! I'm not made of glass, and I know how to take care of myself, but …" She sighed, and nodded, clearly deciding that over protective males were the cross she was going to have to bear. "I promise, okay? Someone with me all the time. Someone I *know*," she added, at the look he was giving her. "And trust. Sheesh," she added with a quiet grin, "If I'd known spawning would stir *this* kind of protective shit, I'd have seriously considered parthenogenesis."

"Wouldn't have worked," he shot back with a relieved grin of his own. "I was just as bad with Beverley about Reuben as I was with Molly. And I *knew* he wasn't mine, so…"

She snorted softly, and gave his shoulder a gentle punch. "*You*," she accused with affection, "are a dork. An adorable dork, but … yeah, okay. Mazzy will be good, Dr Holland."

"Thank you," he breathed, knowing there wasn't much more he could do – other than find a way to remove the danger she didn't know about, and didn't *need* to know about. Especially now.

"Marcus?" Pete appeared from around the stand, the anxious look he was wearing relaxing a little as he spotted the pair of them. "There you are." He tilted his wrist and tapped at his watch. "The signing session's about to start?"

Damn. Marcus was no closer to getting the help he needed, and this was going to eat further into the limited time he suspected he had. He'd almost forgotten about his signing session, but he couldn't *not* do it; he was here to work, after all. Vampire hunting would have to wait. At least he'd got a promise of being careful from Mazzy, which was a start.

"Thanks, Pete," he said, "I'll be right there."

— * —

The Dealers' Room had been busy when he and Pete had finally made it through the door. It held the usual mix of bookstalls, along with someone selling slogan printed tee-shirts, the Fan Fund stall and the leaflet table beside it strewn with flyers for other cons, a table offering steam-punk paraphernalia sitting next to Lilith's display of metal jewellery, and – opposite both – Ashera's table, sporting strings of beads, stands displaying bracelets and amulets, various packets of herbs and incense, and a box of papyrus scrolls. Her general theme was Egyptian in style: it matched her stylised make up and the rather impressive wig and beaded collar she was wearing.

He waved at her, and at Lilith as Pete chivvied him past, and they both waved back. Lilith was in full steam-punk Gothic gear, clinched into a tight purple corset, and wearing a smart little velvet hat complete with a half veil. Her make-up included crystal dotted black dagger drops under each eye, and deep purple lipstick. Normally her theatrical extravagance would be a reason to smile; but – for some reason – seeing one of his best friends deliberately disguised as a vampire didn't *entirely* feel … amusing, anymore.

Lilith waved back anyway, probably attributing his vaguely discomforted expression to the size of the queue that had begun to build up at the end of the room. They'd cordoned off the signing area with a line of rope, probably trying to leave plenty of space for the fans to queue without impeding the dealers' business, but it was looking decidedly crowded. There was no immediate sign of Namon, which allowed Marcus to relax a little. The only top hats in the room belonged to a buxom young woman wearing a leather corset over a voluminous skirt in bottle green silk, and Cordell – who wasn't wearing his, but had placed it reverently on the table in front of him. Marcus grinned as he took the seat behind the table next to him; the hat – in a purple plush that matched Lilith's corset, and sporting a decoration of chicken bones and black rooster feathers – had become as much a part of Cordell's presence at a signing as his signature. He'd been presented with the thing at a con in New Orleans, and taken to wearing it for the rest of the weekend, declaring that *If you can get away with Jackson's bowler*, then there would be nothing wrong with him choosing to honour Baron Samedi in the same way.

"I see you brought the hat," Marcus observed teasingly, taking off his bowler and making a show of placing it on the matching corner of his own table. Cordell laughed.

"You always do," he shot back, reaching to brush a non-existent speck of dust from the edge of his hat's brim. "Seen Mazzy this morning?"

The question was casual, but Marcus wasn't fooled. "I have," he said. "I hear that congratulations are in order."

"Oh, man," Cordell shook his head, excitement, pride and a whole lot of worry warring for dominance in his expression. "Scary stuff, you know? Good scary, but – whole new thing for me. And her. Thank the loa for Lilith; I'm not sure we'd be dealing with this without her."

"You'll manage," Marcus assured him, laying his two signing pens – one black, one gold – side by side on the table. "I did, so – it can't be *that* hard. Listen," he said, turning towards his friend with a serious note in his voice. "Mazzy's going to be very vulnerable right now. You keep an eye on her: make sure nobody bothers her, that she's safe, okay?"

The look Cordell threw him held wry rebuke: an *as-if-I-would-do-anything-else* look. He might have said something to go with it, but – at that moment – a con steward unclipped the obstructing rope and the queues surged forward, eager to gain their prize.

Signing sessions were always interesting, no matter where he did them. Bookshops were always good, since most of them would supply him with endless cups of tea, offer biscuits, and be encouraging fans to buy more books. Not that the kind of fan he was meeting *this* weekend needed much encouragement. Cons tended to be less stressful: the awareness of being on public display was balanced with the knowledge that most of the people in the queue really had read the books and were there because they admired his work. Then, the fact that there were other queues, with other authors at the end of them, also pasting on their welcoming smiles and gritting their teeth through over used and – in some cases – over familiar comments and questions, somehow made the effort that little bit easier to deal with.

Besides Marcus and Cordell, this particular session included both Angela Bee, a modest, middle-aged lady, whose friendly smile belied the blood drenched horror of the post-apocalyptic worlds she wrote about, and Karia Duboz, who retold Russian folk tales in futuristic settings. The four of them were all popular that morning, although – probably inevitably – Marcus had the longest queue. The con had restricted signing to one book per person, for which he was very grateful; there had been occasions when fans had arrived with every single one of his books piled in their arms, and while Francis might have thought that good for sales, it had wrought havoc on the readability of his signature.

He'd perfected a faster version now, the sort of quick and casual scrawl that remained vaguely recognisable and allowed him to have time for at least a quick word with his readership. He managed most of them with a smile, accepting compliments and taking the occasional gush of praise in practised style. Some of them had sensible questions; one or two wanted to point out 'flaws' or plot holes they'd noticed, while others tried to dispute the facts used in his non-fictional works. Most of them however, just wanted to say thank you, and he accepted those with slightly embarrassed grace; it was still hard to believe sometimes that people actually *liked* what he did. He'd started writing as an escape, seeking refuge from dry academic texts and even drier academics back in his student days. He'd always liked his subject, and he'd never quite understood why some of the so-called experts who'd taught him seemed to think it duller than dishwater. That first book – he smiled as he signed a first edition copy for a long-term fan – had really been a piece of fan-fiction, a tribute to all those much better fantasy writers who'd got him interested in folklore and myth in the first place.

The next group to step up were some of the younger members of the convention: fresh faced and filled with bounce and enthusiasm. The young man – his tee-shirt had dragons on it – had his arm round one of the two girls, and he smiled at her as he handed his book over to be signed. She was wearing a blue velvet dress that had far too many frills and ruffles to qualify as 'Goth'; Marcus thought it was rather fetching, and said so, earning himself a shy smile. "Told you," the young man – his name badge had 'Mason Lane' written on it – said with a hint of exasperation. The third member of their party – another young woman who, even if she wasn't Mason's sister was almost definitely related to him – rolled her eyes.

"She was *aiming* for Faerie Queen," she said, "but – really – I think it's just way too Disney."

"Oh, come on, Cyn," Mason protested. "Don't listen to her, Shelley. I like it. Dr Holland likes it. What's not to like?"

'Cyn' – her name badge labelled her 'Cynthia Lane' – snorted. "Boyfriend's opinions don't count," she said. "You're biased."

"And *you're* supposed to be her best friend," the young man shot back. "What happened to supporto-gal?"

"She turned into a third wheel and rolled away." Cyn's response was a muttered one, not really meant for the ears of the other two. Marcus felt a surge of sympathy for her; there was clearly a lot more to this particular disagreement than a difference of opinion over a dress.

"Just leave it, Mason," Shelley advised, turning to Marcus with an apologetic smile. "Don't mind them, Dr Holland. Cyn never agrees with Mason on principle – him being her brother, you know? The dress is *meant* to be like the one you gave Eloise, but I don't think it's quite right..."

"Oh." Marcus glanced down at the book in his hand, realising it was a copy of *Fair and Faerie*, the tale he'd written that had drawn heavily from Spenser's *Faerie Queene*. "Her gown, sky blue and velvet soft, draped around her like drifting clouds, wrapping her in simple eloquence ... That one, right?"

"Right." Her response held a note of relief. "Did I get it right?"

Too Disney, Cyn mouthed from behind her, and Marcus had to swallow down the urge to laugh.

"I think you make a charming Eloise," he said instead, reaching for his gold pen and using it to autograph the volume. He avoided pointing out that the character concerned was a slender, half-starved waif at that point in the book, and was doomed to die, loveless and abandoned by the Fae knight she'd chosen to follow into the wilderness. The whole point of the book was about avoiding being seduced by surface appearances – that the Fae did 'fair' in order to use and manipulate the foolish – but Shelley had probably missed that in among the helpless romance of the young woman seeking the love of a man she had only ever seen from a distance.

"Thank you" she said, clutching the book back to her velvet draped bosom and letting Mason lead her away. Cyn dropped her own copy of the book in front of him.

"She doesn't get it," she said, resignedly. "But she's always been a would-be princess, and... I guess he likes that in her. I'd rather be Brineld, myself. But I don't look good in armour."

He gave her a thoughtful look; her hair might be cut even shorter than her brother's, but there was no way she'd be mistaken for a man. "Armour's over-rated," he said, signing the book – in black – 'To Cyn, may she only do so in good cause' before scrawling his name. "And knightly deeds don't always require a sword." He handed it back to her; she examined his words warily – and then favoured him with a warm and delighted smile.

"Oh, that's ... *thank you.* Thank you *so* much."

She left, still smiling, which Marcus thought was probably a good sign. He turned away from the queue for a moment to ask Pete if he'd mind getting him a fresh bottle of water, and when he turned back, Isiah Namon was standing in front of him.

The good mood that the encounter with Cyn had left him with froze and shattered instantly. His heart rate tipped into overdrive as adrenaline surged through his veins. It took every effort he had not to leap to his feet and back away; he forced himself to take a slow, deep breath instead, trying very, very hard, not to let the terror show.

Fortunately, his smile had frozen along with the rest of him; it stayed on his face just long enough for him to recover a little from the shock, and he schooled it into neutral lines as best he could. Namon wasn't actually looking at him when he did so; his eyes had drifted sideways to glare at Cordell for some reason.

"Mr Namon," Marcus greeted him, with as friendly a note as he could manage. "I didn't know you were a fan."

"I read your book," the vampire purred, placing a hardback copy of 'Blood on their Lips' on the table. "I found it – fascinating."

I bet you did, sprang to Marcus' mind, but he managed to keep the thought to himself. "Really? It's – uh – a little more scholarly than my fiction, of course, but – I tried to keep it readable. Purely academic papers can be … heavy going, sometimes."

"So I've heard. I prefer the classics, on the whole, but some of the more modern works can be enlightening. And times change, as your work so clearly shows." His smile did not reach his eyes, but he seemed genuinely amused all the same. "Perhaps you should have entitled it 'From Monster to Movie star'."

Francis had suggested something like that, and Marcus had rejected it with fervour. His history of vampirism was not about what the film industry had done to elevate them to revered status. It had been meant to put the record straight; to clarify what Stoker had romanticised, used to push his own political and cultural spin.

"Movie Stars don't kill people," he said, bluntly, then added – since he could see amusement starting to widen the monster's smile, "Not as a general rule, anyway. For vampires it's part of the job description – in the blood, you could say."

"So you could." Namon's eyes started to narrow, and then he glanced sideways again, shifting uncomfortably as if he had an itch somewhere, distracting him. "But even in this – " His fingers tapped the book's cover. "– while you suggest that blood is the vampire's only sustenance, you do point out that not all of them … kill."

"Not all of them spread the plague, or turn into bats, either," Marcus pointed out. "There are many kinds of vampires, Mr Namon." *Which one are you?*

It was easy, now he knew, to realise just how people made *space* for the monster in their midst. Most of it was probably unconscious, some unspoken instinct giving him a slightly wider berth than most. Some of it people undoubtedly rationalised, deferring to the gentleman, stepping back from their elders, remembering their manners. Nobody invaded his personal space; people stepped around him, like shoals of fish swimming in warm currents and avoiding sudden cold eddies.

Namon clearly glided through them all like a shark.

"Who should I sign it to?" Marcus asked, pulling the book towards him, and trying to keep that professional smile on his face. "Isiah? Or John?"

He froze as soon as the question had left his lips. That was *stupid*. Up until then, the two of them had been playing, skirting round the amusement – to Namon – of the false truthhood, the game they were both meant to be playing. Marcus was supposed to be in on *that* joke. But that was going to hit too close to home, to suggest, to the previously oblivious vampire, that Marcus knew more than he should.

Dark eyes, shadowed beneath the brim of the hat, widened in a moment of surprise – then narrowed in calculated anger, studying Marcus with an intensity that made his blood run cold.

"My father," the vampire said tightly, "called me *Isiah*. He was always saying: *In quietness and in confidence shall be your strength.*" He leaned forward, putting out his right hand and laying it deliberately over Marcus' own. His fingers and palm were dry and cold. Something – a sense of heat, a shiver of energy – reacted to the touch, pulsing down Marcus' arm and into that contact, warmth and vitality draining from skin and muscle alike.

"Do not underestimate me, *Dr* Holland," Namon hissed softly, leaning close enough to whisper. "Your facts are merely tissues of lies, and your expertise is fatally flawed. What you know is *nothing*. I have no reason to fear you. And you," he leaned even closer, a knowing smile on his lips, "have every reason to fear *me*."

He let go and straightened up again. Pins and needles flooded into Marcus' fingers, replacing that brief discomfort of cold, and his fingers clenched in a moment of disconcerted pain.

"Isiah, then," he managed to stutter out, his attempt to cover his reaction with a laugh tinted with a note of hysteria. The vampire nodded benevolently, his entire demeanour once again cloaked in mannered humour and charm.

The pen felt like lead in his hands, but Marcus managed to sign his name with most of his usual flare. The *To Isiah* that he scribbled above it lacked conviction, but Namon accepted the book's return with gracious thanks and started to glide away. Two steps, and then he stepped back, turning hastily away from his intended path to head back into the crowd, pushing one or two of them aside as he went. Cordell glanced up as he did so, looking across the top of the Baron's hat to stare at the retreating figure in a moment of puzzlement.

"Guess he didn't want my autograph," he joked to the people gathered round his table. They laughed. Marcus didn't. He was too busy trying to disentangle the idea of a vampire who would happily quote scripture at him – yet turn tail at the sight of a purple hat draped with bones.

"You think *he's* the vampire?" one of the fans standing in Marcus' queue asked, staring after Namon's departing back.

"Nah," his friend countered. "Too obvious. Besides," he added, stepping up to place his own book on the table. "What kind of vampire would be daft enough to threaten Marcus Holland? He knows all their tricks. Right?"

Marcus stared at him. "I wouldn't say that," he responded. Still feeling dazed. Then he shook himself and found the man a wan smile. "I'm just the author," he pointed out. "There are probably a few tricks I don't know about yet."

Pete brought back the requested water, which Marcus gulped down gratefully. He massaged some of the feeling back into his hand, and returned to work, smiling and signing, and making small talk as the queue gradually grew shorter. Eventually, he signed one last book, smiled at its owner's thanks, put down his pen, and took a moment to flex his fingers. It had been an hour since the confrontation – if you could call it that – with Namon, but that odd sense of cold and the pins and needles had never entirely faded from his arm. Add that to the number of books that had passed under his hands, and it was no wonder that he was beginning to feel the burn of long repetition eating into his bones.

A shadow fell across the table. Someone reached down and gently encircled his aching hand with elegant fingers. He nearly flinched at the touch, but relaxed as the warmth of the contact registered. He looked up, feeling the ache and the last of the chill wash away, replaced by a faint tingling of energy.

Ashera was standing there, smiling at him. There was no-one else left in the queue, and the background bustle of the Dealers' Room had died away to a slow murmur as hungry attendees left in search of lunch.

"You need a break," she purred, her voice as smooth and sweet as honey. "Let's get some fresh air, shall we?" She leaned in a little closer; the scent of rich spices, warm resins, and a top note of flowers and herbs wafted over him. Her eyes were serious; her look quietly concerned. "I think you and I need to talk."

Chapter Eight

They left through a door at the back of the room, one hidden behind the heavy curtains that draped across the entire wall. Behind them was a wall of glass that looked out onto the hotel pool: Ashera held the curtain aside and ushered him through, letting the fabric drop down behind them to conceal their exit. Marcus found himself standing in sunlight: the angled glass roof above the full-sized pool sent it dancing across the surface of the water to reflect and shimmer on almost every surface.

"We are safer here," she said, "but walls have ears – as do the staff." She nodded towards an attendant, who was busy picking up a sprawl of towels on the far side of the facility. There was nobody in the pool that time of day, but there were still members of staff in evidence, seemingly engrossed in their work. "This way."

She led the way along the side of the pool and out onto the paved patio at the back of the hotel. The gardens fell away ahead of them, a gentle slope of grass, studded with winding paths and clumps of ornamental trees. Some distance away the sun gleamed off the surface of the canal, its serpentine sweep ending, off to Marcus's right, in a circular basin, more than big enough to allow a full length narrow boat to turn round in it.

He snorted, softly. This was a setting straight out of one of his books. He could just see Jackson Hobbs mooring the *John Barleycorn* on the banks of the canal, and the man himself, bowler jammed onto his head, starting the trudge up towards the house, passing the walled off graveyard on the way...

"This was a happy house, once," Ashera remarked, moving

to sit on a nearby bench. He followed her slowly, feeling decidedly out of his depth – and, like Jackson, somewhat wrongly dressed for his surroundings.

"Who are you?" he asked, then – a little more puzzledly: "*What* are you?"

She sighed and patted the bench beside her, inviting him to sit down.

"Why do people *always* want to start there?" she asked the general air. "They can be hunched in a burning building, surrounded by harpies screaming for their blood, and when you hold out your hand to help? They ask *who are you?*" She threw him a patient look, and he realised he was still standing, despite the obvious invitation to join her.

He grimaced apologetically and took the proffered seat, joining her in staring out across the sunlit grounds. "Perhaps," he ventured warily, "because... when the whole world has just shifted out of shape? You don't feel like trusting a stranger. No matter how... trustworthy, they may seem."

"Yes. *Yes*, I can understand that," she said, turning to smile at him. She wasn't wearing a wig, he realised distractedly. She'd braided her hair, weighting the end of each braid with a line of tiny blue and gold beads. "It's never easy, finding out that there really are monsters, lurking in the dark. Even if you knew the stories were true, when you meet the real thing? The tales never quite... match that first experience."

"Tell me about it," he muttered, rolling his eyes at the understatement. Ashera's laugh was soft and sympathetic.

"I was sixteen," she said. "And that was a very long time ago. A man came across the desert, and asked for shelter in the temple. The High priestess invited him in – and he slaughtered her and her sisters as if they were caged doves, placed upon the altars as a sacrifice. He struck me down without hesitation and left me there to bleed, among the corpses of the only family I had ever known. He didn't bother to drink from *my* veins," she added, distantly. "He was already sated by his savage feast."

Marcus stared at her. There was no hint of horror, no echo of *victim* underlying her words, but there was truth in every syllable, a conviction in her tone that defied any possible denial.

"He – *it?* – left you for dead?"

"I *was* dead." She wasn't looking at him, but out, at the green and gold of the world. Her voice had dropped almost to a whisper. "The pain dragged me away into darkness – and after that there was no pain. Just a bright, warm light … Right there, on the threshold of death, with Anubis waiting, I hesitated. There was no-one else left. No-one to stop him. No-one to warn the villages, or carry the cry to the soldiers. No-one to bury my friends, my family, no-one to avenge our deaths…"

She paused for a moment, turning back from distanced contemplation to seek his puzzled eyes. "So I came back. I took strength from that light, and I brought it back to the world. I chose to stay. Not from fear of what lay beyond – but because I could not abandon what lay behind to the horror, to the *hunger*, that had sought to destroy me.

"It was a hard choice. Don't ever think otherwise of me. But I could not leave, while he remained. I rose from the dead, and I hunted him down – and I have been hunting his kind ever since, walking the world, holding on to the memory of that light, seeking to help and to heal."

She reached to catch his hand, holding his gaze with gentle conviction. "I am Ashera, who was Isetnofret, priestess of Isis, in the days of the Prince Khaemweset. I was born in the lands of Kush, but was gifted by my father to serve the goddess in the great temple on the banks of the Nile. I am chosen by Heh the endless, one of the most ancient of gods, to serve in the circle of the *Shen:* one of the eternal protectors of mankind."

Her hand was warm against his own, a far cry from Namon's bitter and chilling touch. She didn't look as if she were thousands of years old, although there was something – somewhere deep in her kohl-lined eyes – that conveyed both wisdom and experience.

"Wow," he said, after a moment or two of stunned silence. "That's... oh, *wow."* If she'd told him that story the day before, he'd have found it hard not to laugh at her, would have assumed she'd adopted a persona to cosplay and gotten herself a little too deeply into character for the weekend. But he'd seen – or *not* seen, Namon's lack of reflection, and he'd felt the vampire take something from him, a warning to stay away, to not interfere with his game. He knew that the monster was real. He'd also seen – caught a glimpse – of how *she* had reflected in the antique silver the night before; how her image had danced and flickered, as if it echoed multiple souls ... multiple *lives.* If vampires did exist, did that mean everything *else* mentioned in folklore and myth did? Why shouldn't there be some kind of immortal beings wandering around, keeping the monsters in check? "So," he asked with a hint of hysteria, "you're an ancient Egyptian priestess. What's next? Do I start looking round for a mad scientist and his monster? I mean, I've got the vampire and the Mummy, so maybe I should complete the set... "

"You are not going mad, Marcus," she told him firmly, smiling at his expression. "You have seen Isiah Namon for what he is. Suffered his touch. I have trusted you with my secret, and you can trust *me.* I have been hunting the source of his contagion for a long time; he needs to be stopped, and I think you can do it. I think you need to do it – because, if you did not have the heart for it, you would have left, last night. Wouldn't you."

It wasn't a question. And she was right. His sense of self-preservation had nearly sent him fleeing into the night – and he might have listened to it, too, were it not for some greater sense of duty and obligation. His own life was important to him – but not as important as the lives of his friends and the safety of his children. "I chose to stay," he paraphrased, sharing that understanding with her. "Not because I would not believe, or had no fear – but because I cannot abandon my friends to the horror, to the *hunger*, that lurks at the heart of this place."

"We will find a way," she promised. "You and I together. You asked me to help you and I will – as much as I can, anyway. A long time ago – a *very* long time ago now, I would have fought him, face to face, and brought him down myself. But the fires of life burn within me, and their flames have grown brighter every century. He does not know my kind, but he senses my presence here, and – while he is drawn to human warmth – my fire is far too brilliant for him to face. He would turn away and seek escape should I come too close for him to bear. And if I were to force a confrontation? He and I would burn together; he is dark, and his corruption is deep. I could not be sure of surviving such an encounter. I will do it if I must, but …"

"No." Marcus interrupted her with determination. "Nobody dies. Not if I can help it. You're right. We'll find a way. Damn it, I've killed enough vampires in print!" The declamation was fierce, but the thought that followed it was bitter realisation. "Oh, goddess, *that's* stupid. He said … he said my facts were lies, and my expertise was flawed. How can I apply the things I think I know? Why should I trust *any* of my research?"

"Because *he* lied." Ashera's words were confident. Reassuring. "You don't know everything, Marcus. Neither do I. But you know enough to make him fear you. That's why he struck as he did – to put you off balance; to warn you off. He's very dangerous, but he isn't invulnerable. He can be destroyed."

Marcus nodded thoughtfully. That made sense. He'd

made a stupid mistake letting Namon know he was aware of the truth behind the joke – and instead of feigning ignorance, or laughing at him, the vampire had lashed out. Warned him to back off, to leave him and his 'game' alone. Which meant that he could be a threat. If he could only figure out *how*.

"Okay," he considered slowly. "He has to have some kind of weakness we can exploit. I know he doesn't like holy symbols … What kind of vampire is he, anyway? He's walking around in the day, he doesn't seem to have been buried anywhere, and … I don't think he's drinking anyone's blood."

She shook her head, her fingers playing with one of the beaded bracelets around her wrist. "He doesn't need to. It's warmth and soulfire that's feeding him. And he wasn't buried, because he's refused to die. His kind are much rarer than the blood hunters, the walking corpses, or the lost souls caught between this life and the next. Do you know why the Christians identified seven deadly sins? Because there are certain – obsessions – attitudes and actions that don't just corrupt a soul but, taken to extremes, can literally destroy it. Namon is one of the Hollow Men – a creature whose mortal soul was first corrupted and then consumed by desires and passions that left no room for any virtue. He died from the inside out, leaving him nothing more than the husk of a man, an empty shell that may walk and talk and *appear* to live – but, in reality, exists only by stealing life and warmth from others. He feeds an emptiness that cannot be filled, and he does so without care or concern for his victims. His touch chills the heart, tears at the soul, and leaves an echo of his corruption in the wound, like a bitter poison – a contagion that, untreated, can fester and corrupt even the strongest of hearts."

Marcus shivered, thinking about vulnerable orphans, wounded soldiers – and young women who drowned themselves in hotel pools. "That would explain a few things," he said. "I was hoping he was just a hungry spider, but it sounds like he's more than that."

"Much more," she agreed. "He's a disease. And he's been festering here for centuries, spreading sorrow, despair, and some of his hungers across the entire country. I've dealt with blood hunters that have carried his taint, and had to deal with hundreds of wounded souls bearing the scars of his attentions. I have life to give away," she pointed out, in response to his questioning look. "And I do, constantly. If he's the disease," she said waving vaguely at the hotel behind them, "then I am – a white blood cell, trying to repair the damage it causes."

"Oh, don't look at me like that," she went on, amused at his reaction to the analogy. "Just because I was born in ancient Egypt doesn't mean I haven't learned a few things since. I'm a healer, Marcus, and I heal – *have* healed, down through centuries of pain and suffering, and I've seen all sorts of medical breakthroughs. I'm actually a qualified doctor – several times over and in several different disciplines. I've studied at numerous hospitals, and I've worked with more patients than I could possibly count. My current specialty is psychiatry, because – well, wounds to the soul rarely show on the skin. I have been hunting *this* contagion for decades, and this weekend is the best chance I have to finally deal with its source. I came here hoping to find a way – and then *you* asked me to help you, and *that* allows me to intervene."

She paused for breath, suddenly aware of how passionately she'd been speaking. "Vampires like the Hollow Men care only for their own desires," she said, her voice returning to a more measured tone. "They take without asking, and they impose their will without concern for consequences. But *we*, the Shenuheh? We have to be asked, before we can act. The older I get, it becomes harder and harder for me to step in – even to deal with a monster like Namon – without a direct request for help."

He thought about that for a moment, trying to imagine what that might be like – to be aware of evil and yet be unable to take any action against it until, or unless, someone *asked*. When most of the people at risk, the innocents who needed the most protection, were going to be unaware of any danger in the first place. "I only asked you to help me up," he said slowly, remembering the moment all too well.

"I know," she said, smiling one of those wise and knowing smiles. "But sometimes that's all it takes…"

– * –

He left Ashera in the sunshine and walked back round the pool, making his way through the hotel gym and sauna and into the main part of the house. The bracelet she'd insisted on slipping over his wrist curled over the skin beneath his cuff with reassuring weight and warmth; each bead was cut into the shape of a tiny scarab beetle, a carefully scribed hieroglyph carved into its belly. It was, she'd said, a prayer to Anubis, requesting that the Lord of death and rebirth watch over him, and keep his hounds at bay. Marcus had already seen how Namon recoiled in the presence of sacred symbols, and – while he could not explain how, or why, that might be – the knowledge that he carried some additional, but discretely hidden, armour against the vampire's attack, gave him a little more confidence about returning to the depths of his lair.

Ashera had given him a lot to think about. Not just the immediate problems, and the implications of how his understanding of his life's work had suddenly taken on a whole different perspective, but also *her* story, the suggestion that there might be *something* working to counteract the evils that the old tales had described, and which he'd just discovered to be horrifyingly real. '*Don't try to act precipitously,*' she'd advised. '*Observe and learn. Let him*

*think you are respecting his warning. He will be arrogant
enough to think you powerless, and afraid. Discover his
weaknesses. Find yourself allies if you can.'*

He knew she was probably right about needing allies, but
the last thing he wanted to do was drag more people behind
the curtains of ignorance to see the nastiness he'd never be
able to unsee.

His route led him past a long line of display cases, each one
facing the glass walls of the leisure suite in ostentatious
array. They contained a plethora of antique objects: Chinese
porcelain vases, Wedgwood plates, ivory figures, and
silverware jostled together beside carved inkwells, tiny,
intricate cameos, snuffboxes, and other souvenirs of a bygone
age. If they were genuine – and he had no reason to doubt
the fact, then the entire collection was probably worth a
fortune. *Isiah*'s fortune, he realised, pausing in front of a
striking pair of silver candlesticks, each a good eighteen
inches high. A note from his early morning's research sprang
to Marcus' mind. John Wellmore had been reputed to be a
miser, a man who'd responded to his father's profligate
spending by sacking staff and closing down most of the
house. There'd been no records of him ever selling *anything;*
his whole life had been focused on profiting from insurance
and property deals. What if he'd invested in other things as
well? Expensive art and furnishings, like the ones on display
on the second floor. Rare items and expertly crafted
silverware. Hand crafted mirrors, and crystal chandeliers …

Marcus took a step backwards, glancing along the line of
cases and taking a moment to catch his breath. *This* was
what had planted the seeds of corruption in Namon's
hollowed out heart. *Consumed by his desires and passions …*
The sin of avarice – the rapacious pursuit of material
possessions, the desire to own and keep *things* of value,
without ever valuing their use or beauty. It would explain
why the monster was still in residence – still bound within

the house that he owned, clinging to his past and to a collection that he could not bear to abandon. He had found a way to deny death because to die would be to give up *everything* he owned.

"Oooh," Marcus breathed, relishing that sudden understanding of his foe. "You must have *hated* every penny you needed to spend: all that rebuilding and having to commission endless refurbishments ..." How the monster must have wrestled with impossible choices: should he spend his greedily hoarded cash, or watch his precious collection rot and decay? How much had his hunger contributed to those dilemmas? Had he found justification for the investment in his property, in his need to feed? His need to sustain his unlife in order to hold on to the things he thought he loved?

The history of the house made more sense now, too. The rapacious miser, trying to find ways to bring suitable prey into his lair without spending too much of his money, having to avoid drawing attention to himself or his victims. The orphanage would have provided him with an easily exploited supply of abandoned and helpless souls. The military hospitals – paid for, no doubt, by the War Office – would have given ample opportunity for him to stalk the corridors in search of sustenance, and the asylum ... well, who would believe the rambling words of lunatics, afraid of monsters that came in the dark and sucked out life and soul and breath?

Turning the place into a hotel, though? That was twisted genius: creating an on-going supply of visitors, ignorant of any danger, and never staying long enough to become suspicious, or concerned. His victims simply carried the damage he caused away, unknown and possibly even unnoticed most of the time. Until the wounds he caused, slowly festering and spreading their contagion, blossomed into despair, depression, madness, or death.

Ashera had said she'd dealt with blood hunters who'd

carried his taint. Could Namon's hunger sometimes plant seeds of similar desires? Was one of his legacies a quiet plague of true vampires, consumed by a need for blood? How many people had passed through Westeringford's doors over the years? And how far had the Hollow Man's contagion reached, spreading out across an unknowing world?

Too many questions, centred on one monstrous, twisted travesty of a man.

One Marcus had to find a way to stop.

He walked on, past a number of doors marked 'staff only,' then back to carpeted corridors and the main hotel lifts. Mary was busy manoeuvring her chair into one, and he paused to give her a hand, stepping up to hold the lift door before it tried to argue with the chair.

"Stupid lifts," she muttered, smiling at him with appreciative thanks. "They need to update the sensors on these things. Thanks, Marcus. Have you had lunch? I'm told the paninis they're serving on the mezzanine are worth dying for."

"I hope not," he responded, torn – for a moment – between amusement and alarm. No sandwich was worth dying for, no matter how good it might taste, and in Namon's lair, the casual joke might turn out to be more literal than anyone could imagine. "But I am hungry. I've got an hour before my next panel, so – can I buy you a drink? Coffee? Tea?"

"Tea would be lovely," she agreed, beckoning him to join her in the lift. "Are you enjoying the con so far?"

He stepped in and let her hit the relevant button, wondering how to answer that. If it wasn't for the business with Namon, he would have been answering with an unqualified *yes* – but he could hardly say that. Or could he?

"Apart from having this… ancient vampire wandering around somewhere? Yes, I think so. How about you?"

"I'm more upset about these damn lifts than I'm worried

about vampires," Mary said, with feeling. "They've tried to make this place chair friendly, but I'm wearing my wheels out travelling back and forth all the time. And I had to miss a reading because if I hadn't I'd have been late for the panel I wanted to see. Other than that," she concluded philosophically, "It's been pretty good so far."

That was a cheering thought. Somewhere, in the back of his mind, Marcus had been worrying that the vampire's presence would fall across the convention like a dark shadow. But fans were resilient; they'd come to have a good time, and that's exactly what they'd have, just as they had done for many years. There'd been bad cons: he'd been to a few of them, but they'd almost inevitably been saved by so many people finding adventure in disaster and solidarity in survival. The conventions that stuck in the mind were the ones where things had *happened*: the fire alarm late at night, the sudden requirement to move the entire convention from one set of rooms to another because the hotel had double-booked. Conventions where the decorators were still desperately trying to finish a refurbishment – and the one where the lifts had notoriously misbehaved, and heroes had had to rescue panicked claustrophobics with the help of the local fire brigade.

Having a vampire around might be a little bit more than the usual challenge, but that wouldn't stop the filkers from singing, or authors from congregating round the bar and swapping tales about recent reviews, the cluelessness of certain publishers, and the complications lurking in contracts.

"Good," he said, smiling at her. "Glad to hear you're enjoying yourself."

He left her to find a suitable table in among the lunchtime bustle of the mezzanine, and went to put in their order: two cheese and ham paninis, and a pot of tea for two. By the time he brought the loaded tray across, she'd acquired company, a fair-haired woman not *exactly* in costume, but dressed with a large hint of Ann Bonney out of Jules Verne. She looked vaguely familiar, and it took him a moment or two to realise she was one of the two ladies he'd seen talking to Namon the night before.

Her badge said her name was Janti Sales, but Mary introduced her as *Jane:* they'd met at a Worldcon a couple of years before, when Jane had taking part in the Masquerade, and Mary had managed to half strangle her by parking her chair on the end of her long scarf. Marcus thought it was an interesting way to make a friend, but Mary and Jane had obviously found enough in common for them both to dismiss the incident as something amusing, rather than traumatic. She'd actually come over to ask Mary if she'd be willing to help her with her gown for the Midnight Masque, but there was a fair amount of small talk and friends catching up to get through before she could formulate her question. Marcus poured tea and munched on panini while the two of them chatted, nodding agreeably – he hoped in the right places – whenever the conversation seemed to demand it.

He was actually observing Jane with some concern, not sure if the slightly feverish look in her eyes was simply the result of lack of sleep – not uncommon among convention goers – or had a more sinister cause. He felt decidedly guilty at not having stepped in and rescued the two from Namon's clutches the previous evening. Not that there would have been anything he might have said or done that wouldn't have made him look like an idiot; '*I don't like him*' would have simply sounded rude, and if he *had* known then what he knew now, announcing '*Get away from him, he's a vampire,*' would have sounded insane.

"I thought Sharon would be helping you," Mary was saying, since Jane had finally got round to her request. Jane sighed.

"So did I," she said. "But she had a funny turn last night, and she's still feeling miserable and whoozy because of it.

Mr Namon was so helpful. Stopped her from tripping over the gravestones, and practically carried her back to our room." *I bet he did*, Marcus thought angrily. The hot cheese and bread in his mouth suddenly tasted like dust and ashes. So much for '*if he took anything it can't have been more than a taste...*' "I'm a little worried about her, actually. I thought she'd just had a little too much to drink, but it seems to have triggered a rather nasty migraine. Do you think the hotel will be able to call someone? I've given her some painkillers, but they don't seem to be helping very much."

"Migraines can be nasty," Mary agreed. "I've probably got something a little more powerful than 'off the shelf' but..."

"Here." Marcus had plucked Mary's notebook out of the side pocket of her chair, torn off a sheet of paper and had been hastily scribbling a note on it. "Take this down to the Dealers' Room and give it to Ashera. She's the lady in the Egyptian get up. Tell her I sent you. She'll help you."

"With what?" Jane frowned at the folded note in puzzlement. "I saw her earlier. She's just selling new-age-y trinkets, isn't she? I suppose one of those essential oil mix things might help a bit, but Sharon doesn't really believe in all that stuff. Not sure that I do, either."

Marcus bit back a bark of annoyance, and forced a smile instead. "This isn't a prescription," he said, "or a shopping list. It's simply a request. Ashera's a qualified doctor. She's not formally working this weekend – " *Not at her day job, that is.* "– but I know she'll be happy to help if she's asked. *This*" he tapped the note with his pen, "is just me asking."

"Oh." Jane looked down at the paper in surprise. "You didn't have to do that, Dr Holland."

Yes I did...

Vague regret at not intervening the night before had been overwhelmed by serious guilt. He *should* have said something, and a young woman had been hurt because he'd been afraid to voice his concerns. He was going to do his best to make up for that. If he could.

The note simply said: *Namon helped this lady's friend last night. Please, if you can, help her today.* He'd taken a moment to encircle his signature with a *Shen*, so that it looked like a small cartouche. He didn't think Ashera would misunderstand the substance of the message, but it never hurt to be sure – and he was beginning to appreciate the power of symbols, in a way that all of his previous rune studies and research into ancient alphabets had never quite achieved.

"You're welcome. So's Sharon. Tell her to come find me when she's feeling better, and I'll buy you both a drink."

Jane's face lit up. "*Thanks*. We will. See you later, Mary."

Mary waved as Jane left, waiting until she'd vanished down the stairs to turn to him with a knowing smile.

"What?" he asked innocently, and she laughed.

"You're a dark horse, aren't you," she said, her eyes twinkling. "If you did that to stop me from handing out prescription pills that I shouldn't, then I thank you. And if you didn't do it for that reason, then I'll thank you again. I didn't know Ash was a doctor – but it doesn't surprise me. She was handing out free massages at the last con I was at, and she's really, *really* good at those."

She paused, glancing up with a faint frown. Marcus followed the line of her gaze, his face creasing down into similar disquiet as he spotted the figure that had caught her attention, Namon, his top hat set at a slightly dandified angle on his head, was weaving his way through the lunchtime crowd, pausing to greet acquaintances and exchange pleasantries, the way that any gentleman of his chosen era might.

"That guy's a real creep," Mary observed sourly. Marcus tore his eyes away from the vampire's stately progress to raise a questioning eyebrow in her direction.

"Yes, he is," she defended, clearly misreading his

expression. "I know he *sounds* charming, but then so does a fakir's flute. Have you seen the way he touches people? As if he's Lord High and Mighty, and they should be grateful he's deigned to notice them. That's the way *bad* dog owners treat their pets. If he ever does it to me, I'm going to smack him one."

The thought of Mary – bright, determined, and full of unquenchable fire – trying to face down Namon, made his blood run cold. *Yes* to the impulse, but … the Hollow Man would drain her dry. Take every drop of her stubborn spirit and leave her as empty as he was.

"I bet he was the one pouring drinks down Sharon's throat last night," she was saying. "I heard him. Didn't you? *Would you like to see the graveyard by moonlight*, indeed! What kind of pick up line is *that?*"

"A bad one," Marcus muttered. "Listen – Mary. I know you. I know you all too well. Someone may need to take that man down a peg or two, but don't you go doing anything that you might regret. I don't want you hurt – and he's not worth you getting into trouble. No matter how tempting it may be."

She gave him a long, considering look. "Why, Dr Marcus Holland," she pronounced with relish. "I do believe that's the nicest thing you've ever said to me! Don't you worry your heart," she assured him warmly, reaching to squeeze his hand with affection. "I'm not about to *start* a fight. And I doubt he will either. He probably won't even notice me. Men like that are looking for luscious legs and tits that bounce like water balloons; they look straight over the chair. If he ever *does* touch me, it'll be to push me out of the way as he stalks by."

"And as for you," she said, fixing him with a steely eye. "Don't *you* go doing anything you might regret, either. I'm looking forward to your next book, and I want you around to write it, okay? You're a writer, a scholar, and a gentleman.

Three things he will never be."

"Dr Holland? Marcus?"

Pete was hastily jogging towards them, trying to weave around the tables, and only just avoiding making contact as he did so. People leaned sideways, or grabbed plates and glasses as he passed, frowning at his passing intrusion. "Sorry. Uh – sorry ... oh, I'm really sorry ..." He made progress, arriving beside the two of them, and panting a little for breath.

"There you are," he said, managing a slightly breathless smile. "I lost sight of you just after the signing ... Henry's looking for you. For the panel, later?"

"Oh, right." Marcus hadn't forgotten about the panel, but he had forgotten about the preparation pre-meet. "Sorry, Mary. Duty calls. See you later?"

"I'm expecting a dance," she shot back, waving him generously on his way. "And thanks for the tea!"

Chapter Nine

" … so," Henry Mayne was saying as both his panellists and their audience settled into place, "my name is Henry and I write mostly short stories. A lot of them are about technology that goes wrong, but not all of them. Sometimes the AI is right!"

There was a scattering of laughter at that. Henry's stuff tended to be quick, clever and punched to the point, which was why he'd been struggling to sustain anything even novelette length, let alone a full-blown novel. But his short tales were well liked, and his writing style had been good enough to win him a couple of awards.

"I'm your moderator for this session, which is entitled 'Stake it, Solve it, or Save it?' Our panellists are here to discuss their favourite ways to deal with monsters, and why they prefer that approach."

Marcus was carefully taking off his hat and putting it on the table in front of him. He'd thought the topic to be an interesting one when he'd been pitched it, several months before. He'd even done some research to back his arguments up. But they all seemed a little too academic now. Especially with a real monster sitting in the audience.

"Let's start with introductions, shall we? Marcus?"

Namon was sitting in the front row, right in the middle of the room. He'd taken off his top hat and was holding it on his lap, one thumb idly polishing the shine on its crown. He had what everybody else probably saw as a quiet, attentive smile on his face, but Marcus could read him better now; the look in his eyes turned it into smug confidence and arrogant amusement. *Go on*, that look challenged, knowingly. *I dare you…*

Marcus suppressed a shiver, and hitched himself a little closer to the microphone. *You can do this*, he told himself sternly. It was just like swimming with sharks, or dealing with the wasp in the room; you just had to stay aware of where they were.

At least with Namon sitting there, he knew he wasn't somewhere else, indulging his appetite.

"Afternoon, everyone," he said. "For those of you who don't know me, my name is Marcus Holland. I'm a lecturer in European folklore and mythology, and – if you don't count my academic work, I've written around sixteen books to date – some under my own name, and a few others as 'Ned Landers.'"

The audience applauded that; he acknowledged the reception with his usual embarrassed smile and pushed the microphone towards the woman sitting next to him. She smiled – both at his reaction, and more generally at the crowd.

"Wow," she half laughed. "How do you follow that? Well, my name is Lyn Rivers-Wylde, and I've only written three books – so far. My work is mostly set in a Gothic version of medieval Europe, with mad nobles pursuing arcane power in order to indulge in corrupt pleasures, while the Inquisition hunts down dissenters and heretics. Every day tales of everyday folk," she concluded with another smile.

Marcus had read her latest book, and he'd offered her some vague words of praise for it during their pre-meet. It was far too dark for his taste, with unpleasant people doing unpleasant things for unpleasant reasons, but it was well written, and the fate of her central characters had implied a certain karmic morality that redeemed her approach a little. There was certainly a readership for that kind of stuff, although he'd never dream of writing it himself.

Dark destinies and grim fates were not his cup of tea.

Lovecraft may have thought the world deserved to drown in madness, but he tended to side with the skalds; even after Ragnarok, there had to be hope for a new world.

The rest of the panel introduced themselves, the number of books written and published jokingly reducing until the final speaker – who happened to be David, the Fan Guest – blithely admitted he hadn't written *any* books. But he had read every one of everyone else's.

The audience laughed at that. Everyone but the dark haired girl who was sitting at the back of the crowded seminar room. She was the same girl who'd so firmly refused to surrender her Ankh at the opening ceremony, and she was staring – not at the members of the panel, but at the back of Namon's head. The stare was disguised with a carefully indifferent smile, but the eyes above it glinted with such determined hatred that Marcus was surprised that the vampire hadn't physically felt it.

"So ..." Henry picked up the conversation, directing it with admirable skill. "How do you deal with a monster? Is it just a matter of firepower, or should it be more complicated than that? What role do monsters play in your stories? Lyn?"

Lyn argued the definition of 'monster' and whether that was different from being 'monstrous,' suggesting that human beings can be far worse monsters than the traditional idea of some kind of supernatural – or simply ravenous – creature that wanted to eat you. There were, she suggested, far worse fates.

Marcus picked up the theme as he'd offered to do, only too aware of the vampire's amused attention. He questioned whether someone, or something, that had consciously committed evil deeds could achieve redemption, especially if the reason for their attempt to change was born from fear, or a sense of self-preservation. Lyn agreed, but offered the exception where an entity had been trapped by circumstance and forced to act in a negative way – such a creature, she argued could be redeemed – 'rescued' from their monstrosity if, and when, the trap that held them was destroyed.

But there has to be regret, David had interjected. A monster that is proud of their monstrousness, he said, will always *be* a monster.

"What about vengeful ghosts?" Henry had then prompted, spawning another round of examples and arguments.

Had this been a normal convention, Marcus would have been enjoying himself enormously. The complexity of the morals and ethics that lay behind the question, the opportunity to challenge assumptions made in the underpinning concepts, and the detailed examples that the panel cited to illustrate their points, turned what might have been a superficial regurgitation of favourite monster moments into a rich and fascinating discussion.

But there was a man who should have died centuries before sitting among the audience; a predator that had become one by discarding his humanity in the pursuit of purely selfish desires. There was nothing tragic or romantic about Isiah Namon; he pursued no higher aims. He merely indulged his appetites and preserved his own existence by callously stealing the life of others. It was obvious that he had no interest in his victims beyond what they could offer him. He either took control and prolonged their torment by using them as slaves and servants, or else he simply threw away what was left, leaving them to fester and rot from the inside out. He didn't care who he hurt, or who he damaged. For him, it was all about power and possession.

Ashera was right. He wasn't a lost soul in need of redemption, or a tormented ghost that needed help to move on. He wasn't even the victim of a destructive and all-consuming disease. He *was* the disease.

Marcus needed to wipe him out.

"Final vote!" The timekeeper at the door had signalled that

they needed to wind the discussion up so Henry was calling them to order. "Stake, solve, or save? David?"

"Save," David voted, having firmly declared himself to be on Godzilla's side.

Torri Vetla voted 'solve; because she'd always wanted to join the Scooby Gang, and Lyn voted 'stake – but save Spike and Angel' because, she said, she'd rather join *Buffy's* scooby gang.

"Marcus?"

"Stake," he said firmly, unable to help glancing at Namon as he said it. The vampire merely smirked, carefully lifting his hand to dust a non-existent speck from the crown of his hat. He was clearly amused at the idea – which made Marcus wonder whether someone might have tried to do just that, somewhere in his long unlife.

How do you stake someone in the heart – if they don't have one? he wondered, watching as Namon stood up to leave. Behind him the girl, having spent the entire session trying to mentally bore a hole in the back of the vampire's head, quickly turned away, clearly not wanting to be spotted, let alone recognised. Marcus, who'd been politely waiting for Henry to pick up his papers and lead the panel out, pushed back his chair, grabbed his bowler, and hastily made his way down through the crowd to where she was sitting.

"It's okay," he murmured, trying not to loom over her protectively, while making sure that Namon really had left the room. "He didn't spot you. He's headed back to the central mezzanine, I think."

She turned and looked up at him with narrowed eyes. "Was I that obvious?" she asked with a decided growl. A sane man – or a coward – might have tipped his hat to her and quietly walked away – but Marcus had decided not to be a coward where Namon was concerned.

He wasn't entirely sure if he were all that sane, either.

"I'm afraid so." The people who'd been queuing outside

were starting to spill in, taking up emptied seats in preparations for the next panel's session. He jerked his head towards the door. "Want to talk about it?"

She hesitated for a moment, her posture indignant and wary, then she let her tension go with a sigh, slumping forward so that her hair hung down around her face. "Oh, god," she breathed, a painful hitch in her voice. "Do I? I do. I guess I really, really do…"

— * —

Her badge declared her name to be Deyath, although Marcus was pretty sure that wasn't the one she'd been christened with. The look was almost perfect: black tee-shirt and jeans, dark make-up framing her eyes and deepening her lips, the long, straight dark hair – and the silver ankh, firmly and defiantly pulled out and left to hang between her breasts. She wasn't quite pert or pretty enough to be mistaken for the original, but she came close; close enough to make Gaiman smile, Marcus thought. He did – smile, that is, and gave her the space she clearly needed, leaning on the balcony rail and looking down into the currently empty ballroom. Empty of formal program, that is: the tech guys were busy swarming around their equipment, taking an available moment to move it safely aside before the evening's events.

The minstrel gallery itself was empty and quiet: the door into it had offered a convenient escape, taking the two of them away from the milling fans in the corridor while staying far away from Namon's languid drift among the attendees. Marcus had lingered at the door, making sure he'd seen the gleaming top-hat vanish around the corner before he'd slipped in after the girl. She'd found a seat halfway along the balcony, and was sitting in it, her legs kicked out and her head tipped back so she could stare at the ballroom's ornate ceiling.

"He killed my sister," she announced, as Marcus approached. "I know he did. I don't know how, but…" She sighed, and lifted her head to stare at him with an odd mixture of challenge and vulnerability. She couldn't have been much over eighteen – younger than most of his students – and she reminded him, heart achingly so, of Molly, and how she might turn out in a few years time. "Not that anyone believes me. *She* killed herself, they say. Drank too much, and jumped in the fucking pool…"

"No evidence of any foul play," he said gently, making it a fact, not a question.

"Nope!" She held the 'p' so that it popped between her lips, a punctuation mark of anger and disdain. He sighed.

"There wouldn't have been, though, would there." His suggestion was equally gentle, but she jerked at it, a hint of her earlier growl starting to curl her lip. "Because he'd already done the damage. Used her and thrown her away."

Her eyes widened. "You – you believe me? The police wouldn't listen. They said… they said, she hadn't been… touched. But she wouldn't have… Susie was so full of *life*. She had everything to live for. And she didn't drink. Not that much." She turned and stared out at the chandeliers, wrestling with grief and anger. "We came to the ball to have a good time. It was going to be *fun*. Everyone was all dressed up, and you had to wear the masks until the Clock struck midnight … and then *he* asked her to dance, and he whirled her away, and … I never saw her again. Not until…"

Marcus moved to sit next to her, weighing up suitable actions before carefully offering her his hand. She looked down at it, up at him, and then grabbed hold, squeezing it tightly enough to hurt. "Thank you," she murmured, trying not to look ashamed at shaking so much. He squeezed back, easing some of the sudden pain in his fingers, and she found a watery smile.

"I'm sorry," she said. "But it hurts so much. And you said

– you do believe me? He is responsible. Somehow."

"I believe you." He wasn't sure she was going to believe *him* when he told her why, but he needed help dealing with Namon, and this young lady, so full of anger and hate against him, might at least listen to what he had to say. "Deyath – can I call you Deyath? Or is there anything else ..?"

"Deyath will do," she said, shrugging the question away. "Susie was being Desire that night. We loved all that stuff. And I guess – *that* guy, was enough like Morpheus to charm her into a dance. She said she knew him," she added, as if trying to explain why she hadn't protested her sister's choices. "I'd not done the Halloween ball before, but Susie was older than me. She'd been two, three years running. Had so much fun, she wanted me to have that too. And it *was* fun. Until she left with him, and didn't come back."

"Why are you at the Con?"

She grimaced. "To see *him.* Talk to him... oh, I don't know. I wanted to scream at him and make a spectacle so everyone would see, but – I couldn't. I *can't.* He scares me, and I don't know why. He owns the hotel. Did you know that? I know he's all dressed up like a fan, but ... *he's* the vampire round here. Leeching off everyone: charging the earth for lumpy beds and cheap food, and – probably taking most of the registration money, too. Susie booked us the places," she explained. "Last year. It was going to be her treat to me, before I vanished off to University. And yes," she added, suddenly shy, "I am a fan. I do know who you are. I've got all of your books. Well ... most of them. I'm waiting for *Wolfkin* to come out in paperback."

"November," he said, distractedly. "Probably. If they approve the cover I've just acquired..."

A momentary smile danced across her lips – just for a second, but enough to light up her entire face. "Cool."

"Deyath," he said again, wondering how to say it, wondering how best to frame something that – the longer he thought about it, the more insane it became.

"Yes?"

"I know how he killed your sister, but… I'm not sure you'll believe me. I'm still not sure *I* believe it."

Empty mirrors. A dead sister drifting in the pool. Another young woman weak, and wrestling with a migraine after nothing more than a moonlit walk. A sense of chill searing his arm as his warmth and strength was leeched away…

He believed it.

Would she?

"Isiah Namon may be *playing* a vampire this weekend. The same way he plays one every Halloween. But – he isn't pretending. That's the joke. The bad joke. He really is one."

"For real?" Deyath eyed him warily, glancing down at where their hands were still entwined together. "You're shitting me."

"I wish I was. I – *know* this sounds insane, but – I saw, or rather didn't see, him in the old mirrors. The silvered ones. It's the silver that reflects the soul… and he doesn't have one."

"A reflection? Or a soul?" She was listening, but her expression was wary, and he didn't blame her.

"Both. Or maybe neither. He's… *hollow*. Empty. Eaten up from the inside so there's nothing left but an echoing shell. He may look, and walk, and talk like a man, but I don't think he's been one for a long time."

"Okay… " Deyath said slowly. "Dead guy walking, yeah? I get that. I think. But – Susie wasn't… there wasn't a mark on her. No bites or cuts, or anything. Aren't vampires supposed to drink your blood? Drain you dry?"

"Not all of them." Marcus retrieved his hand so he could reach to massage the back of his neck. There was a dull headache beginning to build up inside his skull, and a sense of weariness had begun to nag at him. He hadn't had much sleep the night before, and his frantic early morning research session was starting to take its toll. "Namon's hungry for *life*, not blood. I doubt he's got anything more than dust in his veins by now. He fed off Susie's energies; he stole her joys, her hopes, her dreams. He drained her soul of all the things that make it worth living. That make you want to live... and so she didn't. He left her empty and echoing, just so that he could *feel* for a moment or two, could carry on clinging to a life he should have abandoned centuries ago. I don't think he drinks that deeply, most of the time, but once or twice ... it must be hard to resist the temptation. Susie ... " He hesitated to articulate his thoughts, conscious of the young woman he was speaking to. She was already carrying more than she should have to bear. "She almost certainly didn't understand what was happening to her. She – she probably threw herself into the pool to stop the pain."

"*Shit*," Deyath hissed softly, the sound coming straight from her soul. "I'll kill him. Find me a way to kill him," she demanded, grabbing at Marcus's arm and sinking angry fingers almost bone deep.

"I'm working on it," he answered, suppressing a yelp of pain and hastily reaching to disentangle her grip. "I need – *ow...*" She'd let go, and the blood in his arm had rushed back into place, his muscles protesting and his nerves sparking with indignant complaint.

"Sorry," she said, not sounding entirely sincere about it. She flopped back into her seat, shifting nervously, filled with so much energy and reaction that she didn't entirely know what to do with herself. "But if all that's true... the bastard violated – soul-raped my sister. And she wasn't the first, was she."

"No." He cautiously rubbed some of the feeling back into his arm. "She won't be the last, either, unless we can stop him. I think he's learned how to graze; I've seen him feeding off the staff, and he probably does the same to the guests. Touching and tasting; taking advantage, leaving his victims discomforted and not knowing why. And when he does drink deeper, he seems to… take control. Somehow."

"Maybe they're just afraid to speak. Afraid he'll hurt them again if they do. It's not like he's leaving a mark, is it. Who'd believe them? *My boss is a vampire*. You said it yourself. It sounds insane."

"I know." Marcus thought of Spanner, and how he seemed to be actively co-operating with Namon's twisted plan. Removing the potential for his guests to defend themselves, sowing seeds that would allow him to move among them, disguising his nature with a truth wrapped up as a lie. "I think it's a little more than that, but – you may be right. We have to plan this," he realised, remembering Ashera's advice. "He's cunning and he's dangerous. He's already warned me off, and I'm hoping he thinks I took the hint. I have friends here, Deyath. People I don't want to get hurt, and – you just got added to the list. I don't want him to hurt *anybody*, but I need time to figure out his weaknesses. To find a way to stop him once and for all. And I need to get some *sleep*," he realised, fighting down a sudden yawn. "I – uh – didn't get much, last night."

She gave him a wry look. "So that's how the great vampire hunters work, huh? Point at the bad guy – and then go take a nap? You want me to keep any eye on him while you get your beauty sleep?"

He was too tired to argue with her sass – and if he were a few years younger he might have been able to shake off his fatigue and soldier through, the way that heroes in the movies did. But he was just a middle-aged academic, for whom 'working-out' was a day spent in the University library, carting around massive, leather-bound tomes. Namon was less of a threat during the day: there were too many people about, too much going on to allow him to single out the vulnerable from the herd. But night was coming; there'd be revelry and drunkeness, and attendees drifting away to seek sleep. Only the brave, the bold, the gamers, the filkers, and the late night drinkers would remain awake into the small hours – and the predator would be prowling for prey, seeking a little more than the quick sip or the hastily snatched taste.

Marcus knew that he'd never be able to protect *everybody* that night, but he could certainly be around to thwart some of Namon's games. Provided he could get some sleep before it started getting dark again.

"Would you? I mean – you want in on this? I'd understand if you just – packed your bags and left. I almost did…"

"I'm in." Deyath's expression was a determined one. "I can keep an eye on him this afternoon. I'll keep a low profile doing it, though. Stay out of his way, you know? *I'm* not the expert on vampires. I'm only in this for the revenge – and I can wait for that. Just one thing," she added as he started to get to his feet. "I believe you. It makes – sense of some stuff. But… if this turns out to be some sick joke, some way of playing on that stupid idea of Spanner's? I'm going to make you wish you'd never been born. You hear me?"

He found her a tired grin. "I hear you," he said. "It isn't, I promise. And before you go charging off to take up your watch, there's someone I think you ought to meet…"

– * –

Ashera was back at her table in the Dealers' Room by the time he led Deyath into it. He waited until she'd finished serving her latest customers, before introducing the two of them. Ashera smiled at the delicate ankh, which Deyath had forgotten to slip back under her blouse, and reached under her table to extract a small white box.

"Yours is lovely," she said, handing the box to Deyath. "But I think you might find this one a little more useful this weekend."

Deyath frowned, and opened the box. Inside lay another ankh – this one twice the size of the one she was wearing. It had lines of delicate hieroglyphs stamped, or cut on the back, and while the decoration on the front was minimal and didn't distract from the sheen of the silvered surface, its loop and extended arms were marked with a twisting cord, adding a shenu to the overall design.

"Is this real silver?" Deyath asked, lifting the ankh from its box. A line of chain spilled down, revealing a number of small, additional charms hanging from the links. Marcus spotted an eye of Horus, and several tiny icons of gods, Isis and Anubis among them.

"Of course," Ashera answered with amusement. "I would never propitiate the gods with mere plate. They'd spot the difference right away. Silver, being pure, and sacred to the Moon," she explained, "provides additional protective properties over and above the way the piece is shaped. Please – wear it. And put it safely away for the moment, along with the other – otherwise some zealous con-gopher's going to confiscate it. And I'd rather not have to ransom it back."

"Wow. Thanks." Deyath dropped the chain over her head and then carefully tucked both ankhs away, out of sight. "Dr Holland," she asked warily, glancing round to see if anyone else was close enough to hear the question, "does she know about... you know?"

He leaned forward a little, helping to keep their conversation from being overheard. "Ashera is more of an expert than I am. If you need help, and I'm not around? Find her and ask for it. Come to that," he added dryly. "If I am around, I'm probably going to be looking for her too."

Deyath gave Ashera a wide-eyed look of respect. Ashera laughed.

"He knows more than he thinks he does," she noted warmly. "And is still willing to learn, as a good scholar should. I will be here until six, when the room closes. After that, look for me on the mezzanine and – later – in the games room. I have promised to teach some new friends how to play Senet properly. They were admiring my boards, earlier."

There were, indeed, a couple of Senet boards at the end of her table: lovely things cut from polished woods. The boards themselves were marked out with intricate inlays of darker wood and strips of mother of pearl. Ashera pulled one towards her, demonstrating how the game pieces were packed into a small drawer that lay concealed at the end of the board.

Marcus turned one of the tiny jade scarab beetles over in his hand. A momentary smile touched his lips as he imagined Jackson Hobbs, sitting in the prow of the *John Barleycorn* and playing Senet with an old friend. "Maybe you'll teach me, sometime," he suggested, and she smiled.

"Maybe I will. How about you young lady? Do you play games?"

"Yeah." Deyath had been browsing round her stall, her fingers lingering on strings of beads that Marcus suspected her sister would have loved. "Sometimes. Susie was seriously into Shadowrunning at one point. I'm more of a Pathfinder person, myself. I like the setting," she said, glancing up to offer Marcus a smile. "Fairies and knights, and noble deeds. Speaking of *which*," she realised, as if suddenly recognising that she was letting her guard down, "I need to go do my duty. I'll see you later, Dr Holland. Ashera." She hastened away, waving back to acknowledge Marcus's quiet '*Be careful*', as she passed. Ashera sighed.

"So young," she noted a little sadly. "Youth should not be robbed of its dreams too early, nor left to founder in the world's ills."

"Her sister was the girl that drowned," he said, still watching as the girl in black vanished through the door. "At

Halloween… " He turned with determined cheer, not wanting to linger on those thoughts for too long. "How's Sharon?"

"Better for my care," she answered confidently. "Thank you for sending her friend to me. The damage was less than it could have been, but might have festered if unattended."

"I thought that might be the case. I could have stopped them," he admitted bleakly. "*Should* have stopped them. Last night."

"No man can save the entire world," she told him tartly. "And sometimes you have to ignore the smaller wounds in order to stop arteries bleeding. I learned that lesson a long, long time ago. Not that that means deliberately putting the innocent in harm's way," she added, with equal asperity. "You must be on your guard tonight."

"I know. I intend to be." He lost the fight against another yawn, and threw her a sheepish smile. "*After* I've managed to get some sleep, that is. I was awake a little – early, this morning."

"I rose with the sun," she announced, smiling at potential customers who'd come to see what she had for sale. "But then I always do. Rest well and rise refreshed."

"I intend to," he said, and left her to it, heading for the stairs and the irresistible lure of a bed.

Chapter Ten

Marcus slept with the windows open, letting in the warm summer air along with the soft wash of afternoon sunlight. Daylight turned his slightly gloomy and faded room into a quiet haven, and the warm caress of the sun made him feel a lot safer than he had the night before. It didn't stop him refreshing his protective runes, though, especially as the maid had been by to make the bed, replace used coffee cups and top up his sugar bowl. He wasn't quite paranoid enough to think that Namon was using the maid service to spy on him, although he wouldn't put it past the man to question the maid about his habits if he thought it necessary.

He was too tired to dream, dropping into a deep and refreshing slumber almost as soon as his head hit the pillow.

His alarm went off two hours later. He awoke with a groan, taking a moment or two to orientate himself. The sun was lower on the horizon, but not yet below it. Somewhere below him, the Clock struck six, and he rolled off the bed and into the bathroom, conscious that he had work to do and that he needed to be both awake and ready to do it.

He dressed in his evening finery: a deep purple shirt and scarlet and gold waistcoat replaced the white and silver he'd worn during the day. He checked that Ashera's bracelet still encircled his wrist, and remembered to unbutton his Ticky and place it – along with his silver pentagram – into the relevant pocket, letting its watch-chain loop across the scarlet silk.

Then he made his way out of his room – checking that the door locked behind him – and into battle.

Pete nearly ran into him, halfway down the hall.

"Marcus!" he gasped, as out of breath as usual. "Abigail was worried about you – thought you might miss the Kaffeeklatsch."

"On my way there now," Marcus smiled, tilting his head in an invitation to join him. Pete nodded, looking relieved. "I'm looking forward to a decent cup of coffee."

He'd only slept for two hours, but he felt a whole lot better for it. He still wasn't sure what his plan of action needed to be; he had no idea as to how Namon might be dealt with once and for all, and – until he did – there was little he could do except dance around him, finding ways to warn people away, or to distract him from his victims. Even that was going to be tricky, and undoubtedly dangerous. He didn't want to get the vampire so frustrated or angry that he'd move from subtle tasting to outright attack, and he could hardly arrange to be everywhere in the hotel at once.

On the other hand, neither could Namon – so as long as he kept an eye on where he was, and who he might have targeted, he had a chance to minimise some of the damage he might cause.

Some, not all of it. Marcus was under no illusions that he could protect the entire convention, and he knew that there would be people who'd suffer the vampire's touch that night. Hopefully, none of them seriously so, and with Ashera on hand to mitigate the impact a little, there might be a chance that they'd suffer no long-term effects from the experience.

What the hell am I doing? he wondered as he made his way down the spiral stairs and onto the hotel mezzanine. He was about to spend his entire evening running interference between an oblivious crowd and a very old and cunning vampire – and the only help he had was an ancient Egyptian priestess that he had to keep in reserve – and preferably far away from the creature she'd been trying to hunt – and an angry and grief-stricken young woman for whom, he suspected, her desire for revenge might take precedence over her own safety.

This wasn't one of his books. He didn't have *any* control over the plot, let alone the characters – and he was just as much in the dark about the end game as he always hoped his readers were going to be.

"Kaffeeklatsch is in seminar three, I think." Pete had paused to check one of the program notices stuck to a nearby notice board. There were a scattering of con newsletters on the table next to it, and Marcus picked one up, interested to see how the convention was looking to those who remained oblivious to the danger in their midst. The newsletter headline was '*Keep those shutters closed',* and was followed by a reminder about taking care to not expose the hotel's collection of antiques to sunlight. Under that was a jokier piece with several quick candid shots of attendees and the question 'Is this the convention vampire?' None of the pictures, he noted wryly, were of Namon.

"Pete?" he questioned on a sudden whim as the man waved him in the relevant direction. "Do *you* know who Spanner asked to play the vampire this weekend?"

"Mm? Oh – uh … no, I don't. I'm not even sure if all the committee know. He's been very secretive about the whole thing."

"I suppose that's the point."

"Yeah." Pete's expression took on a thoughtful caste. "I can't decide whether it's Malcolm Jarvis or Mr Namon. Malcolm's been drifting about looking romantically tragic and trying to chat up girls, but he does that at most events. Mr Namon's really got into the spirit of the weekend though. His costumes are superb – and he's got this whole 'Mr Manners' thing going. So polite and charming, you wouldn't *mind* him taking a quick bite. He's really good at lurking in the background with a knowing smile on his face. He's been sitting in on some of the panels, and I've seen him watching the audience in the ballroom, so he's been around all day."

"Has he now," Marcus noted, giving Pete a few points for having noticed, even if he didn't know the truth of the situation.

"Yeah. Don't think I've seen him in the Art Show, or the Dealers' Room, but he can't be everywhere." Pete added with a happy grin. "He has a hotel to run, you know?"

"Yes, I know." A thought occurred to Marcus – a potential opening ploy in the game of 'mouse hunt cat hunt mouse' that he was going to have to play. "Would you do me a favour? Would you find Mr Namon and ask him to join me in the Kaffeeklatsch? He probably deserves a good cup of coffee more than I do. Oh – and, once you've done that? If you see a young lady hanging around? Long dark hair, all in black, badge saying 'Deyath'? Would you tell her she needs to eat and take her up to the Mezzanine so she can grab a panini or something. Get something for yourself too," he added, reaching for his wallet and tugging out a ten and a twenty. "On me, okay?"

Pete looked a little stunned. "You don't need to buy me – " he began, but Marcus interrupted him, putting a friendly hand to his shoulder.

"Pete," he said, with the voice he'd perfected getting Molly to co-operate on her more stubborn days, "I need Deyath to eat. If you just give her the message and the money, she'll probably forget. Buy her a sandwich, and have one with her, and that way I'll know she's taking care of herself. Now, run along, because this needs to start, and Namon won't be in time to get his cup of coffee unless you hurry."

He ran, a lanky lope full of *Excuse me's* as he darted through the lines of attendees leaving and entering the seminar rooms. Marcus set his shoulders, plastered a friendly grin on his face and went to schmooze with eager fans, would-be-authors and publishers, and those among his peers who, like him, knew the value of a hot cup of mocha at the end of a Saturday afternoon.

Namon arrived about ten minutes later, insinuating his way into the gathering with a congenial smile. He made his way over to where Marcus – large coffee mug in one hand – was listening to a fan expound yet another theory on Jackson Hobb's parentage. This one was somewhat better than most, even if it followed a number of red herrings and had missed the vital point: the lady concerned was clearly familiar with the related research, and Marcus' inner author was busy muttering *That's a good idea. Why didn't you think of that…?*

He briefly turned and smiled – a little tightly – adding a nod to acknowledge Namon's presence, then turned back, responding to the lady's arguments with a series of non-committal mms, uhuhs, and a *Yes, I see where you're going with that,* before she ran out of steam.

"I like it," he told her warmly. "It's not right, but I like it. You're quite close as it happens, but you've made a couple of unsubstantiated assumptions, and missed one vital clue. And no," he added with a mock glare, "I'm not going to tell you which one."

She pouted at that, but her annoyance lacked heat; she held it for a moment, then grinned at him. "It's all there, isn't it?" she said, and he nodded.

"Everything you need," he assured her. "Although, you do realise that – even if you do get it right – I'm not going to confirm it, one way or another. Not until Jackson does." *Which may be never*, he reminded himself. Francis might be waiting a long time for those three books…

"I'll look forward to it," she said. "That – or whatever you decide to write next."

"I'm working on – some ideas," he said noncommittally. Not entirely a lie, but definitely an evasion. She smiled and moved away, leaving him – for a moment – the sole focus of a dead man's attention.

"You summoned me," Namon said quietly, sounding a little annoyed about it. "I was on my way to change. For the ball?" The last few words were pointed: he was clearly a man that didn't appreciate having his plans disrupted.

"I thought you might like a coffee," Marcus replied, lifting his cup to emphasise the idea. "Since you've been working so hard today. Being – " he glanced round with deliberated conspiracy. "You know."

Namon's tight smile turned into a glower. "I warned you, Dr Holland," he hissed, his hand clenching around the top of his cane. "Do not think you can play games with me."

Marcus put down his cup and faced him, meeting his glare with stern determination. There was, he realised somewhere in the back of his mind, no real life to be found in this creature's eyes; beneath the vague hint of cultured charm that he'd adopted, there lay a cold, empty stare, barely cloaked in a mimicry of human expression.

They say that the eyes are the mirrors of the soul ...

He already knew that Isiah Namon didn't have one; the silvered mirrors had refused to reflect him. Now, standing close enough, with the layers of pretence momentarily abandoned, he'd caught a glimpse of the true nature underneath. Namon was hollow – empty of everything, except for hunger and desire.

"That's just it," Marcus said, dropping his voice to match the low, quiet tones of his adversary. "This is nothing but a game – one you started, the moment you understood what Spanner was offering you. All these people – immersed in the joys of make-believe, taking the opportunity to play and explore in worlds that never were – and you, tempted to join the fun, to wear, as a cloak, the mask of your true nature. Such a clever disguise. If I were to raise my voice, right now, and accuse you, all I'd get was a round of applause."

The crowd was murmuring all around them, their voices adding no more than another quiet layer to the general hubbub; no-one was paying them any attention – and even if they did, they would leap to erroneous conclusions, not understanding that what they heard was literal truth, rather than mere literature.

Namon stared at him as he spoke, his dead eyes narrowing in calculation – and then he laughed, finding a moment of real amusement in those quiet words.

"Oh, Bravo," he murmured, his lips curling with pleasure. "The author speaks – and reveals the trap that has snapped shut around him. This may be your world, Dr Holland – but it has entered my domain. You may try all you like, but you have no power to truly hurt me, no way to thwart or threaten my existence. And yes, tonight I will play and I will take tribute from my guests as I always do. You may – if you wish – play the white knight and intervene, if you can. But you are not your heroes, and you cannot win this game."

Namon leaned forward, and Marcus had to fight the instinct to retreat, had to force himself to stay right where he was, with a fake smile plastered on his face. He aimed at making it *brave* – but he suspected the best he managed was a hint of indigestion.

"I seem to remember you mentioning," the vampire purred, practically in his ear, "that Mr O'Toole will need you to present the awards tomorrow. Try not to upset me too much before then, will you? I would be a very poor host if I were to kill the guest of honour before his speech, wouldn't I?"

"Yes," Marcus managed to say, his mouth suddenly dry and his heart pounding in his chest. Namon wasn't joking. "You would. A *good* host," he suggested warily, "wouldn't kill anyone at all."

"True," Namon agreed, leaning back a little and giving him some space to breathe. "But then, I rarely do. When there's a banquet spread in your honour, even the hungriest man can be satisfied with a taste from every dish."

He glanced around, studying the gathering around them with a thoughtful eye. "We are surrounded by temptation, Dr Holland," he noted with indulgent amusement. "How many do you think you can save?"

– * –

He'd needed another cup of coffee – one that came both strong and very black – after Namon had left. His hands had been shaking, and it took a serious effort of will to keep them still enough to shake hands with the Kaffeeklatsch guests when they departed at the end of the session. It was nearly seven o'clock by then – just enough time to catch up with Ashera and Deyath up on the mezzanine and hopefully come up with some sort of plan for the evening. Namon was right: there was no way he could protect everybody, but he could at least try to keep the vampire off balance and away from the most vulnerable.

Somehow.

He'd already made the mental note: *Try to keep him amused, rather than annoyed.* He didn't want to end up like Susie, face down in the pool. For one thing, Molly would be extremely upset with him if that happened. And Beverley, because she was still mentioned in his current will, would almost certainly get a cut from his royalties. Which would be galling, especially as he'd fought so hard to keep them out of her hands when they settled the divorce.

"You okay, man?"

Cordell – who had clearly been waiting out in the corridor when his guests began to leave – poked his head, crowned by a gleaming white version of the Baron's hat, through the door when Marcus failed to follow after them.

"Mmm? Oh – hi Cordell. Yeah. Yeah, I'm fine. Just – um – wool-gathering for a moment. How's Mazzy?"

"Mazzy fine. Lilith fine. Baby come-lately fine. We're fine. We're all fine. How are you?"

Marcus threw him a pained look at the mangled quote, and Cordell laughed. "Boring conversation, anyway. Come on – I owe you another beer. And that lovely lady friend of yours has been holding court on the mezzanine without you. She's definitely a find, Marcus. You should hang on to that one."

"She's not – " he began, then abandoned any attempt at *that* argument. He did quite like Ashera – but it was going to be hard to feel anything other than respect and awe for the ancient Eygyptian priestess who'd lived through all the intervening centuries. Besides – given the lady's nature, she probably loved everybody, and there was no way he could explain why that might be a problem. Especially not to Cordell, who would never understand why it would be one. "Never mind. A beer sounds like a great idea."

The mezzanine was buzzing. Fans were gathering for the evening, some of them snatching the chance to get something to eat, others starting to take advantage of the Real Ale bar. There were even some elaborately gowned cosplayers moving among the crowd, ready for the coming Masked Ball. Lilith and Mazzy were among them; the two ladies were dressed in matching outfits that flowed from bare shoulders, through close fitting, figure hugging elegance at breast and waist, and tumbled out at the hip before falling to pool at their feet in a rustling froth of silk and spiderweb lace. Mazzy's gown was red and gold, Lilith's was black and silver; with Cordell – who'd gone all out and was wearing a suggestion of the Baron's skeletal make-up to complement his white and silver touched outfit – making up their trio, they looked stunning.

"Wow," Marcus said, and meant it.

"My last time to dress up for a while," Mazzy grinned, leaning in to greet him with a kiss to his cheek. "Like this, anyway. Goodbye corsets and tight lacings. Hello hippy kaftans and dresses like yurts."

"You're going to be a great mother, Mazzy," he assured her. "And beautiful, no matter what you're wearing. You're certainly looking good right now. You too, Lilith," he added, accepting the matching kiss on his other cheek. "How do you do it, Cordell?" he asked warmly. "Surround yourself with such beautiful people, I mean."

"I sacrifice to the loa of love, every day," Cordell laughed. "And I put the evil eye on negative thinkers." He pressed his left forefinger under his left eye in a theatrical gesture, and stamped his cane against the floor with a short sharp *snap*.

Somewhere behind him Marcus heard Ashera laugh.

"Using the power of positive thinking again, Cordell?" she

called with amusement. "Hello, Marcus. How did the Kaffeeklatsch go?"

The ex-priestess of Isis was, indeed, *holding court.* She was sitting in one of the antique armchairs that were scattered around the mezzanine, her presence turning it into a regal throne. Somewhere between the time he'd left her in the Dealers' Room, and now, she'd discarded her Egyptian look for a caught back hair style and a simple, yet elegant, dress in midnight blue. Deyath was sitting on the floor at her feet, still dressed in black, and Pete was sprawled on the low slung sofa next to her; he was carefully nursing a drink and all too obviously trying *not* to look down at Deyath. Marcus solved that problem by chivvying him to move along the couch so he could sink into the space he left. That meant the younger man was far enough away to watch the young woman with more covert interest, and far less likelihood of embarrassing himself. Marcus didn't blame him for paying attention: had he still been Pete's age he might well have considered the girl worth looking at too.

"It was – interesting," he murmured, responding to Ashera's question. A glance towards his other friends reassured him that they were unlikely to overhear anything else he had to say; Cordell was heading towards the Real Ale Bar, and his girls were busy showing off their gowns to a group of fans who'd stopped to say hello. "Namon – showed a little of his true colours," he admitted, still keeping his voice low. "I was given a challenge – and a warning. He knows I *know.* He also knows I can't call him out, because no-one would believe me. He'll tolerate a little interference, provided I keep him amused – but push too far, and someone's going to get seriously hurt. It might even be me."

Ashera curled her hand over his, offering reassurance. "Sometimes," she said, her voice equally soft and low, "you have to allow your opponent to think they have control of the board. When they think that, they become complacent and pay little attention to where you are placing your pieces. Let him nibble at the feast. He has survived centuries through cautious guile and low cunning. He will not be foolish enough to draw attention to his deeds. If he takes only little bites and shallow sips, I can replace what he steals. What *you* must do is watch him – watch that he does not overstep his own limits, the way he did at Halloween. The night is *his* time. Anyone truly vulnerable may be a temptation he can't resist."

"He takes them out into the dark, alone," Deyath interjected, close enough to follow their conversation. "That's how he got to Susie..."

Marcus nodded, reaching to give her shoulder a sympathetic squeeze. "Standard predatory behaviour," he muttered. "Separate the chosen target from the herd... Okay," he said, taking a deep breath. "He's expecting me to *try* to intervene in some way. If I can keep him on his toes, keep him looking over his shoulder all night, maybe that will be enough.

"Enough to limit the damage, at least."

Cordell was looming into sight, a large pint glass in either hand. "Cheer up," he told Marcus, handing him his beer. "It's Saturday night, and it's time to party!"

– * –

The ballroom had been transformed: the tangles of technology had been packed away. The chapel door was shut, and another curtain had been drawn across it. The theatre-style rows of seats had vanished leaving a clear, open space in the middle of the room, and a well-polished wooden dance floor in the middle of that. Down the length of the room on either side, a series of large, round tables had been placed, white cloths thrown over them and chairs placed around them, creating seating and space for conversation. At the back, behind a cluster of smaller tables and chairs, the hotel had opened up another bar. One of the platforms in front of the Clock now supported a DJ and his decks; the dais on the other side, closest to the curtains over the French windows, provided a platform for two more of his huge speakers, the cable running between the two was carefully secured underneath a thick rubber strip.

They'd opened the doors at precisely eight o'clock – by the Clock, which obligingly struck the hour as a cheer went up from the gathered crowd. Marcus had surged in with the rest of them, to be greeted by the bouncy notes of Voltaire's 'Day of the Dead' as the DJ started up his set. It was, he supposed, a good way to start the party, or would have been, had there not been a genuine spectre intending to join the event – and to feast, with the unsuspecting revellers providing the creature's repast.

Minimise the damage he reminded himself, watching Cordell, wearing a white mask, swirl a red-masked Mazzy onto the dance floor. At least he wouldn't have to worry too much about that particular trio tonight. The three of them would be thicker than thieves, taking the opportunity to celebrate their good news – and with Cordell practically channelling Baron Samedi, it was unlikely that Namon would try to insinuate himself into that closeness, no matter how tempting that first new spark of life might be. If he'd backed away from the mere display of the Baron's hat, he was hardly going to consider even approaching Cordell that evening, not given the way he was currently dressed.

For the briefest of moments, Marcus found himself seriously considering whether his friend might be willing to *actually* call on the Baron's assistance for help against a man who had defied the lure of the grave – and then he shook his head and dismissed the thought with a wry grimace. It was a long mental leap from *'Vampires are real'* to *'Let's summon up the loa to deal with one'*. Cordell might well have some faith in his grandmother's Vodun powers, but Marcus had no idea of how to convince him of point one, let alone moving on to point two – and no guarantee that trying it would do any more than persuade the world that they'd both gone stark raving mad.

He wasn't entirely sure that he'd convinced Deyath, and she had good reason to be suspicious – not to mention a deep-seated hatred of the man the vampire was pretending to be.

He made his way to the bar, ordered himself a diet soda, and picked a quiet table where he could sit and bide his time. He was still buzzing a little from the rich, dark beer that Cordell had bought him, and he sipped the soda slowly, knowing that he had to be both focused and sober when Namon walked through the door. The sound of conversation and laughter was building under the joyful thrum of the music; he'd have been enjoying himself, if he wasn't knotted up with anxious anticipation. He was under no illusions. For all his taunting words and his history of cautious, secretive survival, Namon was still an unpredictable, and very dangerous creature.

He could probably slaughter the entire convention, if he wanted to.

It was another half hour before the vampire made his appearance. He had gone from smart Victorian to full Georgian dandy, in tan britches, calf hugging button up boots, a deep maroon, high cut tail coat, a gold striped waistcoat, and a cascading cravat of silk and lace. He had been, Marcus remembered, recalling the portraits he'd found, quite a striking man in his youth; seeing him standing there, framed in the ornate doorway, you could still see echoes of that earnest young man behind his mask, the ambitious investor who had been seduced and corrupted by the lure of money and the security he thought it gave him. *He made more than enough to buy anything he wanted...*

He'd been clinging to it ever since.

He didn't make a grand entrance, or draw attention to his arrival. Marcus might not even have spotted him if he hadn't been specifically watching and waiting for him to appear. He merged into the crowd with studied ease, greeting those he'd come to know over the course of the day with casual nods and deliberated touches. For most of them, those gentle sweeps of his fingers across a woman's shoulder, that simple touch of his hand to a man's, even the friendly drape of his arm across an acquaintance's shoulder, were nothing more than a moment's contact, sometimes ignored, occasionally shrugged off, and – once or twice, reacted to with an annoyed or indignant glare. He smiled, and he laughed, and he apologised – politely – and then moved on, his progress barely a ripple through the general hubbub, his momentary intrusions lost in the beat of the music and the enjoyment of the crowd.

Marcus wasn't fooled for a moment. That offhand intimacy, excused in the bustle of humanity partying in close proximity, was the calculated prowl of a predator, taking the opportunity to test, to taste, and to savour his place among his prey. Those brief beats of laughter were as much of a disguise as the simple mask he was wearing. It was as much of an antique as he was, at a guess, since its contoured and supple fit were a far cry from the gaudy paper and plastic variety that the doorkeepers were handing out to anyone who hadn't brought their own.

Marcus hadn't bothered to put his on. He was the Guest of honour and everyone there knew exactly who he was.

He downed the last of his soda, regretted – for a brief moment – that he hadn't gone for a good stiff whiskey instead, and got to his feet, determined to make himself the vampire's shadow for the evening. His plan was not to be too obvious about it, but to follow him as closely as he could, lurking in his vicinity and being ready to step in to distract him from whoever his chosen target might be. It might well work the first couple of times, but after that? Well, he'd just have to improvise. As long as he stayed a minor irritation, he'd be fine. He might even amuse Namon with his efforts to come between him and his prey. But he'd have to watch how he did it. If he became a major annoyance, the vampire might decide to change the game...

Chapter Eleven

The evening felt interminable.

Namon was clearly in no hurry to do more than drift among the revellers and enjoy the general energy of the event. There was a reason, Marcus realised, after about an hour of equal drifting and standing on the edge of conversations, why the vampire didn't linger long in any one place. He'd be drawn to vivacity; to laughter and light-hearted talk, or to fervent discussion and passionate engagement. He'd stand, or sit, at the edge of a group, echoing the laughs, or dropping the odd word into their talk, and after a while, the laughter would die down. The discussions would become less focused; anger and irritation would begin to stir among the voices, and Namon would smile – and move on.

The effect of his presence was never enough to completely take the edge off the atmosphere but, as the night drew on, the general sense of joy became muted and weary. The dedicated drinkers drifted away from the music in search of better tasting ale and less hectic company. The filkers left to share their own music, and the gamers started to go back to their dice and their late night campaigning. Namon had asked several women to join him in a dance over the evening, and Marcus had tensed every time he'd done so – but they had simply danced, and afterwards he'd returned them to friends and partners – sometimes looking a little flushed, or else grown a little paler behind their masks.

Marcus had only seen the need to intervene twice so far. The first time he'd been concerned that the vampire might be targeting a well-on-his-way to drunk fan, trying to separate him from his friends. He'd stepped in with a cheery greeting and a friendly round of *How are you enjoying the ball? And the weekend?* Namon had almost immediately faded away into the background and then moved on, throwing Marcus an amused look as he did so. The second time he'd been less obvious, but his adversary hadn't been fooled by that intervention either; he'd smiled and nodded, and paused to tap Marcus playfully on the chest with the top of his cane before he sauntered away. The cane was made of wood and ivory; if he hadn't been wearing his waistcoat the tap would have been hard enough to bruise.

Midnight edged closer. The mood of the entire party was turning sombre by then, as if overlain by an unseen cloak of vague gloom. Cordell had passed by, proffering his good nights; he and the girls were usually late night, late morning people, especially at cons, but they'd decided to go early for once, making sure that Mazzy would get a good night's sleep. Marcus had watched them leave with a sense of relief, glad that they were moving out of the immediate danger zone.

Deyath drifted by, Pete in tow. She was also watching Namon, although from the happy expression on Pete's face he probably thought he was on a date. Marcus sent him to the bar, to buy a round of drinks and spent a moment or two comparing notes. Deyath suggested that now the crowd was beginning to thin, she start keeping an eye on the bathrooms – just in case Namon decided to follow a lone straggler into one. Marcus nodded at the idea – mostly because he thought that would keep her from drawing too much of the vampire's attention – and when Pete returned with her rum and coke, his beer, and another club soda for Marcus, he'd accepted the drink, wished them a good evening and went back to being a lurking shadow, following Namon as he headed towards a table on the far side of the room.

Shelley and Mason were sitting at it, along with Cyn and two or three others, similarly dressed. Shelley had exchanged her blue velvet for silk and leather in a much deeper hue. Her tightly laced corset suited her much better than the earlier frills, and went well with Mason's Byronic look, all snug leather trousers and voluminous white silk shirt. Even Cyn had abandoned her tee-shirt and was dressed in a snazzy combination of cog-wheel printed leggings, a wide leather belt adorned with a slew of buckles and studs, a low cut blouse, and a military style jacket, complete with red braid and gold frogging.

Namon walked round the table, having approached it at an angle; his route allowed him to indulge in more of that brush-stroke touching that made Marcus' skin crawl. Cyn looked up, and shifted slightly in her chair to shrug him off. The man beside her probably didn't even feel the gentle contact, because he didn't appear to react at all. Mason jumped and shifted the way his sister had, giving Namon a sideways look as he passed. Shelley shivered and leaned in towards Mason, whose sideways look turned into a small frown. Nobody actually said anything. Nobody had all night, despite the fact that some of the interactions had been disturbingly close to intimate. They had, perhaps, been a little too subtle to be called a caress, but then Namon had had many years to master his technique; nevertheless, anyone who'd bothered to watch him closely – as Marcus was doing – would have soon realised just how deliberated they were.

The chair next to Shelley was empty. Namon pulled it out and slid in to join their company, asking a polite *Mind if I sit here,* before laying his cane across the table and putting a half full glass of wine down in front of him. He'd been nursing the same glass for most of the evening. Marcus hadn't seen him take a sip from it once.

Marcus warily slid onto a chair at the next table, using the excuse of finding a resting place for his own, now half-empty, soda glass. He was wondering if Namon had started to forget he had a shadow; either the vampire was getting more than enough of what he wanted from those tiny, casual thefts, or he was still looking for the right victim. If it was the latter, then he was either being very particular in his choices, or else had been trying very hard not to be too obvious in his hunting. Marcus hoped that his persistent attention might well have contributed to the monster's caution: he couldn't afford to assume that the danger was passed, or that everyone was safe. Not yet.

There was only one other person sitting at the table he'd chosen, and his attention was turned towards the dance floor, where couples were drifting in gentle intimacy, lulled by the slow, smooth music that the DJ had started to introduce about half an hour before. That left Marcus free to lean back and listen in, close enough, this time, to hear the dandy's voice as he insinuated himself into the conversation.

The group were talking about a panel they'd attended earlier in the day; one in which the guests had apparently been talking about the difference between books and movies. In among all the other discussions around pace, viewpoint, and the slow reveal, someone had made the suggestion that movies were a better media for horror, because while a book might scare their readers, only a movie – or a video game – could actually make them jump. Mason was prepared to accept the point, but was arguing that too many movies relied on shock effects and ignored the more subtle horrors that a good writer could employ. This had spurred a slew of amused suggestions round the table concerning movies where the first half was filled with tension and suspense – and then the second half had been laughable since, once you'd actually *seen* the monster, you just couldn't take it seriously anymore.

Namon seemed content to listen, rather than participate at this point. Marcus found himself wondering just how many movies a Georgian vampire might have seen, and then rolled his eyes and pushed the thought away. Namon might have been born long before film was invented, but that hardly meant he was going to be ignorant of modern culture and technologies. The hotel had cable and a pay-for-movie TV installed in every room, for a start – it wasn't as if he'd just stepped out of his father's drawing room, no matter how accurately he was currently dressed.

Cyn was countering her brother's argument with a point about *Alien*, saying that no writer could have conjured up the nightmares that Giger's art had inspired. Someone else in the group agreed, but pointed out that while *Alien* and *Aliens* were good movies, no-one had yet managed to capture or convey horror the way that Lovecraft and his followers could. Namon had leaned forward at that, unquestionably sensing a chance to turn the conversation to his advantage. The movement also allowed him to slide his hand closer to where Shelley's lay on the tabletop: either an opening move for another stolen touch, or the preamble to something more sinister and dangerous.

"Lovecraft is overrated. Madness and despair no matter which way you turn. *True* Horror," Namon was saying, "is much more subtle. Something slow and seductive. Something to be… savoured." There was a hint of amusement in the observation, a wry acknowledgment of personal knowledge that most of his audience had no way of understanding. "None of this – slash and scream nonsense that seems to consume the modern expectation. Fear is… primal, of course, but alert and alarm, a few moments of panic and… then death? Terrifying, perhaps. But horrifying? Never. Horror has to creep up on you, crawl in with a slow sense of inevitability. It is not death that chills the soul, but *dying*. The onset of age. Of disease. Of helplessness and impotence, creeping over you with each tick of the clock. The fear of losing all you have. All you've worked for. Of failing, simply through living, day by day."

His smile held a hint of quiet triumph, and Marcus shivered, all the way down to his soul. If *that* was the horror that Namon had sought to avoid, then part of him could understand how the man might be able to justify what he'd become. But in his determination *not* to die, his refusal to accept the natural inevitability of life, he had chosen a path which had led to something far more horrifying than his fears could possibly justify. He had invested in his personal survival without thought or care for the impact or consequence it might have on others: he had taken advantage of everyone around him, using them – first to accumulate his wealth, and then *literally* using them to sustain his existence. It was a self-defeating course of action. By denying death that way, by seeking to survive at all costs – he had allowed all the things that made living worth *living* wither away and die, leaving an empty husk that clung to material wealth and power, using it to place himself apart from the mortal world.

"I get that," Shelley said, nodding thoughtfully. "That's some of the appeal of the vampire, right? That they live forever, staying forever young? Who wouldn't want that?"

"Who indeed?" Namon countered, gently laying his fingers over hers – as thanks, she probably thought, for her support.

I wouldn't, Marcus started to think, and then grimaced, realising the irony of the thought. Was immortality a blessing or a curse? Ashera clearly did not regret her choices, but she had turned back in full acceptance of the responsibilities that doing so would bring. To Namon, it was clearly a blessing, even if it had cost him his soul. He was the true horror in the room, a hollow echo of a man, wrapped in an illusion of life and chained by all the material trappings that defined it.

"But there's always a price, isn't there?" Cyn was frowning into her drink, black and gold tipped fingers curling around the stem of her glass. She was drinking what looked like red wine. At a Horrorcon, you could never entirely be sure.

"Hunger," Namon murmured, looking at her with more than a hint of it in his eyes. "Endless hunger..."

His voice had dropped to a dramatic whisper, a sound

enhanced by the dry and dusty timbre with which he delivered the words. His hand had tightened over Shelley's, deliberately capturing her fingers within his own. He wasn't looking at her at all – but Marcus was. He saw the way a wary frown crossed her face, to be quickly replaced by a haunted, anxious look. He saw how she tried to tug her hand away, and how quickly the fight started to go out of her; how she relaxed – not with acceptance or surrender, but into the start of a distanced, and fear-filled slump.

Three things happened all at once: Marcus leapt to his feet in alarm; Mason responded to his girlfriend's apparent fainting fit by turning to support her; and Cyn stood up, leaned across the table – and threw the contents of her wine glass straight into Namon's face.

"Get away from her, you *creep*," she yelled. Namon – startled by his sudden soaking, and with a look of pure fury on his face, leapt to *his* feet, let go of Shelley, and reached for Cyn's outstretched hand instead.

"Hey, hey. *Hey,*" Marcus declared as jovially as he could manage, stepping across to push Namon away from both young women and deliberately put himself between the vampire and his prey. "Let's not start a fight tonight, okay? I think you've made your point, young lady," he said, turning to Cyn and taking a moment to mouth a quick *Let me deal with this* at her. She scowled at him, but put down her glass, not looking at all contrite. "Isiah," he went on, turning back to Namon and hoping – just *hoping* – that the vampire would play along, "I know Spanner asked you to play the vampire for him this weekend, but I think you're getting a little deep into the part. That speech was great, and the – subtle way you captured Shelley's hand was really in character ... but I don't think you know your own strength. That obviously hurt. I think you owe her an apology, don't you?"

Namon had pulled off his wine splattered mask and was glowering at him; if looks could kill, that one almost certainly would. "I do not apologise to whores and strumpets," he hissed. "That bitch..."

"That *bitch,*" Marcus interrupted, throwing an apologetic glance at Cyn, "thought you were hurting her friend. So did I. Now, come on. We're all friends here, right? Just enjoying the night, having a little fun? I'm sorry about your costume – I'm sure the Con will pay for getting it cleaned – but you can't go around playing the monster that well and still expect everyone to know it's just an act."

"Can't I?" Namon growled, half under his breath. Marcus' words seemed to have dispelled some of his anger, though. He glanced down at his soaked cravat and the spatter of staining on his coat, and then up, meeting Marcus' eyes with calculated challenge. "So," he growled softly. "You have outed me, Dr Holland. Did you want to spoil Mr O'Toole's game so soon?"

He reached out with his right hand as he spoke, his fingers starting to close around Marcus' own right wrist – but then his hand spasmed and he surreptitiously jerked it back, almost as if he'd been burned.

"I was trying very hard not to spoil it at all." Marcus was trying to keep his voice even and friendly, which wasn't easy, given the way Namon was now looking at him. He was feeling very, very grateful for Ashera's gift, the knobbled line of beads that still lay tucked under his shirt cuff. "Let's not make more of this than we need to, shall we? Why don't you apologise to the young lady, and – uh – go change out of the outfit before anything becomes permanently stained? The party's almost over, anyway."

Namon glanced round. Despite it still being a few more minutes to midnight, the room had a definite 'end of the evening' feel to it. There were still some couples out on the dance floor, waiting for the chimes of the Clock to tell them to unmask, but the general hubbub of conversation that had underpinned the music had practically died away. There were only a few people at the bar, and many of the side tables were empty. Most of the convention had found somewhere else to be. Marcus suspected that the atmosphere was much livelier up on the mezzanine, but he wasn't about to suggest that to Namon; he was hoping the vampire, his fun disrupted and his dignity affronted, could be persuaded to retire, to slink back to wherever his lair might be so he could sit and sulk for a while.

"Very well," Namon said, after a moment. He picked up his cane, stepped back from the tables, and offered a slight bow to Shelley, who was shivering inside the curve of Mason's arms. "My – apologies, my lady," he said, politely and just a little bit disdainfully. "Be assured, my intentions were merely playful. I was, perhaps, as Dr Holland suggests, a little *too* immersed in my – role."

Marcus caught the slight hesitation and with it the hint of underlying amusement that had begun to creep back into Namon's voice. He was, indeed, playing a part – the wolf pretending to be a sheep, while dressed in wolf's clothing: the incident might have annoyed and irritated him, but he was still very much in control of the game.

"You're the vampire," Mason said, completely unaware of the irony of that conclusion. "Aren't you. I used to do a little LARPing. You're good. Really good. But that – wasn't cool."

"It's okay," Shelley interrupted in a slightly shaky voice. "I mean – I guess I'm okay, so ... no permanent harm done. Really."

She was wrong, but no-one in the group but Marcus knew that. Namon probably did, but then he wouldn't care. He tipped her another slight bow, nodded warningly at Marcus, and turned to walk away, heading across the back of the dance floor and towards the nearest door leading back into the hotel. Marcus started to watch him go, but just as he reached the farside of the wooden flooring, the Clock started to strike the hour. The dancers cheered and threw their masks into the air, their swirl of resurging enthusiasm, sweeping across his line of vision. By the time they moved away, Namon was gone.

"Come on," Marcus said, turning back to Shelley and offering her his hand. "We need to get you some help. Right now."

"She's fine, Dr Holland." Mason was holding her closely, probably instinctively aware that she needed protection, but not knowing why.

"No, she's not," Cyn snapped at him, slipping round the table to hunker down beside her friend and place a reassuring hand to her arm. "He did something to her, didn't he?" She directed the question at Marcus, who sighed.

"Yes," he said. He glanced round warily: the few people who might have overheard the discussion with Namon had moved away, drawn by the midnight celebration and the lure of last orders at the bar. That only left Cyn, Mason, and Shelley in hearing distance. His next few words were still quiet ones; he didn't really want to be saying the things he had to where they might be overheard. He had just managed to reveal that Namon was Spanner's special 'guest' in front of a wider audience – but that had been a hasty, and probably not entirely sensible, choice to defuse a dangerous situation.

The truth was going to be much harder to explain, especially when, moments before, he'd been the one reinforcing the lie.

"Mr Namon isn't – acting," he announced. "He really is a vampire. Or something like one, anyway."

Shelley's eyes went wide. Cyn was obviously willing to give him the benefit of the doubt, and reacted with a slightly puzzled frown. Mason, on the other hand, rolled his eyes in immediate disbelief.

"Oh, come on," he reacted. "Are you working on a new book, or something? There's no such thing as a vampire. Any more than there are Immortals wandering around cutting each other's heads off, or – werewolves, running around in London."

"I don't know about the werewolves," Marcus countered sharply. "But I do know about Namon – what he is, and what he does. He feeds off other people – steals their life and their energies to sustain his existence. And he doesn't care about what that does to his victims. Doesn't care about anyone other than himself. Don't be deceived by Hollywood, and don't let his look and his manners deceive you. He's not some angst driven, tragic, romantic hero." He paused to take a breath, then added: "He's a monster. Taking what he wants without concern or consent."

"This is bull…" Mason began angrily, but Shelley silenced him, putting her hand up to his lips.

"Mason, don't," she requested, her voice cracking a little. "Dr Holland's right. That man – *did* something, when he touched me. I couldn't – I – I wanted to pull away, and… I was just – *frozen*. My hand's still numb. *I* feel numb. Shaky. Like I want to cry… " she concluded, her face crumpling in unspecified distress. Mason stared at her.

"Really?" he asked, and she nodded, catching back a small sob and burying herself in against him for comfort.

"I don't know," Cyn said, looking at the two of them with anxious concern, "what that creep did, or why he did it, but he did *something*." She threw Marcus a challenging glare. "You said something about getting help, didn't you? Let's do that, and worry about… vampires and the other stuff, later. I think she needs it, Mace," she went on in a softer tone, seeing her brother still looking reluctant.

"Maybe," he agreed slowly. "But what kind of help are we talking about, here? I may like reading about magic, but I don't actually believe in it – so if you're talking about conducting exorcisms, or some new-age-y crystal and candle stuff, forget it."

Marcus found him a wry, if weary smile.

"My friend is a qualified doctor," he said, reassuringly. *One,* his inner writer insisted on pointing out, *who happens to be several thousand years old...*

— * —

Ashera, it appeared, had finished playing Senet for the evening. The board was sitting beside her on the table, but the dice and the playing pieces were all carefully packed away. She, and the small group of gamers still wired enough to be playing anything that late at night, had clearly moved on to card games. When Marcus led the way into the Games Room, she was calmly laying down a handful of colourful cards next to an equally colourful board and announcing: "That's the set, so that's sixteen points – and – um – am I right? I get three more for having a token on *this* space?"

"She's right." The man next to her – a portly figure with an impressive beard and a very large tankard which sat next to him on the table – grinned at the other players, most of whom immediately put the rest of their cards down on the table. "That's another round to the lady – unless anyone has a triumph card they haven't used yet?"

"I have," the last active player announced, putting the relevant card down with a reluctant flourish. "But that only gives me eighteen points, and I have to give up any tokens in the city to play it, so I won't get the city bonus. She still wins."

"You sure you haven't played this before?" The question was amused, rather than accusatory. Ashera laughed.

"This? No. But I have played many games in my life, and I have learned a lot by playing them ... Marcus?" She rose to her feet as soon as she saw the look on his face. "Excuse me, everyone..."

"This is Shelley," Marcus said as Ashera hurried over to join him. Shelley had managed to walk the short distance from the ballroom to the Fan rooms, although she'd clung to Mason the entire way. The impact of Namon's attack had become more pronounced with every step; she'd kept her head down and had struggled to breath, trying to fight off the impulse to burst into tears. She hadn't been all that successful: she'd started to gulp down sobs as they'd passed the archway into the lobby, and they'd become more frequent and desperate, heart-rending to hear, even over the raucous chorus that drifted out of the Filker's room as they passed the half-open door. "Can you help her? She needs…"

"So I see." Ashera swept in with motherly concern, holding out her arms. Mason took one look at her face and handed his girlfriend over without a word, gently untangling her from his shirt and passing her into the Shenuheh's embrace. Shelley gulped in one last, painful sob, then breathed out a shuddering sigh. "It's all right," Ashera murmured. "I've got you. You're safe now." She looked up, over the shivering girl's head, and fixed Marcus with a questioning look. His own sigh sounded almost as weary as Shelley's had done.

"He was just – touching and tasting, most of the evening, and then… " He shrugged. "I don't know. Maybe he was getting tired of the game. Maybe he usually takes more than my watching him allowed. And maybe he just – liked what he found, when he held her hand."

"Where is he now?" she asked, guiding her charge to a nearby sofa and helping her sit down.

"I'm not entirely sure. Cyn here threw half a glass of wine over him. I'm hoping he's gone to clean up and nurse his indignation for the rest of the night."

"He was *hurting* her," Cyn said, hotly. "I don't know how, because all he did was grab her hand, but… I had to do *something.*"

Ashera nodded distractedly, focused on soothing Shelley with gentle touches and an equally gentle embrace. "Not everyone would have seen that," she murmured, conveying quiet approval. "And not everyone who did, would have taken action to prevent it. Creatures like the Hollow Men rely on the wilful blindness that protects mankind from awareness of their horror, while making the innocent vulnerable to their attack. There," she smiled, having managed to coax Shelley to relax a little. "Has that helped?"

Shelley nodded wordlessly, her head tucked down against Ashera's shoulder. Mason stepped a little closer, staring down at the two of them with a mixture of concern, anxiety, and angry disbelief. "Are you really a doctor?" he demanded. "Because she needs one, and I'm hearing way too much of this bloke's bullshit to be confident…"

"Sit *down*, young man." Ashera's voice didn't change in volume, but – just for a moment – she spoke with complete and utter command. It was a tone, Marcus noted, that would have commanded Pharaohs and gods alike – and probably had done so, at some point in her long history. Mason sat, dropping bonelessly into the nearest easy chair as if he'd been poleaxed. "Thank you. Now," she went on, fixing him with a firm but sympathetic eye, "this young lady – your friend? Lover?" Mason nodded a vaguely shell-shocked agreement to both suggestions, earning himself a wry and knowing smile. "I thought so. She has just been savagely attacked and violated, and she needs help – a help only I can give her, since her wounds are hard to see, and even harder to heal… You may not have believed that there are creatures capable of inflicting this kind of damage, and you may not *want* to believe it, but I have been dealing with this kind of poison for many years. She has been touched by a corruption that – untreated – will fester and spread until it taints her entire existence. And unless you want to watch her be dragged away from you by despair, consumed by self-loathing and eaten up by a guilt she cannot understand, you will let me do my work and let me save her soul. All right?"

Mason nodded, still looking shell-shocked. Marcus didn't blame him. Cyn moved round to perch on the arm of her brother's chair, watching her friend, rather than the woman that cradled her.

"Can you help her?" Cyn asked gently. Ashera smiled.

"I can. You brought her to me quickly, and I have already countered some of his poison. There will be scars, but only faint ones. This will be a nightmare that will quickly fade. Unlike some he has inflicted over the years," she added, sharing the thought with Marcus, who heaved another sigh.

"Yeah. And he'll go on doing it, unless I can figure out some way of stopping him."

One of the gamers left his friends packing the game boards away and came across to see if he could be of any help: Ashera assured him they had everything in hand, and wished him, and his friends a good night. There was a short round of mutual *Great games today, see you in the morning* chatter, and then the room emptied, leaving Marcus and Ashera alone with a still shivering Shelley, her disconcerted boyfriend and his sister.

Who, as soon as the door closed, fixed Marcus with a steely stare.

"If you knew Mr Namon was a vampire – a *real* vampire, that is, why you haven't you stopped him? You're the expert, aren't you? I thought all it took was a stake through the heart, or something."

"He's not *Buffy*, Cyn. Nobody is." Mason had rallied a little, possibly helped by the wan smile that Shelley had found for him, just as the gamers were leaving. "That's just tripe the TV people try to sell you – so they can make money selling you other stuff. Dr Holland isn't some mythical 'chosen one.' He's not even a Watcher. What do you think would happen if he tried to stick a stake in someone?"

"I suppose…" Cyn thought about it for a moment. "It's not that easy, is it."

"It's fucking mental, that's what it is." Her brother's response was tight with anger; it was hard to tell if it was with her, with Marcus, or simply with himself. "*Nobody* goes round sticking stakes in people, because if they tried, they'd end up in jail. Or the loony bin. There are no such things as *vampires*. I don't know what that bastard did to Shelley, but I didn't see any fangs, or – anything that would make me think 'woo hoo, vampire attack!'" He waved his arms in frustrated helplessness. "Now, this lady is very nice, and she's being kind, but – I am still not buying this bullshit, and…"

The door flew open with a bang. Everybody, except Ashera, jumped. Marcus turned, in time to see Deyath push Pete into the room, take a good look up and down the corridor and then follow him in, hastily reaching to shut the door behind them.

"Oh, thank god," she breathed, seeing first Marcus, and then Ashera behind him. "You're both here." She stepped forward, barely in time to stop Pete from falling over as his legs gave way. "We couldn't see you in the ballroom, Dr Holland. I thought he might have – done something, or… I don't know." Adrenaline was abandoning her, letting events catch up in a way she was struggling to deal with. "He attacked Pete," she explained, grateful as Marcus took the young man's weight from her to half push, half carry him over to the sofa. Pete slid into the seat with jellied legs and a wan smile; Ashera, still encumbered with Shelley, immediately reached out and gathered him in.

"I was in the ladies," Deyath started to explain, then hesitated, seeing Mason and Cyn both staring at her. Marcus glanced at them, and grimaced, tellingly.

"They know – well," he added for accuracy, "I told them. I don't think Mason's entirely convinced as yet. What happened?"

Deyath grabbed a chair and sank into it, running a hand

through her hair. "Like I said, I was in the ladies – the ones down past the Breakfast bar? I was keeping an eye on a lone straggler – and Pete was waiting for me out in the hall, down by the doors to the gym? When I came out, that *creep* had him pinned up against the wall and – well, I think he was probably whispering something to him, but it looked... I'm not sure what it looked like," she admitted reluctantly. "But I was scared and I didn't know what else to do, so I pulled out that ankh Ashera gave me, and I charged in and waved it in his face." She demonstrated with the silver ankh, her fingers clenching round it fiercely enough to bruise. "He – he reared back, and *hissed* at me. But he let go of Pete, so I grabbed him and I told him to run. Which we did. I don't think he followed us. I kept looking back, but I didn't see him. Oh, *god,*" she concluded, letting the ankh drop to the end of its chain and burying her face into her palm. "I wasn't sure I believed you, Dr Holland, but – that look on his face... He was *so* angry. If I hadn't had the ankh – I think he might have killed me."

Chapter Twelve

They decanted to Marcus' room, which – while probably no safer than the space they left – at least had the advantage of a bed to tuck Shelley into while she slept and recovered a little of her strength. Ashera settled Pete on the chaise-longue, which Marcus and Mason dragged out of the bathroom and into the bedroom so that she could keep an eye on both of her patients more easily. Pete, while shaken and disorientated by the assault, had not taken as much hurt as Namon's earlier victim. Namon, it appeared, had recognised Marcus' messenger from earlier in the day, and had paused in his indignant retreat to leave his adversary a cruel and pointed message.

He said, Pete had recalled as Marcus and Deyath had helped him into the lift, *'I don't touch coffee, but do thank Dr Holland for the nightcap.' I didn't understand what he meant. But then I felt really cold and everything started to swim…*

If Deyath hadn't charged in the way she did, it was probable that Namon would have taken a lot more from Pete than he had.

Mason had still been extremely suspicious and sceptical of the whole business, but he wasn't about – as he said – to leave Shelley in the hands of lunatics, so he'd tagged along anyway, earning himself a cynical look from his sister and a grateful smile from his girlfriend. Shelley had clung to Ashera the entire way, which might have helped convince the young man that there was *something* going on that didn't fall into his neat view of the world. They'd used the lifts to avoid having to deal with late night stragglers on the mezzanine, which also meant taking the longer walk from the lift shafts, through the rotunda and down the passageway to reach Marcus' room.

Every single one of the antique mirrors they passed flickered with multiple reflections as Ashera moved into and out of their frames. Now he knew to look for it, Marcus was fascinated by the effect: it was like catching a glimpse of some artful motion capture footage, but presented in real time rather than the exaggerated slow-motion that such things usually employed. The Shenuheh's reflection was surrounded by shimmering echoes of herself that lingered for a moment as she moved past the glass. They formed an odd contrast to the reflection that Shelley left behind. That was not as clear as perhaps it should be: the edges of her image were faintly blurred, as if she had somehow started to become translucent.

Not transparent though, a fact for which Marcus was deeply grateful.

Just after they'd passed the rotunda, the sounds of late night laughter drifting up from the mezzanine below, Mason had dropped back to pace beside Marcus, who was helping Pete stay upright at the back of their hasty convoy. He glanced at Marcus, then nodded at the mirrors, somehow managing to include Ashera in the gesture. "Is she..?" He clearly didn't know how to articulate his question, and Marcus allowed himself to drop a slight hint of a smug *I told you so* into his answering grin.

"Anti-vampire," he told him, deadpan, then corrected himself with his usual academic rigor for accuracy. "Actually, vampire anti-body, in a manner of speaking. Long story, not mine to tell."

Pete, focused on putting one foot after the other, almost as if he were drunk, rather than had been drunk *from*, looked up, blinking – first at the two of them and then past the nearest mirror and on to where Ashera nursed Shelley's progress, the same way Marcus was marshalling his own. "Cool," he decided, adding: "Why don't *they* get mentioned in the stories and legends and stuff?"

"Because we are very, very rare," Ashera's voice floated

back to the three of them, "and we like to keep a low profile. Besides," she added, glancing back to flash Marcus an amused grin, "I doubt that Bram Stoker would know how to write about a woman who knew more than his hero did – let alone a black one. To him women were either helpless damsels, or seductive creatures of the night."

Marcus suppressed a small wince. The first Nettlestone book had committed that particular sin – at least before his editor had got hold of it. He'd learned to be better than that – knowing Mazzy and Lilith had helped after his earlier experiences with Beverley – and Jackson Hobbs had avoided falling into the trope by being generally unimpressed by the human race as a whole. An early critic had once suggested that Jackson was a hopeless misogynist – an impression immediately countered by any number of his female fans pointing out that the character's curmudgeonly attitude extended to anyone and everyone, no matter what sex, race, or sexual leaning they might have.

He'd mellowed a little, after four harrowing adventures, but he was never going to become Mr Congeniality. There were principles at stake.

Once they'd reached the room, they'd taken a moment or two to sort themselves, Ashera dealing with her patients, and Cyn commandeering the kettle to make tea and coffee for everyone. The suite – being a suite, rather than a standard room, had a whole drawer of cups in the unit under the kettle, and there was a fresh half-pint of milk lurking in the tiny fridge. The maid must have replenished that when she came in to service the room – Marcus had used up the one from the day before, getting through several cups of hot milky coffee during his early morning research session.

The reminder of that was useful, though. He pulled out the laptop and showed Mason, Cyn and Deyath what he'd been able to find: the history of the house and its owners, along with the portraits, and the more recent newspaper reports. He didn't open the article that mentioned Susie, but Deyath added her story to ones he had shared, explaining about her sister's untimely death, and why she believed Namon to be responsible for it.

"Bastard," Mason had growled once she'd finished. "You're right, Marcus." They had gone from formal modes of address to first name terms somewhere around the early twentieth century – in-between considering orphanages, and the impact of bringing shell-shocked soldiers into the sphere of Namon's influences. "This – monster – needs to be dealt with. Any idea how?"

"Not really," Marcus admitted, wearily. He had less than a day left. If he couldn't figure something out before the closing ceremony, he would have to leave – and leave the vampire smirking at the heart of his carefully constructed web of lies. It had been hard enough to convince Mason – who'd witnessed the attack against Shelley, as well as seeing its aftermath. It was going to be impossible to get anyone official to even listen to him, let alone take action against a perfectly respectable hotel owner.

Especially as the evidence he'd used to convince Mason wouldn't prove anything to anyone who hadn't actually seen the monster that lurked within the hollow shell of the man.

"There is a process I have seen in many mystery novels," Ashera suggested softly from the bedroom doorway, "Where the protagonists review the evidence and consider the clues. Even your heroes, Marcus, take time out to reconsider what they have learned. Perhaps it would help if you summarised what you have gleaned so far."

Marcus opened his mouth to respond to that, then closed it again. She was right, of course. He'd been so busy trying to convince others of the danger they were in, that he hadn't found time to examine the additional data he'd been gathering, let alone review his research in the light of what that data might reveal. "She's right, you know," he said, with a touch of chagrin. "Trouble is, when I'm working as a *writer*, I'm always adjusting the clues so they point to the outcome I'm wanting to happen, not the other way round. So I've not been thinking about this the right way at all. When I work academically, I try to focus on balancing fact against interpretation, so as to avoid unsupported speculation – and you should always revisit the interpretation if the facts contradict the current theory…"

"Do we have a current theory?" Cyn asked, passing him the cup of coffee he'd requested.

"I don't know," he answered thoughtfully, his mind slipping gears and winding up some of the critical thinking skills he'd been trained to use. "But let's see if we can come up with one."

He fought down a sudden yearning for a white-board or pad of flip-chart paper and headed for his laptop case, tugging out the battered notebook he always kept tucked inside the front pocket. A few flipped pages, and he was looking at a pristine sheet, covered in neat lines. "Who wants to take notes?"

Cyn put up her hand – and then lowered it again, a little sheepishly. "I will," she offered. "But – are we safe in here? This is his hotel, right? He'll have a key, and…"

"You are safer here, than you would be in your own room." Ashera drifted round behind Marcus to trace out the invisible runes Marcus had earlier marked on the door. As her finger followed the lines, Marcus could have sworn that the faint traces from the oil he'd used flared with a momentary hint of light. "This place has some protection, and my being here will add to that. I will warn you, if I sense his presence; he moves like a cold wind, swirling and drifting at the edges of my awareness. I will know if he draws near."

"She feels the trembling in the Force," Mason noted, visibly relaxing a little. "Early warning system. Nice. I think."

"I think so, too," Marcus said, handing the notepad, and a

pen, over to Cyn. Deyath moved her chair a little closer, changing the angle so she could see over the other girl's shoulder. "Mark that down, will you?" he requested. *"Dark presence can be remotely detected by sensitives.* It's not exactly diagnostic, but it's still evidence."

"Evidence for what?" Cyn paused for a moment, the pen poised to write. Marcus smiled grimly.

"For the existence of vampires. It's as good a place to start as any, don't you think?"

— * —

They worked at it for an hour or two, Marcus wracking his brains to recall everything he might have noticed, while the other three threw questions about vampire lore at him, trying to untangle the modern mythologies from the older, more visceral texts. By half-past two they had covered a lot of ground, but had failed to come to any clear conclusions, beyond the most obvious one: Mason finally voiced it with weary disgust.

"We're screwed, aren't we," he said. He pushed his dreg-filled coffee cup away from him and leaned back in his chair, running a tired hand over the back of his neck. "He's never been buried – as far as we know – so there's no way to deal with him in the grave. He's already hinted that staking him won't work, and while that could be misdirection, no-one round here wants to get close enough to him to try it anyway. He's like a leech – ripping… whatever he rips out of people, with just a touch. So there's no way to grab him, or restrain him, or anything, without risking life and… well, not limb, as such, but yeah – life. So that's out. Right?"

"Right," Marcus agreed with a sigh. The real problem was that Namon was too integral a figure at the hotel, too much a part of modern life to be disposed of in any overt way without creating longer-term problems. The half joking suggestion – that Marcus simply grab a sword from the wall display outside the ballroom and strike the monster's head from his shoulders – was beginning to sound more and more appealing. *If* he could face the idea of being tried for cold-blooded murder, convicted, and spending the rest of his life in jail…

They'd become inventive as the night wound on: Deyath had suggested getting Shelley to press charges for assault, because at least that way Namon might spend some time locked away somewhere. Mason had shot that idea down, pointing out that there had been too many potential witnesses to the incident, most of whom would speak in Namon's favour. Then he'd suggested getting Pete to do it, but the general consensus was that his case would be even flimsier than Shelley's – at least in the eyes of the law, who probably wouldn't accept the idea that the assault had been a metaphysical one. Cyn – in a moment of sheer frustration – had proposed burning the whole hotel to the ground. Then she'd realised that doing so would only work if they could find some way to trap Namon in the building while trying to ensure that everyone else would escape unharmed. Marcus did briefly wonder what would happen if they set off the fire alarm, but dismissed the thought; he suspected that all that would do was annoy the vampire even more than they had managed to do so far. If it did bring Namon out into the dark along with everyone else, he'd undoubtedly make sure he stayed among the crowd while the local fire brigade turned up. Then, as the owner of the hotel, he'd be the one to *deal* with the fire brigade – there'd certainly be no chance of isolating him and dealing with him unseen amongst the furore.

He might even take the opportunity to find himself another victim or two.

"What we need," he said, around a yawn, "is some way to remove him from the picture without raising any kind of hue and cry. For that, we need to know his weaknesses, and – so far – all we have is his antipathy for holy symbols – for religious iconography and – " He lifted his hand and rattled the beads that still clasped his wrist. "Magical protections. And I have no idea how that works, let alone knowing how it might help."

"Do you need to know?" Ashera asked softly. Marcus looked up, to find her leaning against the bedroom doorframe. She'd not taken part in any of their meandering discussion, excusing herself to attend to her sleeping patients. He wondered how long she'd been standing there. "It can take a lifetime – maybe more – to understand even the simplest of magics. Do you know how the lights work, or how a car converts fuel to energy? Of course you don't. You simply know that – when you flick a switch, or turn a key – your technologies will deliver."

"Well, yeah," Mason shrugged. "But that's science. I don't need to know, but someone does. Someone figured it out and invented things. Made them work."

She smiled. "That's true of magic, too. Lights and cars and much of the modern world use electricity as their source of power. These – " She turned her hand so that the bangles she wore turned and glinted in the electric light. "– and that – " Her finger pointed at the silver ankh that hung around Deyath's neck. "Draws on belief and faith. The silver helps," she added, wryly. "Like copper and electricity, some things – conduct and direct power more effectively than others."

"But science is – well, *science*." Mason glanced at his sister, looking for support. "Magic is just – superstition, isn't it?" Cyn shrugged.

"I don't know," she admitted anxiously. "I didn't use to believe in vampires, but now…"

Ashera sighed, drifting across to sit next to Marcus and regard them all with sympathetic eyes.

"There are many unpleasant and dangerous things out in the world," she said. "The Blood Hunters and the Hollow Men are not the worst, although they are probably the most commonly encountered. Behind every myth and dark tale of horror, there may lurk an even darker truth – one concealed by the way that names and natures and explanations have, over millennia, become blurred by time. Memories of that truth can be lost and changed in endless re-tellings, and what might have been understanding becomes coloured by the anticipations of terror and the garbled words of damaged survivors."

"Witnesses can be notoriously unreliable," Marcus observed. "As can myth, and folklore. There can be endless variations of the same tale, some that agree, and some that contradict. But tales like that are generally seen as metaphors for something else. Means of transmitting and sustaining culture. When they're not just antiquated versions of the urban myth..." He'd spoken out of habit, regurgitating the commonly held perspective that underpinned the meat and drink of his profession. But Ashera was watching him, her eyes dancing with a hint of laughter. "Oh," he realised, a little sheepishly. "Yeah. Vampires are real. So other things may well be real, too. Metaphors reflecting older realities, I suppose. Fact and fiction interlaced, and the truth so wrapped up in the myths that it's impossible to untangle it."

She reached to lay her hand over his, her touch both warm and reassuring. "I think you had to be there," she murmured with a hint of amusement. "People tend to sleep more easily in their beds if they can dismiss the demons that haunt the night," she considered, a little more loudly. "Turning those terrors into tales, where heroes prevail and the innocent can be saved by faith, is one way they've found to shield themselves. The development of civilisation and the rationalisation of science is another. The modern world scoffs at the warnings of ancient lore and delights in the echoes of lurid tales.

"But science cannot yet explain everything, nor can it always protect the vulnerable from the old hungers that still lurk in shadows and silences. Sometimes it can be safer to sleep with protective runes, or holy symbols painted on your window frames."

"Any holy symbol?" Deyath was studying the silver ankh, turning it over in her hand. "Even if you don't believe in it? What makes a symbol holy, anyway?"

"Belief," Ashera countered, smiling at her. "It's a – feedback loop, I suppose. One feeds the other. A symbol is just that – a symbol. But symbols have power, the same way words do. They represent an idea, a concept, perhaps an unseen power of some kind. Affirmation of that idea, or faith in that power, inspires belief, which then invests further energies into that particular symbol – which then, in turn, magnifies the power of that belief. In the end, the symbol itself becomes a conduit for that power. So, no, you don't have to personally believe in that particular god, or that ideal. The investment of centuries will have already imbued that symbol with sufficient significance to repel the kind of creatures we're talking about. But if you *do* have faith – that's *true* faith, not some book taught belief, or a superstitious reflex – then in your hands, that symbol can become a potent weapon. To be protected from the dark, there has to be a light – a light bestowed upon a symbol by the faith of generations – or a light within you that burns with deep conviction. I believed in my gods once. An indoctrinated belief, filled with awe and terror. *Now* I understand that they are merely aspects of a greater whole. All gods are one god – and yet, there are many, and they work in mysterious ways. Call them incarnations – personifications, perhaps – of energies that lie beyond the simple grasp of human thought. Those energies serve this world, and link to worlds beyond it in ways – ways that you and I will never understand. But, in giving them shape, in recognising them, we can call upon them, and engage with them as conduits to a deeper truth.

"I have seen the light. My faith lies in understanding that – one day – I will see it again."

"And because you have faith in – *something*," Cyn said warily, "your amulets – that ankh – have power to repel something like Namon?"

"Oh, my dear," Ashera laughed, "I wish I were that strong. If I were, you would not be sitting here and Marcus would be worrying about his next book, not his next breath. Yes, my faith – my understanding of who and what I am – gives me strength. But the symbols I use ... thousands of souls, for hundreds of generations have invested their belief in the power they represent. It would take a very dark creature indeed to deny that kind of power. A symbol's power can be redirected, of course." She sighed. "Namon might be repelled by a swastika, given his history, but I wouldn't want to rely on it. Not in Europe, at least."

Mason winced. "Don't," he said. "Having to deal with one Georgian dandy is bad enough. Facing down Nazi vampires...? I don't want to go there. Ever."

Marcus' inner author had been busy taking notes: he quashed that final thought with grim determination. "I think I get the theory," he said, slowly. "But... "

"Doubt is good," she said. "Doubt avoids foolish convictions and thoughtless adherence. This isn't about finding anything abstract to believe in, even if some achieve it that way. This is about believing in yourself and in what you think is right." Ashera's smile was kind. "In the end, that's where all faith lies."

– * –

Marcus woke slowly, emerging from a cocoon of drowsiness to focus, blearily, on the soft grey light of an early dawn. The room was filled with smoky shadows, the last lingerings of the night. That – and soft snores from where Mason lay sprawled in the other overstuffed armchair in the corner. They'd all had to admit defeat somewhere shortly after

Ashera re-joined the conversation, exhaustion creeping up on them with inevitability. His mind had felt thoroughly fuzzy by then, his body a little too wired to succumb easily to the promise of sleep, but the rest of him far too exhausted to make sense of idea or argument. He'd shooed Cyn and Deyath into the bedroom to find space on the sprawling bed beside Shelley, while Mason had bagged one of the armchairs, and Ashera had considerately plumped the cushions on the other. He might have argued with her – might have tried to be a gentleman – but she'd merely smiled and pointed commandingly, and he'd obeyed, falling over into the welcome embrace of the chair. Sleep had ambushed him immediately, dragging him down into haunted dreams.

Something had been nagging at him all night: an idea, a thought, a missed moment … something too elusive to grasp, but still too insistent to ignore. It was still nagging him as he woke, some hint of *something* rising, like the sun, tugging at his memory, demanding attention even though he couldn't quite pin it down.

"Good morning." Ashera greeted him warmly, sounding far too perky and awake for whatever hour in the morning it was. She was standing at the window, watching the light pearl across the lightening sky. "It's going to be a lovely day."

"No it isn't," he grumped, hauling himself to his feet and walking over to join her. He fought down a yawn and stared, blearily, out at the dawn. "There's a bloody vampire lurking somewhere in this hotel, and he's won. Because I have no idea how to stop him doing what he does. And I have to stand up and give my grand speech this afternoon, knowing that he'll be sitting there, right in the front row, laughing at me…"

He ran a weary hand through his dishevelled hair. "I'm sorry," he said. "I said I'd find a way, and I haven't. But if I leave tonight and he's still here, helping himself to the staff and feeding off the guests as they check in … *Goddess*," he swore, feeling angry and impotent. "I can't – maybe I should

just kill him. All those lives, those hopes, those dreams …
stolen, corrupted … Maybe that'd be worth the sacrifice…"

"There may be many things in this world that would be
worth the offer of your life, Marcus," she said gently. "But
he is not one of them. If you cannot find a way to do this,
then I will confront him. Because this disease, this source of
corruption, has to be ended. One way or another."

"No," he protested, reaching to squeeze her arm, to keep
her at his side. "You can't. You mustn't. The people here
need you – Spanner and the others. The staff – everyone he's
touched. They'll need your help to heal. If you face him…"

"If I face him, it will be done." Her voice was soft, but her
announcement was firm and determined. "I should thank you,
though. For thinking of the others." She leaned over and
placed a soft kiss on his cheek. "So many, in the past, have
sought to hold onto *me* – me, who was Isetnofret, and priestess
of Isis, subject to no man, and mistress of my own destiny. I
make my own choices – as much as I can, these days."

"I should bloody well hope so," he growled, warmed but
disconcerted by the kiss, which had managed to sweep every
last hint of fuzz from his brain. Much more effectively than a
jolt of double espresso would have done. "Funny," he said,
turning back to the view of the garden and the way that
colour was awakening in the world outside. "Thinking of
him living in this place – all these wonderful windows and he
keeps them shuttered up day and night. I bet he never stands
like this to watch the sun rise … *Shit!*"

That nagging persistence, that sense of having missed
something, reared up and hit him right between the eyes.

"Marcus?" Ashera was looking at him with concern. "Are
you all right?"

"I'm wonderful," he declared, sweeping her into his arms
and waltzing across the floor with her. "I'm a bloody genius!
Look!"

He'd found the paper he'd been looking for, tucked into the

pocket of the waistcoat he'd hung over the back of the office chair, at some point in the night. He'd picked it up just before the Kaffeeklatsch and stuffed it into his waistcoat pocket to read later – except he hadn't. He'd almost completely forgotten about it.

"I saw this yesterday," she said, mystified by his happy grin. "I don't see what..."

"It's been nagging at me *all* night. Why, *why* would it be a big deal if people were opening the shutters in their rooms? *This* room, maybe. It's got some of the antiques that all those precautions are supposed to be protecting, right?"

She nodded, clearly not seeing where he was going with this.

"Well, *this* is a special suite. For special guests, and probably wedding parties. It's all part of the mystique – the shtick he uses to lure in his prey. But I seriously doubt that Namon would be willing to risk putting any of his priceless possessions in the hands of the general hoi polloi. I bet the decorations *they* get are all fakes and reproductions. Which have no *need* to be protected from the sun. He told me, the first time I met him, that the shutters were there to preserve his interests and protect his investments. He was most insistent about how insistent he was about it."

She still looked puzzled. "But the place is full of antiques," she said. "I remember seeing some of these things – or things like them – when they were new. Sunlight can certainly damage paintings and furnishings. Museums spend vast amounts of money keeping it out. Why would that...?"

He waved the con newsletter at her. "Because there is only *one* antique that actually moves around the hotel, and might be found in one of these guest rooms. Namon himself."

Puzzlement turned into a wary frown. "I suppose," she began, and he interrupted with enthusiasm.

"No, no – it gets better. I don't know *why* I missed this. The shutters are there to protect his investment, right? So why are the most expensive pieces – the silverware, the porcelain, all his snuff boxes and the candlesticks – stuck out in display cases along the corridor that faces the glass roof over the pool? They get a full dose of sunlight every day!"

"Sunlight doesn't fade silver," she said, but her protest was a half-hearted one. There was a beat, and then she realised what she'd just said. "The silver," she breathed. "He'd never the let the silver go. His greed would never allow that, but – it wouldn't be something he'd gloat over. It might even hurt him to touch it. Much safer tucked away in cabinets …" She looked up, the light in her eyes a match to the dawning light outside the window. "He's avoiding the sun."

"He's not just avoiding it." Marcus almost laughed at the idea. "I think he's *terrified* of it. Yes," he went on as she half opened her mouth to protest again, "I know Namon clearly walks about in the daytime. So he's not some – *creature of the night,* or a grave bound revenant … Even if he were, that whole thing about Vampires going *poof* in the sunlight? I've always thought that that was something Hollywood made up for dramatic effect. But," he said, with growing confidence, "there are *some* references in the literature that must have influenced that particular myth. About sensitivity, about monsters that prefer the night, that lurk in the shadows and only venture out in the day in cloaks and heavy coats. I was wrong to dismiss vampires as mere myths. I dismissed the promise of sunlight in the same way. What if Hollywood is right? What if the Hollow Men are the ones particularly sensitive to sunlight? You said they were much rarer than the other kinds. You also said you've never faced one as old as Namon is. What if it gets worse as they get older? So – in the early days, he *might* go out in the day, but he'd prefer not to. Then, as his power grew, and his soul withered, it got harder and harder – until the sunlight – a traditional source of purification, yeah? Rejected him."

"Namon must hate the summer," he concluded with relish.

"Those late night walks in the cemetery may be the only fresh air and exercise he ever gets."

"You can't be sure of this, Marcus." Ashera was thinking through what he'd said. "You've no proof that the sun will hurt him."

Marcus shrugged. "If it doesn't work, we're just back to square one again – with egg on our faces perhaps, but only egg. Not police warrants. I don't think there's a law against exposing someone to the risk of sunburn."

"Deadly exposure," Mason interjected blearily. He blinked and stared at the two of them with early morning confusion. "Did I hear that right? You're planning to turn into Peter Cushing, and drive the villain into a shaft of sunlight? Good luck with *that* idea," he said, stretching out his cramped limbs. "This place is shut up tighter than Fort Knox – and anyone trying to open any of the shutters gets leapt on by the con police. I – uh – nearly got thrown out, yesterday morning," he explained, sheepishly. "I didn't know. I do now. There's nowhere in this damned hotel that you could get to open up any of the shutters without someone noticing. And I seriously doubt you could figure out how to drive him all the way through the lobby and out the main doors. Even if you *were* Peter Cushing. Or Jackson Hobbs, for that matter. No offense," he added, as if suddenly realising who he was talking to.

"None taken." Marcus was still buzzing, ideas and plans bouncing around inside his head. He glanced out of the window again, seeing the sun slowly inching its way above the horizon, the early rays of light catching the edges of the chapel roof and gilding its battered weather vane. "I think there's somewhere much closer than the lobby that we can use. And as for keeping him there?" He let a smile curl onto his face. "Wake the others," he suggested. "I think I have an idea…"

Chapter Thirteen

The Guest of Honour's speech was scheduled for two o'clock, right after lunch and just before the traditional award ceremony, when new and rising authors would be acknowledged, old and established ones recognised, and any number of publishers, agents, and hard-working fans would get a few moments of fame in front of their peers. The awards – a set of stylised and ornate candlesticks – were already set out on a small table in front of the tech station at the back of the ballroom. Marcus, having entered the room through the rearmost door, walked round that way and spent a moment examining the table's contents, picking up one award and examining it with distracted attention.

He already had two such ornaments, which stood in pride of place on the mantelpiece in his study, back home. The first had been a 'best novel' award, for *Dwellers in Destiny* and the first appearance of Faulkner Nettlestone. The second had been awarded three years later for *The Stones at Dawn*, and was probably the one he was most proud of: it had, after all, been the first fiction piece he'd felt confident enough to have published under his own name.

"All right?" Pete asked, strolling down the central aisle to join him. Marcus put down the award and turned to greet him with a smile.

"Well, I'm a little nervous," he admitted, "but this all looks good. How are you feeling?"

Pete shrugged. "I'm okay," he said. " I think. A little jumpy, but Ashera says that's a good sign. Still a lot of fight left in me. Apparently."

Marcus clapped a friendly hand to his shoulder and walked with him back towards the chapel door. "Are we all set?"

"Everything's ready." Pete grinned. "Just waiting for the guest of honour to arrive."

"He'll be here." Marcus was sure of it. He'd seen Namon lurking around earlier in the day – long enough to earn himself an amused and arrogant glance before being dismissed and ignored. The vampire had plenty of reason to feel confident – and was currently being feted by the fans, since the rumour mill had been working overtime all morning. There'd been sufficient witnesses to the previous night's incident to turn speculation into confident assumption – and since Namon could hardly deny the role that Spanner had arranged for him to fill, he'd been making the most of his sudden notoriety.

Marcus had been busy in other ways. He'd managed to grab a shower while Ashera took it on herself to escort his guests back to their rooms so they could get cleaned up and change. Then he'd rung room service and ordered breakfast for seven; they'd held their council of war over crisp bacon, hash browns and hotel fried eggs, after which they'd scattered to carry out their assigned tasks. The only ones who hadn't ended up with a specific job for the morning were Ashera and Shelley, and that was mostly because Shelley was still very shaky after the night before. Ashera had taken her down to the Dealers' Room, sitting her behind her stall where she'd be well protected by the merchandise. Marcus – having remembered to attend his second signing session – had been relieved to see Shelley busy serving customers with something more like her usual smile on her face. Ashera had offered him a soft nod of assurance when he'd left, and he'd returned to his own tasks with renewed determination.

The thought – the *possibility* of Namon remaining at Westeringford like the hungry spider he was – had been fuelling his sense of righteous anger ever since the revelation about the vampire's potential weakness had come to him that morning. *No-one* should be subjected to the kind of soul-shaking violation that Shelley had endured – the same violation which had driven Deyath's sister to take her own life, and which had tainted and twisted the lives of so many others over the years. His mind had, inevitably, substituted Shelley's gentle smile for Molly's equally innocent one, and the idea that his sweet, confident and creative child might one day face *anything* like Namon's arrogant hunger was firing his blood and helping keep both nerves and doubt away.

Spanner wandered in, looking a little lost and bemused. Marcus intercepted him before he reached the chapel, steering him back towards the left hand dais, where the lectern had been replaced after the DJ had packed his equipment away. "You okay?" he asked solicitously, knowing that the answer was probably no, but that the man might not be able to articulate it, given how subtly Namon seemed to be exercising his control.

Spanner sighed. "I'll be glad when this is over," he said, wearily. Marcus suppressed the almost automatic *me too*, and gave him an encouraging smile instead.

"You're doing fine," he said. "People seem to be enjoying themselves. It's been a good Con."

It wasn't exactly a lie. For most of the attendees it seemed to have been just that – your average, kick back, have fun, meet people, indulge your passions, kind of event. It probably didn't rank as highly as some of the events he'd taken part in, but then most of those hadn't had a predatory vampire stalking the halls siphoning off the excess energies and putting a general damper on everything. Most of the people who been wandering around feeling vaguely hung-over that morning would have put it down to actually being hung-over, blaming the Real Ale and the late night, rather than considering the possibility of more sinister causes.

"I dunno." Spanner sighed a second time, leaning against the lectern and trying to drum up some enthusiasm. Marcus wasn't surprised when he failed to do so: it was almost certain that Namon had taken most of it. "It all feels a bit 'off' to me. Too much effort for too little reward. Besides," he added dispiritedly, "you're not seeing the stuff going on behind the scenes: Abigail's practically gone on strike, Johnathan says half the equipment's playing up, and I've had to send Andrew on a treasure hunt, because *somebody's* mislaid the crucifix collection box. We promised to return the stuff. They're going to lynch us if we don't."

"It'll turn up." Marcus had to stop himself from glancing towards Pete, who had taken up position at the chapel door. "Cheer up, Spanner. Everything's going to be fine. There's just me and the awards to go. And I promise you – they're going to be talking about my session for months to come. Years even." *One way or the other,* his inner author muttered sardonically.

"Yeah." Spanner roused himself with an effort, straightening up. "I know you'll do us proud, Marcus. You always do."

At the back of the ballroom, Barry was doing his assigned job as usual, opening the doors and letting the gathered fans stream in to find themselves a seat. Spanner's face creased in a moment of resigned dismay and Marcus half turned, wondering what had triggered that reaction. The answer was, of course, Namon, who was practically leading the charge, strolling into the room with confidence, as if he owned the place.

Which he did, of course.

"Well, he's enjoying himself," Spanner muttered, then leaned in closer and half whispered: "Try not to upset him again, Marcus. We still have to settle the bill."

"Spanner," Marcus announced with a confidence he didn't entirely feel, "I promise you – once this is over, Mr Namon's account will be paid in full."

— * —

"Gentlefemmes and Gentlemen," Spanner announced, his voice echoing loudly through the room. There was a brief screech of amplified feedback, a hasty dive by one of the techs, and Spanner grimaced in general apology. "Sorry folks," he muttered. "Let's try that again.

"Gentlefemmes and Gentlemen, welcome to the Sunday afternoon session here in the main hall – and, hopefully, the event you've all been waiting for. I've known Marcus for a number of years now, and I'm very pleased and proud to have welcomed him here to be our guest of honour this weekend. As 'Ned Landers' he has made a major contribution to both the world of seedy occult detectives and the chronicles of brave and bold gentleman adventurers. Donning a slightly more academic hat, he has introduced us to the dangerous and shadowy lands of Faerie, and kept us informed and educated with his non-fictional explorations of medieval literature and European folklore. It gives me very great pleasure to introduce the creator of Jackson Hobbs, Faulkner Nettlestone, Brineld the Just, Queen Mab the Mellifluous, and innumerable other characters that have entertained us over the years."

The Clock struck two – sharp and sweet notes that rang like a starting bell.

"Dr Marcus Holland!"

Marcus stepped into the spotlight – Tech had arranged a lighting rig to create one right at the end of the aisle, in between the two raised daises – and doffed his hat in an exaggerated bow. The crowd applauded – one or two cheered, and he even got a few whistles from the back of the room.

"Thank you, Spanner," he said warmly, nodding towards the con-chair, who nodded back and headed for a seat at the far end of the front row. Namon was sitting on the aisle seat, right where Marcus wanted him. Somewhere in the crowd, he spotted Cordell, wearing the Baron's hat as he'd asked, along with Mazzy on one side and Lilith on the other. There were other familiar faces dotted round the room, and he made himself relax, falling into the easy, assured manner that years of lecturing and public appearances had helped him to develop. "Good afternoon, everyone."

The tech-crew had equipped him with a roaming microphone, pinned to his shirt lapel and with the battery pack tucked in at the small of his back. That allowed him to pace and declaim, performing, rather than merely lecturing, although it also meant having to speak without notes. Once upon a time, that would have been nerve-wracking – but the only nerves he had to fight that afternoon had nothing to do with his speech, and everything to do with the monster in his audience.

He started with chatty, non-consequential things, aiming to relax the crowd and lull any suspicions that Namon might have had. He had nearly an hour to fill, and he might as well give the rest of the con-attendees the entertainment they were expecting to get. The vampire certainly seemed relaxed: he watched the performance with amused eyes, his top-hat carefully balanced on his lap, and his cane tucked in beside him with the practiced nonchalance that only a man who'd been pretending to be a gentleman for centuries could manage. Marcus made a point of *not* addressing him directly. Not even glancing too obviously in his direction. Not yet, at least.

" … so, while there are still hopes of seeing Jackson make an appearance on the small screen, it won't be with an American accent, wearing a trilby hat, or living in an RV. There are some things," he added with mock growl, "on which I completely refuse to compromise."

The audience greeted that with generous applause. Marcus had been annoyed about the rumours of TV options and potential screen adaptations that had been targeting his work just recently. Most of them were just that – unsubstantiated rumours, set running by media executives with bright ideas and a total lack of morals. The worst one had been started by someone who had clearly never read any of his books, let alone approached their author to discuss rights and other relevant matters. Francis had had to take legal action to shut down the man's website – although it was possible the appalling trailer he'd made was still lurking somewhere on YouTube.

"All of that aside… " He threw a quick glance at the Clock to check his timing. "… what you really want to hear about is what I'm doing next. Right?"

Cheers of agreement. He grinned, walking across to the right hand dais, taking off Jackson's hat as he did so. He placed it – very carefully, on the small side table on the end of the dais – the one that currently supported his glass of water and a half filled jug of the same.

"Well," he considered, taking a moment to gather his nerves and centre himself. "What I'm going to do, is tell you a story."

The door opened at the back of the hall, admitting two shadowed figures. One of them was Shelley, dressed in her blue velvet gown, and the other was Ashera, taking up position just as she'd promised. Any closer, and she'd alert Namon to her presence, but she was there, willing to make a generous sacrifice if his idea – his plan – failed in any way.

He took a deep breath and made himself a quiet promise. Even if it *did* fail, he'd deal with the vampire himself and take whatever followed. The world could not afford to lose the Shenuheh – not if there were others, like Namon, unliving in it.

"The story concerns this house – Westeringford Grange – and the old and cunning vampire that has dwelt in it for centuries." The crowd stirred with interest. Namon straightened in his chair, his face creasing with sudden suspicion.

"I won't say *lived* here," Marcus continued breezily, "although, of course, he did once, spending his early years being brought up by his profligate but stern father, and then later, as an older man, building up a vast fortune and investing it in precious objects, in rare art, and other things of value." He started walking up the side of the ballroom, along the line of the heavily curtained windows, and waving at the general architecture to illustrate his thinking. "The house had been built by his father, remodelled and expanded as the whim took him. Matthew Wellmore didn't really care for money. Only for what it would buy him – friends and fun, and probably wine, women and song as well. John Wellmore, his son, was cut from more puritan cloth. He was an investor, and made his own fortune in insurance. After his father died, he inherited the house and took steps to preserve that inheritance for years to come. In fact," he'd reached the back row and turned down the length of it, nodding his acknowledgment to Ashera, who nodded back with a calm serenity that he wished he felt. Heads were swivelling to track his progress. The microphone made sure that everyone in the room could still hear his words.

"He cherished his money, his *things* so much, that he started to fear what would happen if anything happened to *him*. He grew afraid of dying, of having to give up everything he'd worked so hard to save."

He'd arrived in front of the award table, and he turned to rest himself against it, staring down the aisle at Namon, who was staring back with wary, narrowed eyes.

"By then, of course, he was so eaten up by miserly greed that he'd abandoned most of his humanity. It was easy to slip into true corruption, to find ways of taking life from others in order to preserve his own.

"He's been here ever since, surviving on the 'tribute' he takes from his guests. Lurking in the shadows like a hungry spider, luring in his victims and throwing away their husks once he is done. Ladies and Gentlemen," he savoured, crossing his fingers behind his back and hoping that the vampire would fall into the trap. "May I present – John Isiah Wellmore – better known to you as Isiah Namon – the owner of this hotel!"

He lifted his hand in invitation. After a wary moment, Namon rose to his feet, and gave him a deep and ironic bow. Several people in the audience gasped. Most of them applauded and cheered. The response clearly amused – and reassured – the subject of his revelation. Namon smiled, and bowed again, this time to the general audience. Their applause redoubled, and the cheers took a moment to subside.

"Mr Namon has been playing this role to great effect this weekend, don't you think? Free to wander among you once you gave up your symbols and your amulets. Did you wake with a headache this morning? Snap at your partner? Think that – perhaps – the breakfast lacked taste, or the coffee its kick? The vampire has been stealing from you all – taking a little hope from one person, a little joy from another. Drinking – deeper – when he thought he could get away with it."

They were hanging on his every word, fascinated by his narrative and watching Namon's knowing smirk, his enjoyment at accusations that – oh *yes* – were just part of the game.

"Well," Marcus announced, turning to reach into the array of candlesticks and lift out the two that were lurking at the back. "*I* think enough is enough. That it's time this vampire's reign of terror is ended. Don't you?"

They were heavy, ornate pieces, much older than the modern, reproductions the convention had picked for its awards. They'd probably stood for years in their display case, slowly gathering dust and tarnishing with time. The fluted columns that rose from their sturdy bases now gleamed softly in the artificial light, polished to a bright perfection after Mason had carefully liberated them from their usual resting place. Namon – being, by nature, a miser – hadn't bothered to install any kind of electronic security for his silverware, content to rely on old-fashioned locks and the general security within the hotel.

Neither of which had protected them – or him – in the long run.

Marcus turned back and began a slow pace down the centre aisle, a candlestick dangling casually from each hand. Namon watched him advance, his lips curved in a cruel smile of amusement. *Do your worst*, his expression suggested challengingly. Marcus kept his own expression as neutral as he could. He was, he hoped, going to do just that...

"I'm afraid I'm a poor substitute for Peter Cushing," he apologised to his audience. "He'd manage this much more dramatically than I will, but... nevertheless..."

He swung the candlesticks up, bringing them together to form a solid cross in front of him. Namon's smirk froze. He glanced rapidly from side to side, discovering himself surrounded by an eager crowd of attentive onlookers, before taking a decidedly disconcerted step backwards – and then another as Marcus advanced another step.

"The cross has been a symbol of protection for millennia," Marcus considered, slowly forcing Namon backwards, towards the chapel door. "The Egyptians used the ankh and the *tau* cross – it was a symbol for Tammuz, one of the resurrected gods, and it has appeared as a sacred symbol nearly all over the world in one form or another. It represents the fusion of the human and the divine – the power of the soul within the earthly mantle of the body. And vampires – " he took another step. Namon was glowering at him now, caught in the deception of his own making. "– lacking any soul, except those that they steal and corrupt, fear it, fear its rejection, and their own inability to face a symbol so deeply imbued with the power of faith."

The vampire lurched back another step, his eyes darting wildly in search of some other avenue of escape. The audience were on the edges of their seats, admiring the performance, the way that Namon visibly flinched as the makeshift cross came close. Some of that might be the silver, of course, but Marcus had seen his earlier reaction to religious iconography, and he'd been sure that this would work. Ashera's lecture on the power of symbols had struck a deep chord, and he clung to it with confidence, focused in the moment, rather than on the questions it would raise later. Was it *his* faith that drove the creature backwards, or was it Namon's own, the vampire rejecting the symbol he'd almost certainly been taught to see as the sign of the resurrection, of the life that lay *beyond* death?

Was he driven by the sheer determination in Marcus's eyes, or was it by the engagement of the crowd, caught up in the unfolding moment, brought – by the story-teller's art – to a state of unquestioning conviction? How many of them believed, right there and then, that a pair of silver candlesticks, formed into the ancient symbol of the cross and wielded by a determined heart, would hold the power to defy and dismay a creature of utter corruption?

They all knew the simple laws of literature and Hollywood. *Vampires are repelled by the sign of the cross.*

Against that delighted expectation, Namon's desiccated heart would have little defence; he had spent years stealing the life of others in sips, warming his cold world with the stolen embers of the fire he had lost so long ago. The fire he was facing must have felt like a raging furnace, too strong to use, and far too bright to bear.

Whatever the reason, it was working. Step by step, Marcus drove his adversary backwards, giving him no opportunity to break to the side, or to turn in search of escape.

"Don't be foolish," Namon pleaded, clearly torn between the need to play along and the more pressing need to avoid the pain the cross was causing him. "You've made your point. Let's end the game. You cannot – *truly* hurt me."

"Watch me try," Marcus growled. He nodded to Pete, who reached to push open the chapel door then stepped back, watching as Namon stumbled past him and into the space beyond. The vampire crossed the threshold with a snarl, resenting every backward step. Marcus followed at the same pace, pressing his advantage, and taking his audience with him with his words.

"Step by step," he extemporised, as caught up in the moment as Namon was, "the monster is driven back, forced to enter the place he fears the most – the consecrated chapel, and the light within that he cannot bear!"

A forward thrust of the makeshift cross made Namon retreat with greater haste. He was so focused on his tormentor that he didn't see what awaited him; so fixed and furious that he entered the trap of his own, reluctant, will.

Cyn and Deyath had worked miracles. The central tables had been pushed together and back to form a makeshift altar, on which now stood Mazzy's masterpiece: the god upon the world tree looked down with knowing eyes, his blood dripping onto the soil beneath him and his arms held out in willing sacrifice. Around him, the faith of the world was on display. They'd used the contents of the appropriated box to decorate every single surface they could find. There were angled crosses hanging from hooks and nails. Glittering pentagrams and ankhs and stars of David were scattered across the smaller tables which had also been pushed to the sides. Some of Ashera's paper banners hung beneath them, breathing praise to ancient gods, while a few of Lilith's ornate pieces, sacred and profane, crowned the display.

Namon staggered to a halt in the middle of all of it and fell to his knees, wide eyed and shivering.

"How *dare* you!" he snarled, a low-pitched howl of pain.

"How dare we?" Marcus echoed back, pinning him in place

with the makeshift cross and giving his team a hasty nod of acknowledgment. "How dare *you!* How dare you defy the natural cycle of life? You defile everything you touch. You averred the joys of living long ago. You are nothing but an empty shell, subsisting on the life of others, stolen moments, someone else's allotted years, taken without their consent. But you don't benefit from that theft. You don't really feel the warmth you take, or the delight you seek. You devour all joy, all delight, and all meaning from them, leaving nothing but darkness and despair. You didn't find a way to live forever. You died inside long before your allotted time had passed."

"And now your time has finally come."

"I don't think so." Namon had rallied a little, possibly realising that – while the situation was painful for him, it didn't seem to be doing any permanent harm. "You may hold me here, but I am in my own home, and here *I* hold the power. You will tire, and so will they – " his nod was directed towards the inhabitants of the ballroom, perched on the edges of their seats. "And then I will be free to take whatever I like. This was a good try." His chuckle was forced, but he was genuinely amused. "But it will fail. You cannot hurt me, Dr Holland. I am not one of your literary creations, vulnerable to stake or spells. You do not have the power."

"No." Marcus favoured him with a feral grin, knowing he had one more trick up his sleeve. "*I* don't. But you know what? I don't think you keep the curtains closed just because the sunlight might fade your precious *things*. And I don't think you prefer stalking around in the dark simply because the night suits your character better. I think I know your weakness. Shall we test my theory?"

He gave a second nod, this time in Cyn's direction. She nodded back and started to tug at the nearest curtain cords. On the other side of the chapel Deyath started to do the same.

Namon laughed.

"Oh, very clever," he hissed, starting to lift himself back to his feet. "But foolish. The curtains are merely cosmetic. Every window in this house is shuttered from the outside."

Marcus took a step back, bouncing a little from all the energy that was thrumming through his veins. He was going to enjoy this.

"They were," he agreed. "But you gave me the corner suite. Right up there." He waved a candlestick in the relevant direction, then hastily slammed it back where it came from as Namon started to lurch towards him. "This morning? I climbed out of my window and took a little stroll on the roof."

The curtains swung open with a jerk. Sunlight streamed in from either side, bright, piercing shafts of it that haloed Marcus like a frescoed saint. With the first set of side windows revealed, Cyn and Deyath raced to the next set of cords, pulling at them with frenzied strength. At the back of the chapel, Mason wrestled to pull aside the largest curtain, the one that hung over the stained glass panes behind the altar space. More light streamed in as the girls uncovered the remaining side windows, this time bathing the makeshift altar and its tribute to the resurrected god in glorious fire.

Namon screamed.

He had jerked back from the first shafts of light in horror. The new assault sent him reeling sideways, only to be driven back to the centre space by the symbolic display on the walls, which was glittering and gleaming as the rays of the sun overwhelmed the softer electric illumination.

His skin, Marcus noted with surprising disconcertion, had begun to smoke.

It was a faint effect to start with, a soft wisp of vapour that drifted upwards, to dance, like dust motes, in the now brilliant air.

"No," the vampire muttered, shaking his head and lifting

his hands to stare at them. Smoke curled from his fingertips, adding to the haze. "I won't. I *can't...* "

He spun round to confront Marcus again, his face distorted with horror and pain. He seemed to be crumbling in on himself, the light stripping him of substance, his flesh shrinking against his bones. "You," he hissed, taking a step forward despite the hasty forward thrust of the candlesticks. "You don't *understand.* You can't do this to *me...*"

He reached out, his hands and arms extending to seize his foe and – perhaps – to take what he needed to survive. Marcus' heart leapt into his throat and he stepped back, holding the cross in front of him, trying to avoid that suddenly skeletal lunge.

At the back of the room, Mason finally won his battle. The curtain swung back. Light, filled with colour and glory, pierced the painted glass for the first time in decades. It flooded across the room, sweeping every last moment of shadow from it. Namon's forward lunge became a lurch, his knees crumbling beneath him and his head falling back as the weight of his skull dragged it from his rapidly decaying body. What hit the floor was a bundle of cloth and bone, and even the bones were crumbling, dissolving into centuries of dust.

Marcus gaped at the sight, open mouthed – then started to cough, wrestling for breath as the last remnants of the vampire drifted round him and then fell, quietly, onto the ancient tiles.

Nobody moved for a moment. All of them simply stood and stared at the way Namon had vanished, consumed by time much faster, and much more thoroughly than any of them had expected.

"Thus," Marcus managed, clearing his throat and suddenly remembering he had an audience, "thus ends the vampire. Dust to dust, and ashes to ashes, just as all men come to end in time."

In front of the altar, Cyn and Deyath collided in an

impulsive clinch of joy and relief – one that turned into a decidedly passionate smooch. Marcus blinked. He hadn't seen *that* coming, either.

Mason walked round them, rolling his eyes at his sister as only a brother could. He clapped Pete on the shoulder with apologetic sympathy and nodded to Marcus as if to say: *Go. We've got this.*

Marcus nodded back, reached to brush a little of the dust from his hair, and turned to stroll out of the chapel as casually as he could manage. His hands were actually shaking and his limbs felt filled with water, but he had a presentation to finish and a reputation to retain. He walked across to carefully place the candlesticks down on the side table, and reached to retrieve his hat. He paused there, catching sight of himself in yet another mirror, this one hanging on the ballroom wall. Taking in his slightly dishevelled appearance – his hair a little mussed and his waistcoat spattered with vampire dust – he allowed a slow and relieved smile to curl onto his face. Then he lifted the hat, took a studied moment to adjust its angle on his head to *just* the right amount of tilt, and then turned back to his audience with a grin.

"Any questions?" he asked.

They rose, almost as one, cheering and applauding with enthusiasm. At the back of the ballroom, Ashera dipped her head in quiet acknowledgment of his victory and he – in turn – offered her a deep, and extremely ironic bow.

Somewhere behind him, the Clock struck three.

Chapter Fourteen

"You could have said something, man," Cordell was saying, eyeing Marcus up and down with amused approval.

"Mm?" Marcus wasn't really listening. He was watching the swirl of fans and volunteers as they milled in the hotel lobby, checking out of rooms, collecting luggage, and wildly praising *best con **ever**,* to anyone and everyone in hearing distance. "About what?"

"About him being a *real* vampire."

He looked up – an inevitability when Cordell was standing right next to him. His friend was smiling at him with a wry and knowing look in his eyes.

"He wasn't – " Marcus began, about to spout the official line about actors and special effects and pre-planning that Spanner had hastily come up with. As the majority of the actual 'effects' had happened out of general view, most people were buying it. A large percentage of them were trying to figure out how it was done, offering wilder and wilder suggestions that would serve to mask the truth for years to come. The amusement in Cordell's eye made him swallow his words with a gulp.

"I didn't think you'd believe me," he said instead, making it an apology as well as an excuse.

"Yeah," Cordell grinned. "Don't suppose you did. But I could have helped. I didn't just learn *stories* at grandma Eva's knee. She taught me a lot more than that."

Marcus heaved a sigh, considering his company with weary affection. "*Next* time," he promised, trying very hard not to re-visit the events of the weekend, the mistakes he had probably made, and the people he might have protected better if he'd had a little more help.

"I'll hold you to that," Cordell laughed, clapping him on the back. "And hey – you were trying to protect my girls. I 'preciate it. You give my regards to your lady friend, okay? She's something special, you know?"

"I know."

Ashera had decided to stay on at the hotel for a while, helping the staff to deal with the absence of their employer, as well as the longer term effects of his 'employment'. No-one at the hotel had expressed anything other than a quiet sense of relief at the vampire's sudden and unexpected absence, although it was likely that there were some of the longer term employees among them so tainted and twisted by his domination that even the Shenuheh might have difficulty bringing them back to reasonable human expectations. The fallout from his years of influence was going to take a long time to unravel, and the impact he may have had on his guests and his business contacts would take even longer to fade. With no evidence to the contrary, it was likely that Namon would go down on record as a missing person, someone who had – for some unknown reason – decided to abandon their life and leave everything behind them. Ashera would do her best to identify and repair as much of the damage as she could. Someone else would have to sort out the other ramifications of his absence: the fate of his physical legacies – the hotel, his treasures, his investments and the other properties he may have acquired – was likely to hang in limbo for a long time.

Marcus was rather hoping that someone would step up to keep the hotel and at least some of its contents secured until those issues could be resolved. It would be a shame for the Grange to fall to rack and ruin after all this time – even if that was exactly what had happened to its owner.

"We'll – be keeping in touch," he said. He wasn't entirely sure how often, or even when that might be as yet, but she'd assured him she would be there if he ever needed her help again. A part of him hoped that he never would *need* her, the way he had that weekend, but he also hoped that she thought of him as a friend, and would not reject the overtures of simple contact and connection that he might pursue with any new friend that he'd made.

Like Cyn and Deyath, who'd effusively promised to stay in contact, or Mason and Shelley, who had already invited him to their wedding.

It wasn't, they'd assured him, going to be held at Westeringford Grange…

"I should hope so," Cordell grinned, probably misreading the thoughtful expression that had settled on his face. "You stay in touch with us, too, okay? I want you at the naming – how do you feel about becoming a godfather?"

Marcus shrugged off his introspection and returned the grin. "Only if I can make you an offer you can't refuse," he said. "But no leaving horses' heads on pillows. I promise."

Cordell laughed, stepping in to give him a friendly hug. "You take care, Marcus," he ordered. "Stay safe, stay alert, and stay out of the shadows, okay?"

"I'll try," Marcus promised warmly. "You too, Cordell. See you soon?"

"Real soon."

Mazzy and Lilith arrived to collect him, adding their own hugs of farewell: Marcus promised to get back about the *Wolfkin* cover as soon as he was able to speak to the publisher, and thanked Mazzy – again – for her generous gifts. Not just the painting of the Wolfraiders, which now lay carefully packed and padded at the bottom of his suitcase, but for Odin on the World Tree, which was currently nestled against it, secured in the same packing. She'd never questioned why he might want to borrow her masterpiece for his speech, but had been happy to hand it over into his care. He'd expected her to reclaim it later. He certainly hadn't expected to have her hand it to him a second time, packed snug and secure beside the painting he had been intending to take home with him.

I can always paint another, she'd said, waving off all and every attempt to either protest or pay. *Molly will love it. Make sure she hangs it in her room.*

That had given him pause – and reason to smile, and say heartfelt thank yous – although he doubted that Beverley would 'love' it, or allow its pagan honesty any wall space in her modern and designer influenced house.   It would, however, hang in pride of place in his own tiny hall, opposite the front door of his flat, providing additional protection for all of his family, whenever they came to stay.

He waved the three of them off, watching as they passed through the hotel's ornate doors. He wondered – a little idly – what Christopher Lee had made of the Grange's owner, back in the day, then shook the fancy out of his head with a wry smile. Namon, he suspected, would have stayed far away from the aristocratic actor – along with the glaring arc lights the studio would have employed to illuminate their filming.

"Leaving us, Marcus?" Spanner was looking a little more like his old self – although it would probably take some time for him to recover from the whole experience – convention *and* vampire, in a handy two-for-one deal.

"Yeah – well, in a moment or two.   Thought I'd rather waste time waiting here, than standing in Moor Street station for an hour. Cordell and the girls have just left – he's, um, picking up an earlier connection at New Street. Will you be staying tonight?"

"Yes, I – uh … yes."   Spanner shivered a little, then shrugged it off with a slightly forced laugh. "Only one more night."

"You'll be fine."   Marcus wished he could be confident about that; Namon had been influencing the man for months, coercing him with subtle machinations that would be hard to shake off, and manipulating him into doing things that were going to haunt him for a long time. He wasn't responsible for what the vampire had done to others, but there was no escaping the fact that – through his inability to fight free of his control – he had worked to enable those deeds. "Ashera's staying on for a bit – buy her a drink in the bar tonight and tell her your woes. She's a really good listener."

"Maybe I will." Daniel O'Toole, Convention Chairman for Coffincon Seven, scrubbed the palm of his hand against his trouser leg and then held it out with expectation. "Thank you, Marcus," he said, with sincerity. "Thank you for coming to the Con. Thank you for being our Guest of Honour. And thank you for... doing what you did. Because you didn't have to."

"Yes, I did." Marcus took the proffered hand, clasping it with firm assurance. The curve of his lips held sympathy, along with a quietly wry twist. "What kind of a writer would I be if I didn't take care of my fans?"

Spanner grinned, returning the grip with gratitude. "A bloody good one," he shot back. "But it's – good to know you're a good man, too. I mean it, Marcus. *Thank* you."

"You're welcome," Marcus said, and smiled.

– * –

He walked down the hotel drive with a much jauntier step than he'd walked up it only two days before. It seemed like a lifetime. His whole worldview had been tipped over, stood on its head, and then shaken firmly just to make sure he'd got the point. He'd spent years professionally denying – debunking – the myths and magic that he'd chosen to write about as a hobby. But if vampires actually existed – rarely, but still reality – and determined souls like Ashera could *choose* to return from death in order to oppose them... then the lore he'd dismissed as fantasy, the myths he'd unfailingly interpreted as mundane, might be far truer records of history than he'd given them credit for. Had his subconscious mind caught those echoes of truth and understood those layers of meaning, bringing them back to light and life through his fictional words?

Or was it just that the world was far more magical and mysterious than he'd allowed himself to believe?

He didn't know. He wasn't entirely sure that he wanted to. One lone vampire, Hollow and hungry, had been more than enough to terrify him. He wasn't about to start looking for other creatures of the night – werewolves, ghosts, ghouls or goblins...

No, he *still* wasn't sure about the goblins. But he didn't think he'd want to meet one if they *did* exist.

He caught the train from Westeringford and waved farewell to the Grange, heading back into Birmingham and a return to the mundane world where he lived and worked, and where vampires were merely myths and metaphors. Unless, of course, you failed to catch a reflection in a silvered mirror as one of the Hollow Men walked by. Or glimpsed in it the coruscating shimmer of a Shenuheh as they moved among mankind, sharing the joys of life.

There were tales he wanted to tell, ideas he needed to share in ways that could – like the myths and the lore he'd studied – warn of the dangers that lurked in the shadows and shine a little light on how they might be avoided – or be defeated, should the need arise. There were horrors like Namon's tale – a history of how greed and unchecked avarice could lead to inner corruptions and the decay of the soul – but also stories of inspiration, redemption, and the triumph of good over evil.

He had met, and fought, and defeated, a creature of true evil and corruption. He'd done so, risking his life and his soul, so that others would be spared that horror, so that the plague it spread could be ended. Or at least curtailed, for a while.

It had given him a totally new perspective on things.

The summer sun was low on the horizon as he left the train

and made his way back to Moor Street to pick up his connection. He savoured the warmth of it as he walked, appreciating why the ancient Egyptians had chosen to worship it as a god – and the power it had to lift the spirit and inspire the soul. It would be late by the time he reached home, hopefully to be greeted by an indignant Malfeasance, and the joys of dealing with all the emails that had accumulated over the weekend. He had plans to make: making sure that *home* was ready for Molly, and all the adventures he wanted to share with her; organising his workload so he could take on those extra students in the new term; and jotting down all the notes and ideas that were dancing in his head, the thoughts and possibilities that were making his inner author rub their hands with glee.

He climbed into the train as it arrived, carefully settled his luggage on the racks, sank into his reserved seat, and reached for his phone.

"Francis?" he said as the familiar voice answered with a hint of puzzlement. "I know it's late, but – I've been thinking about what you said. About the three book deal? Do you think they'd go for Jackson Hobbs dealing with a haunted stately home, Faulkner taking a break from Carpathia and visiting Egypt, and – something about the seven deadly sins? That they're called deadly for a reason?"

"Seven deadly what?" Francis was having trouble keeping up. "Well, it sounds good, but – couldn't this have waited until tomorrow? I've got guests, and we're halfway through dinner…"

"It's all right for some," Marcus laughed. Francis was always calling *him* at inconvenient times. It was nice to be turning the tables for once. "You may have taken a couple of days off, but *I've* been working all weekend!"

< < < < > > >

Acknowledgements

This book could not have been written without the memories of attending innumerable fan run conventions and the many friends I have met and made there over the years. Thanks are particularly directed to the dedicated volunteers who make these kind of events happen – to people like Dot Owens, who was like a second mother in the days of early Star Trek fandom, to Anne Page and Barbie Bowerman, who managed to wield microphones and conduct events with both style and panache, and to every convention chairperson and their committees since.

Thanks are also due to the people who helped make those experiences so good I kept going back. To Helen, who 'invited' me and my mother to take part in the first galactic fashion show, and who has been a good friend ever since. To Marilyn, who joined me at conventions on the other side of the pond. To Miri, and Marion, to Hilary, to Rog, to Cathy, Barbara, Chris, Jack, Carole, Derek, Caroline, Farah, and Sue, and… well, far too many others to embarrass by being listed here.

I should also acknowledge the many writers that conventions introduced me to, and who have inspired and encouraged me to follow in their footsteps ever since. Writers like Anne McCaffery, Ted Tubb, Ken Bulmer, Terry Pratchett, Neil Gaiman, Peter Moorwood, Diane Duane … The list is as long as the index to our library, and I keep adding to it – both the list, and the library, of course.

Speaking of books, I should mention Peter and the folk at Elsewhen Press, who asked to read my stuff, and discovered they liked it. Thanks to them for giving me this opportunity to share my work.

The idea for this particular book had been lurking in my head for some time, but probably wouldn't have been written without encouragement from my good friend Judith, who persuaded me to join her in taking the Nanowrimo challenge that year. So a lot of this is due to her. And thanks too, go to Lynn, who suffered the two of us discussing plots and characters over the lunch and the dinner table for the entire month. Still does, I have to say. Her patience is much to be admired. Both of them belong in that long list of fans up there, but have become family in recent years, and I'm very appreciative of that.

Thanks need to go to my mother, who took me to that first convention, and who dealt with my fannish tendencies by teaching me ancient Greek at an early age, and drawing me dragons whenever I asked her too. She was an inspiring woman, an artist, a writer and a wonderful needlewoman. She gave me much to live up to, and I think she'd be pleased to finally see my name in print.

Lastly, and most certainly not least, I should thank my dearly beloved husband, Robin, who was taken from me far too soon. We met at a convention, of course. He was a hugely influential part of my life and still is, despite no longer being with me. He was my best friend for many years and is probably the reason why I still have so many cats. We shared many interests, and he always encouraged me to follow my dreams. We never met an actual vampire at any of the conventions we attended, though.

At least, I don't think we did …

Elsewhen Press

delivering outstanding new talents in speculative fiction

Visit the Elsewhen Press website at elsewhen.press for the latest
information on all of our titles, authors and events; to read our blog; find
out where to buy our books and ebooks; or to place an order.

Sign up for the Elsewhen Press InFlight Newsletter at
elsewhen.press/newsletter

Urban fantasy by Tej Turner

The Janus Cycle

The Janus Cycle can best be described as gritty, surreal, urban fantasy. The over-arching story revolves around a nightclub called Janus, which is not merely a location but virtually a character in its own right. On the surface it appears to be a subcultural hub where the strange and disillusioned who feel alienated and oppressed by society escape to be free from convention; but underneath that façade is a surreal space in time where the very foundations of reality are twisted and distorted. But the special unique vibe of Janus is hijacked by a bandwagon of people who choose to conform to alternative lifestyles simply because it has become fashionable to be 'different', and this causes many of its original occupants to feel lost and disenchanted. We see the story of Janus unfold through the eyes of eight narrators, each with their own perspective and their own personal journey. A story in which the nightclub itself goes on a journey. But throughout, one character, a strange girl, briefly appears and reappears warning the narrators that their individual journeys are going to collide in a cataclysmic event. Is she just another one of the nightclub's denizens, a cynical mischief-maker out to create havoc or a time-traveller trying to prevent an impending disaster?

ISBN: 9781908168566 (epub, kindle) / ISBN: 9781908168467 (224pp paperback)
Visit bit.ly/JanusCycle

Dinnusos Rises

The vibe has soured somewhat after a violent clash in the Janus nightclub a few months ago, and since then Neal has opened a new establishment called 'Dinnusos'. Located on a derelict and forgotten side of town, it is not the sort of place you stumble upon by accident, but over time it enchants people, and soon becomes a nucleus for urban bohemians and a refuge for the city's lost souls. Rumour has it that it was once a grand hotel, many years ago, but no one is quite sure. Whilst mingling in the bar downstairs you might find yourself in the company of poets, dreamers, outsiders, and all manner of misfits and rebels. And if you're daring enough to explore its ghostly halls, there's a whole labyrinth of rooms on the upper floors to get lost in…

Now it seems that not just Neal's clientele, but the entire population of the city, begin to go crazy when beings, once thought mythological, enter the mortal realm to stir chaos as they sow the seeds of militancy.

Eight characters. Most of them friends, some of them strangers. Each with their own story to tell. All of them destined to cross paths in a surreal sequence of events which will change them forever.

ISBN: 9781911409137 (epub, kindle) / ISBN: 9781911409038 (280pp paperback)
visit bit.ly/DinnusosRises

CAN'T DREAM WITHOUT YOU
FROM THE DARK CHRONICLES

TANYA REIMER

Legends say that tens of thousands of years ago, Whisperers were banished from the heavens, torn in half, and dumped on a mortal realm they didn't understand. Longing for their other half, they went from being powerful immortals to lonely leeches relying on humans to survive. Over the years, they earnt magic from demons, they left themselves Notebooks with hints, and by pairing up with human souls, they eventually found their other halves. Humbled by their experiences, they discovered the true purpose of life and many were worthy of returning to the heavens. But many were not.

The Dark Chronicles are stories that share the heartache of select unworthy Whisperers on their journey to immortality after The War of 2019. *Can't Dream Without You* is one of those stories, in which we meet Steve and Julia, two such heroes.

Steve isn't a normal boy. He plays with demons, his soul travels to a dream realm at night using mystical butterflies, and soon he'll earn the power to raise the dead. Al thinks that destroying him would do the world a favour, yet he just can't kill his own son. Wanting to acquire the power that raises the dead before Steve does, Al performs a ritual on Steve's sixteenth birthday. He transfers Steve's dark magic to Julia, an innocent girl he plans to kill. But Steve is determined to save Julia and sucks her soul to Dreamland. From the dream world, he invokes the help of her brother to keep her safe.

Five years later, Steve can't tell what's real or what's a nightmare. Julia's brother wants to kill him, a strange bald eagle is erasing memories, and Steve's caught in some bizarre bullfight on another realm with a cop hot on his trail looking to be Julia's hero. All the while, Steve and Julia must fight the desperate need to make their steamy dreams a reality.

ISBN: 9781908168924 (epub, kindle) / ISBN: 9781908168825 (288pp paperback)
Visit bit.ly/CantDream

About Penelope Hill

Penelope Hill has wanted to be a writer for as long as she can remember, and her fascination with both futuristic and fantastic worlds has fuelled that ambition ever since. She is an avid reader, a long time role-player and games-master, and loves world-building: designing exotic places, writing mythic histories, and crafting cultures. She's been a costumer and is busy developing her skills as a textile artist, so when she's not writing she can usually be found stitching, knitting, knotting, or exercising other creative skills.

During her working life, she spent many years supporting services in local government, and eventually found herself contributing to the development of both local and national policy, particularly around privacy and confidentiality. The research for her PhD helped influence some of that work, but has also brought new perspectives to both her writing and her world building. While she has published academically, she prefers creative writing, and retirement has given her the opportunity to pursue her long-standing ambition to become a professional author.

She currently lives in Gloucestershire with five cats, a huge library of books, a treasure hoard of fabric and thread, and far too many dice.

Milton Keynes UK
Ingram Content Group UK Ltd.
UKHW011014271023
431432UK00001B/29

9 781911 409618